RIPPER COUNTRY: A COLLECTION

"*Ripper Country: A Collection*"
A short story collection from Jack Harding. This edition published 2022 by DarkLit Press.

First Edition published January 2022 by Blood Rites Horror, an imprint of Blood Rites Publishing.

Edited and formatted by Jay Alexander.

RIPPER COUNTRY

A COLLECTION

JACK HARDING

with original illustrations by
TIM CHILDS

DARKLIT
PRESS

Content Warnings

The stories in this book, while fictional, contain scenes and elements of violence, gore and other graphic content that may upset some readers.

Please go to the very back of the book for more detailed trigger warnings.

Be aware of spoilers.

Tim Childs

"London calling, yes, I was there too
And you know what they said?
Well, some of it was true
London calling at the top of the dial
And after all this, won't you give me a smile?"

The Clash
London Calling

"Lights out tonight, trouble in the heartland
Got a head on collision smashin' in my guts, man
I'm caught in a crossfire that I don't understand"

Bruce Springsteen
Badlands

"And I heard a voice in the midst of the four beasts
And I looked and behold, a pale horse
And his name that sat on him was Death
And Hell followed with him"

Johnny Cash
The Man Comes Around

For Mark

CONTENTS

INTRODUCTION

BY CHRISTOPHER BADCOCK

Allow me, good reader, to speak with you briefly about the frightful fiction that follows, and the man behind this most exquisitely unpleasant of works; a man who signs all of his correspondences with *Jack*.

I fear that I may not be able to sound legitimately Victorian long enough to sustain this introduction, so we'll leave it there. I want to start with the most important thing, and that's a huge congratulations to one of the nicest folk I've had the pleasure of connecting with. Jack Harding, you're a hell of a dude (perhaps even *From Hell*), and you should be incredibly proud of what you've accomplished with this book.

There have been others who've sought to explore this terrifying real-life mystery in a fictional way, but none, in my opinion, have achieved what Jack has with this collection.

What achievement do you speak of, my good man?

Well, lend me your ear (or eyes) for but a moment, and I'll endeavour to elaborate.

We need to head to the big smoke. Not the London of today, mind you. But one with cobbled streets and

3

the dulcet clip-clopping of horse hooves upon said stones. A time of bill-stickered walls and well-worn penny dreadfuls read by gaslight. Of Old Nichol slums, smallpox, and pollution so bad that it turned the grass of royal parks (and the sheep that grazed on them) black with soot. It was an age of industrial marvels, great strikes, pantomime and *Punch*. It was an age of terror, mutilation. And death.

It was the late 19. century: 1888, to be more precise. And a killer was stalking the streets of Whitechapel. This man – for he was surely a man – wasn't just killing his victims; no, he was maiming them in the most deplorable and hideous of fashions. If you feel the morbid need to understand this more visually (and I'd urge you not to pursue this if you're squeamish) search out the official police photograph of Mary Jane Kelly (it appears in Google search images). This advice is given solely as an aid for greater understanding amongst readers as to how iniquitous this man truly was, and with the utmost respect and sincerest condolences to any living ancestors Ms. Kelly may still have.

Mary Jane Kelly was the Ripper's fifth and final victim, though this point is still contested by some, with there being murders of a similar nature that followed before and after the autumn of terror.

At the time, London, and in particular the East End, was gripped by these slayings. People lived in fear, *real fear*, that they, or someone they knew, might be the next victim. Bill-stickers and newspapers only sought to compound this widespread concern, with their posters and rags regularly depicting the Ripper in illustrations as something more than human. A faceless fiend, a ghost or phantom. A beast. A demon. Some believed he was an educated man, perhaps a doctor or maybe even royalty, and others alleged he was most probably a butcher.

What Jack has done here, like no author before him, is manage to show us how the other Jack (the bad one) was all of these things, and none of these things. Each story serves as a potential reality, and although they all conflict with one another, it feels as though they complement each other too. I think this is partly achieved through the author's clear passion for, and understanding of, the subject matter. The works are all peppered with non-fiction, some more than others, and if, like me, you have an interest in the Ripper, you'll find some joy in discovering these details.

There's also a common thread that runs throughout the entire collection: it shows itself in many guises; the clinical, the gentlemanly, the animalistic, and the remorseless. It all amounts to one thing though, and that thing is madness. Because let's face it, no matter who (or indeed, *what*) Jack the Ripper really was, we can all agree on one thing, and that is that he was undeniably and unequivocally, completely mad.

Jack (the nice one) brings all of this together in Ripper Country: the theories, the facts, the people, the madness. He swallows it all up, then spews it all back out into one of the most vividly impressive depictions of Victorian London I've ever had the pleasure (and disgust) of losing myself in.

So join me, mate, if you would, and follow in my footsteps, for I have trodden the dark streets of

Whitechapel that await you, and would be as bold as to contest, that herein you'll find a collection of tales most foul, oh yes, so incredibly uncouth, and yet, most agreeable.

Christopher Badcock
August, 2021

Come and see...

PROLOGUE

Oi, you.

Yeah, *you*. Come 'ere a minute. I know your face.

Oi, don't walk away, come on – come sit over 'ere so I can have a proper look at you. I won't bite, I promise.

What's that?

You're not from round 'ere? Nonsense, you know this place. Everyone knows this place. Well, at least they *think* they knows, know what I mean? Ha. Whitechapel – where pounds and shillings get turned into cheap thrills and crap gin. That's what they say, ain't it? Come on, stop being such a grouch and come sit your arse down next to me for a bit. Come on. It's a beautiful day.

There you go. Sit back and relax a little. The sun's out and everythin'. Probably piss it down in a minute but that's the way it goes in this bloody country, ain't it? Ha.

Yeah, I *know* it's August but it'll be raining cats 'n' dogs before the day is out, you mark my words.

What's that? You can't see the sun? Ha. Yeah, I

know, there's a lot of smoke and shit swirling about, but if you put your mind to it, you can just about see the old currant bun up there somewhere.

Oh don't worry about the smell, you'll get used to it.

Eggs? Yeah, I suppose it does smell a bit like rotten eggs, don't it. That's just all the lovely raw sewage wafting in off the Thames, that is. Can't say I even notice it anymore.

So where is it I know you from, then?

Yeah, I know you said you're not from 'round 'ere, but I must've seen you at some point. I never forget a face, me.

Your first time 'ere?

No? Is it really?

Well stone me. I'm sure I recognise you, but if you swear this is your first time through the old East-End then I ain't about to start calling you a liar, am I?

Yeah, it is a bit crowded ain't it? Been like that round 'ere for bloody ages now. Wasn't this packed when I was a nipper, mind you. They say the amount of people kickin' 'round London has nearly doubled – then doubled again – these last fifty-odd years. Can you believe that? I remember a load of Paddies coming over just after the potato famine and things got a little cramped but it seems to have bloody exploded over the last few years. I mean, you'd think it'd be better – more people about in the community and stuff – but it's a bit too packed for me. Things are as rough round 'ere as they've ever been, and you wanna know somethin'? I've got a feeling they're about to get a lot rougher. I've had this horrible stabbin' pain in my guts for a few days and it ain't the jellied eels or crap gin, I tell you. Nah, something's off. The air just feels kinda different, you know? Dark. Thick. Can you feel it?

Oh sorry, you're not from 'round 'ere are you. I keep forgettin'. Ha. Where is it you're from, then?

Oooh, *very* nice. Anyway, let me tell you somethin', mate – despite what I just said about the feeling in my belly and that – you couldn't have picked a better day to swing through Whitechapel. Just look at her. Ain't she a sight for sore eyes? Ha.

Who?

Which one?

Oh, her. Yeah, that's Lizzie. Tall girl, ain't she? Very pretty. She's from Sweden or Norway, I think. Lizzie Stride, her name is. Apparently she lost her husband and two kids back when the *Alice* went down in '78. You know about *The Princess Alice*, right?

What? You don't? Blimey, you *ain't* from round 'ere are you? Christ, well, let me tell you somethin' mate – it was a bloody tragedy it was. She was one of those big old paddle steamers and, one night, she somehow collided with this massive cargo ship out in the Thames. Went down in less than five minutes, and nearly seven hundred men, women and children all went into the slimy water. Only fifty-odd came out alive. Story goes that poor girl Lizzie was one of 'em. I remember the bodies washing up on the riverbank for weeks after. Just imagine, all those families, all those little nippers on their way back from a lovely day at the seaside and then…

Oh, sorry mate. I still get a little choked up talking

about it. I had a couple of pals on there, you see. Poor bastards. Anyway, where was I?

Oh, yeah. So they say she went down near a load of those great big sewage pipes and the water was black and thick and bubbling with raw shit and piss and god knows what else. You can't even imagine how bad it must've smelt. How it must've tasted. Christ, if it weren't bad enough drowning in plain old water. Makes your stomach turn, don't it? Ten-year anniversary coming up in a few weeks, as it happens. Anyway, a lot of people say poor Lizzie ain't been the same since, and who could blame her? I hear she cleans houses now.

Who?

Oh, him – that's just a cat's meat man. There's a few of them about. Most of them work out of the slaughterhouse over on Buck's Row. They collect up all the shitty bits of meat and gristle from the horses and wheel 'em about town, selling 'em to the dog and cat owners and stuff. Bit of a weird fella that one, though. Never caught his name but he makes me a little nervous.

Same goes for that tall bloke over there, look. The one with the big old 'tash. Evil-looking bugger, ain't he? Look at his eyes. Like two bits of coal. Look at the way he *walks* as well. Almost as if he's floatin'. Makes the bloody hairs stand right up on my neck, he does. Don't know his name either. Not very good, am I? Ha.

'Ere, I know these two passin' by 'ere though. The short one on the left with the dark hair is Annie Chapman. Lovely girl. Got a bit of a brain on her, she has. Think she lives over on Dorset Street, which gets a little hairy after dark. I'd stay away from there if I was you. "Worst street in London," they call it. The one on the right with the curly red hair is Rose… Clarke, I think her surname is. She works in my local most nights. Always proper friendly and that. Got a bit of a mouth on her mind you, but there ain't nothing wrong with that when you look at some of the wronguns we get 'round 'ere. Dog eat dog and all that. People gotta stick up for themselves, you know. Anyway, I think she lives over on Crispin Street. Another dodgy road. You wanna stay away from that part of town if you can, mate. *Spitalfields*, it's called, and you wouldn't catch me there after hours, I tell ya.

Ere, speakin' of Spitalfields, there goes Miss Wright and her two nippers Jake and Lucie. They live over on Dorset street as well, I think. Nice little family unit, them three. Husband was a bit of a bastard mind you, but he took off a few years back. 'Ere, you wanna keep an eye on this bloke 'ere as well. Look.

No not him, that's George Lusk. He's a nice fella. Lost his wife a few months ago. Poor bugger. No, I'm on about that one over there with the fancy top hat and cane. Sticks out like a sore thumb if you ask me. Right spiteful bastard he is. I've seen him on and off the past few weeks and caught him throwing stones at a stray dog the other day over on Hanbury Street. I went to have a word, like, and he started shoutin' at me in old English or something. Madder than a box of frogs he is. Anyway, he pissed off and I've been keeping an eye on the bastard ever since.

Oh, 'ello Ray, morning mate. You all right?

Yeah, survivin' mate, you know me. How's the family?

Lovely stuff. Yeah, I'll swing by later. Have a good one old boy.

Oh that's just Ray Tandey. Lovely fella. Runs a little barbershop over on Commercial Road. I could do with a bit of a trim, don't ya think? Ha.

Yeah, there's quite a few dodgy characters 'round here but there're a few diamonds in the rough 'n' all. Which is the least I can say for these four little ratbags here, look at 'em. Go on, sling your hooks you little scallywags, go on ha ha.

Oh, I'm only messin' about. They're a bit cheeky, them lads, but they got hearts of gold. Boys will be boys, and that. Probably on their way to one of the factories. That's Bill, that's Gordon, I forget the ginger one's name but they call the tall one Fred. Ah, to be young again aye? Ha.

So what brings you through old Whitechapel then?

Oh, that's all right. You don't have to say. I'm only makin' conversation. I get all sorts come sit next to me 'ere on this bench, trust me. Take this one geezer the other week. Pretty excitable he was, but I could listen to him talk all bloody day, I could. He was a journalist or somethin' on his way to a meeting over at the Royal Hospital just down there. Think they were interviewing Merrick again.

Who? You know, Merrick. Joe Merrick. The Elephant Man.

Yeah. We get them all through here, mate. Anyway, this journalist was telling me all about this book he's working on – about this man who sells his soul so he can stay young and handsome forever – but everything bad he does in his life shows up in some oil painting of him or somethin'. The portrait ages and stuff, but he don't. Ain't that the weirdest thing you ever bloody heard? Anyway, he was a clever bastard this chap, and he sat where you're sitting and he chewed the fat with me for ages. Never did catch his name. I'm good with faces, but I'm bloody awful with names I am, ha.

Yep, it's a funny old place. A lot of people, a lot of drink, drugs, and a lot of bloody hurt. Far too many sleeping rough and turning tricks just to get by, you know. Sad really. A lot of locals end up turning to crime and that and I can't say I blame them half the time. As long as they don't hurt no poor bastard. Some people gotta do what they can to survive and earn a bloody crust, don't they?

Yeah, I know it's no excuse. But times are hard, mate. Times are hard. Things ain't as bad just down the road and across some other parts of London, but... I dunno. Places like this seem to be like bloody holding pens for the impoverished, you know. Is that the right word? Impoverished? I dunno, that journalist fella kept saying it. *The poor, the bums, the bottom of the barrel.* Call us what you bloody want. 'Ere, apparently they call areas like this "rookeries". I dunno whether that's some sort of chess reference or somethin', but it ain't no bloody game to us locals. It's just home, you know?

Anyway, thanks for sitting here and listening to me prattle on. You be careful round here all right, and watch your back at night. Like I said, it ain't a *bad* place, but there are a few weirdos floatin' 'round. Jus' try 'n' keep an eye on all those bad eggs I pointed out, yeah?

Somethin's comin'. Somethin' bad. I don't know what exactly, but I got a feeling we'll find out soon enough.

What's that?

Something wicked this way comes?

Ha. Never heard that one before. But I think you're right, mate.

I think you're right.

LONDON, 1888

The following poem was received by the *Central News Agency* at their premises in the city of London on 10th August, 1888. Three days prior, the body of 39-year-old Martha Tabram was found in the communal area of George Yard Buildings just off of Whitechapel High Street. She had been stabbed thirty-nine times.

Experts believe the poem to be a parody of William Wordsworth's *London, 1802* and *Composed Upon Westminster Bridge*. The true origin and authenticity of the poem are debated to this day.

London, 1888

England bares no scene more bleak,
Ignorant of mind who cannot see;
A sight so vulgar in its shame,
A dank stone forest, doth play the game.
Thou hast peered into the the foul,
scorched air;
Tis black, and dank, tis flecked with
embers,

And thou hast glimpsed the best of
Septembers;
A letter, a parcel, a phial, a knife;
The weak shall perish; no trouble, some
strife.
And all that breathes must fall in awe;
The man, the woman, the dog, the whore.
But doth heart cry? Doth mind quiver?
Doth hope sink beneath the river?
The meek shall drown, the fiends must rise,
And they'll ride upon the pale waves of a
pale horse,
And bring henceforth the dead- a flood.
The streets will run red,
The beauty, the blood.

THE CAT'S MEAT MAN

The Cat's Meat Man arrived on Brick Lane just ahead of the storm. It was a grey and sticky afternoon in late August, and the once-faint growls of faraway thunder could now be felt on the crackling wind.

As the Cat's Meat Man wheeled his handcart full of horsemeat down the grimy cobbled lane, his hands and leather apron stained with forty shades of dried blood and filth, he drew a deep breath and looked skywards towards the approaching blackness. His eyes gleamed fiercely. Like piss-yellow diamonds in the dying light. Unblinking. Unwell. The Cat's Meat Man ground his cart to a halt, and put his wraith-like hands on his bony hips. He leant back, stuck out his tongue, and could almost taste the first drops of rain on the slum's foul air and *my, oh my*, didn't they taste sweet?

The Cat's Meat Man smiled.

It was a hideous smile; a sinister smile; a sickening and sadistic smile; it was a rotten sneer, a vile smirk, a wicked scowl; a gum-bearing, shit-eating grin with a pair of thin, cracked lips stretched taut across a set of smashed brown teeth. It was the kind of smile that made women cross the street; it was the kind of smile that gave children nightmares. What the Cat's Meat Man saw on the horizon filled him with twisted excitement: luminous forks of white and violet ripping through a black-red sky, the dying summer sun doing its best to break the clouds of smoke and soot and ash and failing miserably.

The Cat's Meat Man loved storms.

Why? Because most people hated them, and the Cat's Meat Man hated most people. Why? He didn't really know, but if you pushed him for an answer – and the Cat's Meat Man certainly wouldn't like that – then he would probably say there were *way* too many of the stinkin' bastards around these days. Especially in London. Especially in the East-End. Especially in Whitechapel.

Storm's definitely comin', he thought to himself, his callous mind beginning to drift into darkness. *Already 'ere, if what 'appened to that stinkin' whore over on Buck's Row this mornin' is anythin' to go by.*

He chuckled.

The Cat's Meat Man craned his oily neck away from his handcart, cleared his throat, and spat. A congealed glob of pale, brown phlegm hit the ground, instantly lost in a sea of raw sewage. The Cat's Meat Man twisted a skeletal arm behind his hip so he could peel the moist grey shirt from the small of his back. He sniffed. He coughed. He rolled on through the crowd.

*

Earlier that day, the body of Mary Ann "Polly" Nichols – mother of five – had been found on the south side of Buck's Row, no more than a hundred yards from the slaughterhouse where the Cat's Meat Man worked. Her throat had been cut, her face beaten, her genitals stabbed and slashed multiple times. Her stomach had been carved wide open. She'd been covered with a sheet of black tarpaulin and left on the side of the road.

The Borough of Whitechapel was no stranger to violent crime, and a far cry from paradise. But this was different. This was evil; a new and terrifying breed of demonic, mind-bending evil that had slithered into the theatre of the destitute with cruel intentions. Just three weeks ago, the body of Martha Tabram – mother of two – had been found hacked to death on George Yard. She had been stabbed nearly forty times. Were the two connected? Scotland Yard and the local papers certainly thought so, and the Cat's Meat Man had been thinking (*fantasising*) about the grizzly (*brilliant*) killings all day long while he pushed his bloodied cart about the seething city. He wasn't alone – everyone was talking about it; speculating, escalating.

Murdered.

The Cat's Meat Man was intrigued.

Mutilated.

The Cat's Meat Man was excited.

Disembowelled.

The Cat's Meat Man was *inspired*.

"Bloody shame," he snarled with a sour whiff of sarcasm, ripping his deep-set eyes from the charred horizon, that wicked smile never leaving his pale, gaunt face. "Stinkin' whores 'ad it fuckin' comin' if you ask me."

Nobody had asked him a goddamn thing.

Kkkrrrraacccchhhhh! A sudden crack of thunder shook the entire East End of London, and the Cat's Meat Man rolled on.

It had been a long week and an even longer Friday, but the Cat's Meat Man had one last special delivery to make before he could call it quits. As he neared the Thrawl Street junction, frantically steering his cart through a shoal of workers in dirty brown flat caps, his excitement neared its crescendo. Not because of the gathering storm, but because of the cats. They were close. He could sense them.

Can't wait t'see my little babies, he thought to himself as he rounded the turn onto a smoggy Thrawl Street, *'Ope they ain't too scared of this thunder 'n' I 'ope little Jasper's about t'day. I got summit special for him –*

A young boy suddenly crashed into the Cat's Meat Man's precious cart.

"'Ere, mind where you're goin' you fuckin' little bastard!" the Cat's Meat Man roared.

"S-sorry m-mister," the boy stammered, "I... I... d-d-didn't see ya. I'm s-s-s–"

"Didn't see me?!" the Cat's Meat Man roared even louder, cutting the stuttering boy off midsentence. "Didn't fuckin' see me?! You're havin' a fuckin' laugh, int cha?!"

The boy stood frozen and wide-eyed, staring at the rabid man's red right hand.

"You hear what I bloody said, boy? Or you fuckin' deaf as well as d-d-d-dumb?!"

"Uh-uh-uh," the boy was on the verge of tears.

The Cat's Meat Man followed the boy's frozen line of sight and realised he'd instinctively drawn his eight-inch skillet knife from its leather sheath.

He looked at the knife.

Cut him!

Then he looked at the boy.

Gut him!

The Cat's Meat Man's shark-like eyes swam back to the blade once more. They narrowed. They narrowed as he slowly raised the knife, pointing it right between the boy's moist brown eyes, the tip of the blade no more than six inches from his soft, pink face.

The Cat's Meat Man smiled his hideous smile.

"If I ever see your stinkin' face again, boy," he croaked, "I'll cut your fuckin' nose off 'n' feed it to the dogs. Now... *FUCK... OFF*!"

The boy's bottom lip shook violently as he bolted through the sheet of smog towards the safety of the Brick Lane crowd. Crying.

Hahahaha.

The Cat's Meat Man holstered his knife with a chuckle.

"Stinkin' little bastard," he snarled into the thick wall of smoke and embers, "lucky he didn't get the fuckin' red door!"

A severe bolt of lightning tore across the jet-black sky, and the Cat's Meat Man rolled on.

*

The air felt heavy. Damp. The vicious black clouds overhead seemed to lower, and as the storm bore down on the lower west side of the borough, the people of Thrawl Street – and all of Whitechapel, for that matter – moaned and groaned as they hastily made for the discomfort of their homes. The Cat's Meat Man could barely contain his excitement. *Not long now*, he thought, as the first drops of rain began to tapdance on the stone and brick jungle. *Not long now*.

The Cat's Meat Man was about halfway down the quiet street when he caught a glimpse of the first cat – a sleek and malnourished tabby – rubbing its head on the corner of a red brick wall.

"Pss pss pss," went the Cat's Meat Man, "Pss pss pss."

The cat snapped its head towards him. The Cat's Meat Man had its curiosity.

"Ello my darlin'," he said in a high, yet oddly gentle, voice.

"Pss pss pss, come on," he beckoned the tiny creature.

"Pss pss pss, come on, look what I've got 'ere for ya, look." He slowly removed a small strip of dark red meat from one of the drawers of his cart.

He dangled it.

The Cat's Meat Man now had the cat's full attention, and, with that, two more cats appeared from nowhere and swarmed on the bringer of raw flesh – running and meowing and crying and purring – singing and butting his shins and calves with their furry foreheads and faces.

"Ello my luvlies, yes ello, elllllo."

A fourth cat appeared. Then a fifth. Then a sixth, and a seventh, and before long, the Cat's Meat Man was towering over a herd of four-legged friends. There must've been at least a dozen – all twisting and twirling and stretching – begging – for some of that fine British meat. The Cat's Meat Man obliged.

"'Ere ya go my darlins, 'ere yaaaa goooo," he sang in a deranged, broken tune as the cats snatched the rubbery cuts of gristle from his grubby fingers. The Cat's Meat Man's eyes were searching the swirl of fur for little Jasper – his favourite – but he couldn't see him.

There were long hairs and short hairs, and tabbies and toms; there were ragdolls and gingers and Persians, and there was Jekyll, the cat as black as starless night, and Dodger, the fluffy white Ragdoll with the pastel-pink nose. There was Oscar and Fagan and Dinah and Reagan, and a scruffy old shorthair with one eye who the Cat's Meat Man simply called "Mr. Smith".

But there was no Jasper.

"Jasper," the Cat's Meat Man called into the rising wind, "Jasper, boy. Come on, where are ya?" A tremor of concern crept into his scratchy voice.

"Ere mind out my luvlies, mind out," the Cat's Meat Man carefully inched his cart through the sea of ravenous cats, "let's go find 'im, aye?"

With an entourage of furry carnivores at his back, the Cat's Meat Man of Whitechapel made his way down the street in search of the elusive Jasper. He was more like the Pied Piper of Catsville.

Rain pattered softly on the cobbles and felt good on the back of the Cat's Meat Man's hot neck.

"Where is he then?" he asked his army of curious cats as he edged towards the row of terraced houses. "Mus' be round 'ere somewhere."

He searched the shadows.

Nothing.

He stopped and craned his scrawny, wet neck around a darkened alleyway like a hawk.

Nothing.

"Jasper," he called out, "c'mon boy, I got some of your favourite –"

And then Jasper came galloping out of the shadows.

"Jasssper!" Relief rushed over the Cat's Meat Man. "There he is!"

He crouched to greet the long, slender cat. Jasper was an elegant – yet strong – seal point Siamese with a caramel-coloured body, inky black points, bat-like ears and piercing sapphire eyes that could charm even the most obstinate of dog people.

"Ello mate." The Cat's Meat Man rubbed his sleek, lean body with an eager hand. His velvety smooth coat was, perhaps, the softest thing to have ever passed through his rough palms. Jasper looked up at him and meowed. It was more of a wail than anything; so loud, so strong.

"Yessss, yessss," the Cat's Meat Man replied, "I bet I know what you want, don't I?" He stood up, opened one of his drawers, moved his long, yellow fingernails over a bundle of bloodied knives, and removed a light brown packet with the letter "J" scrawled on one side in red crayon.

Jasper wailed again, briefly baring his shiny white fangs and bright pink tongue.

"Yesss mate, yessss."

The Cat's Meat Man unwrapped the packet, revealing two large chunks of raw, moist meat. The other cats suddenly perked up and began to cry, and stir, but Jasper's booming wails drowned out the rest.

"'Ere you go darlin'," the Cat's Meat Man leant forward, handing one of the hunks of rose-red flesh to the impatient cat. Jasper briefly stood on his hind legs, snatched away the offering, and began to gnaw, and grind, and chew.

"Good boy, good boy," he crooned, leaning down to pet the voracious cat, "get some of Daddy's special meat down ya –"

Suddenly the wily Mr. Smith was on the packet of meat in a flash.

"Oiiii," the Cat's Meat Man laughed, "you can't have that, you little rascal, that's Jasper's!"

Mr. Smith couldn't care less as he squirmed and yanked and ultimately won the tug of war with the playful Cat's Meat Man, scampering off into the alley with his pound of hard-earned flesh – the spoils of war.

"Ohhh go-go on then!" The Cat's Meat Man was laughing hysterically now, "jus-jus-just this once –"

"'Ere, whatcha think you're playin' at?" A burly, stern faced woman in a dirty cream dress came stomping over. "What the fuckin' 'ell did I tell you about feeding those bloody cats?!"

The Cat's Meat Man's little flame of joy had been extinguished.

He stood up, glaring at the boiling, po-faced woman.

Stinkin' fat bitch.

"Well?" she asked.

"Well what?" he seethed.

Cut her!

"I bloody told you the other day, stop feeding these fuckin' cats! They ain't all got homes, y'know. They all been 'angin around 'ere waitin' for you 'n' your dogshit meat…"

The Cat's Meat Man stared through the back of the woman's skull. His twisted, skeletal face was a chipped mask full of hate. Full of menace.

"…and they piss 'n' shit 'n' fuck 'n' fight all down the road 'n' who d'ya think has to clear it up? Fuckin' muggins, that's who."

Silence.

"Well? Ain't cha got nuffin t'say?"

The Cat's Meat Man had nothing to say.

"Fuckin' summit wrong with you there is, you bloody skank. Plenty of Cat's Meat Men 'round 'ere. Ours came by earlier today as it happens – woman, she is. Not sure what that fuckin' says about you…"

The heavy-set woman leant forward, prying a still feeding Jasper from the stoney ground. He hissed.

There's nobody about! Fuckin' knife her!

Jasper squirmed in the woman's arms.

Give her the fuckin' red door!

"…I paid her twopence for the cat's food 'n' that was that. You've been down 'ere nearly every day this week feeding my Archie that shit 'n' now he's starting to get all fat!"

The Cat's Meat Man's sunken, yellow eyes widened.

"Jasper," he croaked.

"You what?"

"His name… is Jasper."

"What the fuck are you talkin' about? Summit wrong with you, there is. If my 'usband Johnny were about, he'd give you a fuckin' slap!"

Ha ha.

"Where is he?" the Cat's Meat Man grinned.

"What?" the woman replied, confused.

"Where… is… he?"

"Bloody 'ell should I know? Ain't seen him since Tuesday, but he'll be back soon enough. I'm gonna get him to 'ave a bloody word, I am. My Johnny hates cats but he'd smash your 'orrible face in if he were 'ere, he would!"

Ha ha ha.

"But he's not here," the Cat's Meat Man growled as he moved that red right hand to his leather sheath, "is he?"

Ha ha ha ha!

The woman took a step back.

Give her the red door!

A crack of silver lightning ripped through the angry sky. The pack of well-fed cats scattered in scared unison.

Jasper stirred in the weary woman's arms.

"You're-you're bloody mad," she said, taking another step back.

"We're all mad here, you stinkin' fat cunt!"

"You – you can't talk to-to – you're a fuckin' nut case, you are." The woman was shaking. She turned suddenly, darting back the way she came.

Now!

The Cat's Meat Man took a quick step forward.

Knife the stinkin' bitch!

He stopped.

Get her!

He stared.

Little Jasper was draped over the fleeing woman's bobbing left shoulder, staring back at him with those deep blue eyes. He was licking his lips.

The Cat's Meat Man smiled.

Fuckin' get her! Quick!

"No." The Cat's Meat Man seethed, hypnotised – almost – by the mesmeric cat.

He took his hand from his sheath, returned to his cart, and flung the remaining scraps of stringy meat to the side of the road for his furry disciples. They'd be back.

Fuckin' bitch!

His right eye twitched.

He smiled.

The Cat's Meat Man gripped the handles of his weathered cart, and a monstrous blast of lightning suddenly ripped through the charcoal sky, crashing down no less than a mile from where he stood. It was as if by touching his sacred cart – his ark of the covenant – the Cat's Meat Man had summoned the wrath of God himself. Every last pair of ears in the vicinity were ringing the same high-pitched tune and my, oh my, wasn't it sweet?

The storm had been circling Whitechapel like a famished wolf all afternoon and it was done baring its enormous teeth – the time to sink them deep into this sorry slab of London had come.

Another burst of lightning.

Another roll of thunder.

The Cat's Meat Man craned his greasy head back, took a final look at the angry sky, then swivelled his trusty handcart on its axis before disappearing into the cobbled maze.

The soft rains hardened.

The heavens opened.

By the time the Cat's Meat Man wheeled his now-dripping handcart through the gates of the slaughterhouse, the whole of Whitechapel was fading under the immense thumb of the storm. All the colour – all the life – had been wiped from the streets. Everything was grey and wet and utterly miserable. An occasional flash of bright purple offered something in the way of salvation, but the resulting crash of thunder hammered home the gloom.

Despite the frantic *chkchkchkchkchk* of the rain on the mouldy slate roof, the old slaughterhouse was deathly quiet. The Cat's Meat Man parked his handcart with the others, removed his soaking tweed cap, and wrung it out on the grey, cobbled floor. A dirty cocktail of olive-green sweat, soot and rainwater cascaded to the ground – *splshlshspsh*. The Cat's Meat Man then put his dirtied cap back on and went about securing the precious armoury of knives in his waxed canvas roll bag – they would be needed again tonight.

On his way home, he couldn't resist a short detour via Buck's Row. There had been far too many of the "stinkin' bastards" hanging around there this morning, all crammed together – shoulder to shoulder –

squirming like rotten sardines trying to catch a glimpse of something, anything. Now, though, the street was all but empty and, save for a shambling drunk caught out in the downpour, the Cat's Meat Man had the crime scene all to himself. He was disappointed. Any blood had long been washed away by the black rains. There were no signs of a struggle, no scratches or marks or hair or fingernails anywhere. Nothing. Nothing.

What had he expected?

The Cat's Meat Man couldn't even tell where the gruesome (*brilliant*) killing had taken place. On his rounds, he'd overheard that the woman's body had been found just outside the gated entrance to the stable, but there was nothing to see.

"Bloody shame," he said with a kind of twisted sincerity into the pouring rain, his claw-like hand caressing the stable's wooden door, "S'pose I best be off now anyway. Got us a bit of overtime again t'night, ain't we?" He chuckled.

As the Cat's Meat Man strolled through the sturdy wall of rain, the bag of blades tucked firmly under his skinny right arm, he thought about the killer, and how much he'd like to meet the master craftsman and talk shop.

His sick mind wandered into oblivion.

His pulse quickened.

Another fork of lightning jabbed at the East End, and the Cat's Meat Man walked on.

*

When he arrived at the foot of his terraced house, nightfall was close and the Cat's Meat Man was in fine spirits. Giddy with great expectation, he removed a rusty bundle of keys from his back pocket, hunting and fumbling for the one that would deliver him from the torrential rain that he was, in actual fact, still enjoying. But the thought of what lay beyond the black front door, and – to be specific – down in his basement, was far more exciting.

The Cat's Meat Man found the right key, unlocked the door, and stepped inside.

He paused.

Shut the door.

He turned.

Shut the door!

He took a long, deep breath of the musky air and sighed. *What a week*, the Cat's Meat Man thought to himself, *what a bloody week –*

"SHUT THAT FUCKIN' DOOR!" came a spine-chilling howl from upstairs. The Cat's Meat Man froze. Its ear-splitting volume and sheer guttural force was enough to scare any man stiff. It put the claps of thunder to shame.

"It's only m-me S-Sir," the Cat's Meat Man said, wheeling frantically into the dusty hallway, slamming the door.

"I KNOW WHO IT FUCKIN' IS, SHUT THE STINKIN' DOOR!"

"S-sorry S-Sir, s-sorry," the Cat's Meat Man stammered, numb all over.

"HOW MANY FUCKIN' TIMES DO I HAV' TO TELL YOU, BOY?!"

The Cat's Meat Man's blood turned to black ice. The booming voice seemed to be coming from inside his head. "S-sorry S-Sir. It-it's c-c-closed, it's closed."

Silence.

The Cat's Meat Man had been reduced to the size of a shivering mouse in a matter of seconds. He hadn't heard much at all from Father in recent years. The maniacal old man had virtually shut himself off from the outside world, locking himself away in his miserable lair. The Cat's Meat Man still hated it, though, when Father got angry – even if from a distance. It didn't matter how deformed or decrepit or dormant the senile old man became; he still couldn't stomach his frothing temper, his rabid hate.

The Cat's Meat Man composed himself before inching – sneaking – down the gloomy hallway towards the sanctuary of his basement.

Over the *rrrrrreeeeeeeeeeerrrrggghhhh* of the creaking floorboards, the Cat's Meat Man heard a dull thud from above. He froze, the hairs on his soaking, skeletal arms breaking out in gooseflesh.

He's coming.

Silence.

The basement. Move!

Nothing. Nothing but the static *chkchkchkchkchkchk* of heavy rain peppering the bleak house.

"You best not have that stinkin' animal down there again, boy." Father's ice-cold voice echoed through the gloomy house.

"N-no Sir. N-never again –"

"Because you know what 'appens if I catch you with that *stinkin'* vermin, don't ya boy?"

"Y-y-yes S-Sir."

"Good. Now... *FUCK*... *OFF*!"

The Cat's Meat Man slipped and scurried down the hallway towards the kitchen – he needed a paraffin lamp so he could do his work properly. As he scrambled for a box of matches, he heard several more thumps from upstairs, followed by a faint *eeeeeeeaaaakkk* as Father returned to his bed.

His nerves began to calm.

His pulse eased.

He stopped shaking.

That was the first time he'd heard Father's voice in a while. How long had it been? Weeks? Months? The Cat's Meat Man couldn't be sure. He'd barely heard a creek from the sinister realm above until this past week, and it was strange how he only ever seemed to hear from the old man on trying days like today. When did he even *see* him last? He couldn't remember. What did he even *look* like now? He didn't want to think about it.

The Cat's Meat Man finally found the box of matches, removing one of the tiny wooden sticks with his damp right hand. He struck it against the side of the rattling box – *sssshhhhht*.

Nothing.

Sssshhhhht.

Nothing.

Sssssssshhhhhhhht –

The match snapped.

"For FUCK's sake!"

Quiet!

A sudden bang from upstairs.

Move!

He pocketed the matches, grabbed the lantern, and bolted for the basement door.

"BOYYYYY!"

The Cat's Meat Man was scrambling for the right key when he crashed into the sturdy doorframe with his shoulder, dropping the bundle of cast-iron shapes.

"No!" he cried.

A series of thuds and thumps thundered across the ceiling, fast approaching the top of the stairs.

No! No! No!

The Cat's Meat Man quickly grabbed the keys, miraculously finding the one for the basement first-time as he madly poked and scratched at the rusty keyhole.

Shit! Shit! Shit!

He inserted the key.

thud thud thUD THUD THUD THUD

He turned it.

"I'M GONNA CUT ITS FUCKIN' HEAD OFF!"

The Cat's Meat Man yanked the door open, removing the key and flinging himself into the abyss in one swift move. He slammed the door behind him and fell into it, trembling. Another crash of thunder arrived on cue as if to accentuate the drama of his daring escape.

He bolted the door.

Silence.

Stillness.

Nothing.

The Cat's Meat Man stood at the top of the stairs, peering down into the gloom. *You're safe*, he reassured himself, *you're safe*. And he was, because Father could never – would never – touch him down here. Not in *his* basement, not in *his* lair.

The Cat's Meat Man twisted on his heels and locked the door from the inside. He carefully knelt down and threw the bottom deadbolt across for good measure – *kaachhhha*. The Cat's Meat Man then released the damp knife bag from underneath his skinny right arm and placed it on the narrow landing so he could try, again, to light the paraffin lamp.

Sssshhhhht, ssshhhhht, sssshhht – success. He touched the flickering flame to the wick, and there was light. The Cat's Meat Man shook the match with his forefinger and thumb, retrieved his precious knives, and headed down into the basement.

To say what lay beneath the black house was an abomination would have been an understatement. The Cat's Meat Man's basement was simply beyond imagination, beyond anything. If not for an old wooden table in one corner, and a lice-infested mattress under a few primitive drawings in the other, it would be hard to believe someone – anyone – could spend five minutes in such a place, let alone thirty years. It wasn't a basement, it was a dungeon, a crypt, a hole; a filthy, claustrophobic *hole*; its stained brick walls were plastered with a hundred cobwebs, its concrete floors covered in a thousand spatters. Looking towards the street was a small, high window, caked in a thick layer of old dust and a million dead spiders. At the foot of the stairs - against the wall - were two metal buckets, and behind the stairs, an internal wall ran the width of the dungeon, not quite splitting the entire foundation in half, but almost. There was a large steel door in the centre of the wall. It was closed. It was red.

Then there was the smell; strong, yet difficult to place; it was like a ripe yet fetid mix of rotten eggs, urine, mould and fresh vomit – it was enough to make your eyes water, your stomach twist, your throat gag.

It was the pits. It was death. It was all these things – and more – but to the Cat's Meat Man, it was simply home, and it had been his only home for as long as he could remember and my, oh my, wasn't it sweet?

The Cat's Meat Man shuffled across his sickly chambers towards the table, setting down the lantern and his bag of blades. He twisted the small brass knob on the side of the lantern, and a large orange flame lit the room in a carousel of flickering shadows that somehow managed to illuminate the stench of the place. As the old lamp tossed dull shades of yellow and amber around the space, the Cat's Meat Man began to remove his clothes.

In horrifying contrast to the darkness of the grimy room, the Cat's Meat Man's pallid skin appeared bright white- every last bone in his hideously ghoulish body on display. There were scars – dozens and dozens of scars – that ranged from short, thin threads to great protruding slashes. And they were everywhere: on his chest, his torso, his thighs; on his arms and genitals; but it was his back that bore the worst of the trauma. And it was a sorry sight to behold – like a garish pink road map tattooed on a slab of stained alabaster.

The Cat's Meat Man tossed his soaking wet clothes

to the floor and removed a large knife from his roll bag. It was dirtied with dried blood.

The Cat's Meat Man then moved towards his grimy mattress, leaning forward to grab one of the faded crayon drawings nailed above a single, pale green pillow. He tore it from the brick wall, and then he just stood there looking at it.

Reflecting. Remembering.

"Jasper," he sighed, stroking the blue-eyed cat in the child's drawing with his crimson knife, "I'll 'ave some more of your favourite meat soon mate. That bitch owner of yours is closer to her stinkin' husband than she fuckin' thinks."

Ha ha ha ha ha ha.

In the dripping silence, the Cat's Meat Man heard a series of muffled screams coming from behind him. He slowly turned, and glared at the large red door.

His right eye twitched.

He smiled.

"Evening, Johnny boy."

As the Cat's Meat Man of Whitechapel worked late into the stormy night, a well-fed cat sat staring at his owner while she slept in her lonely bed.

He yawned. He purred. He licked his lips.

DEAR BOSS

The following letter was received by the Central News Agency at their premises in the city of London on 27th September, 1888. Less than three weeks prior, the mutilated body of 47-year-old Annie Chapman was found in the yard of 29 Hanbury Street.

The true origin and authenticity of the letter are debated to this day.

Dear Boss,

I keep on hearing the police have caught me but they wont fix me just yet. I have laughed when they look so clever and talk about being on the right track. That joke about Leather Apron gave me real fits. I am down on whores and I shant quit ripping them till I do get buckled. Grand work the last job was. I gave the lady no time to squeal.

How can they catch me now. I love my work

and want to start again. You will soon hear of me with my funny little games. I saved some of the proper red stuff in a ginger beer bottle over the last job to write with but it went thick like glue and I cant use it. Red ink is fit enough I hope ha ha. The next job I do I shall clip the ladys ears off and send to the police officers just for jolly wouldn't you. Keep this letter back till I do a bit more work, then give it out straight.

My knife's so nice and sharp I want to get to work right away if I get a chance.

Good Luck.

Yours truly
Jack the Ripper

Dont mind me giving the trade name

PS Wasnt good enough to post this before I got all the red ink off my hands curse it. No luck yet. They say I'm a doctor now. ha ha

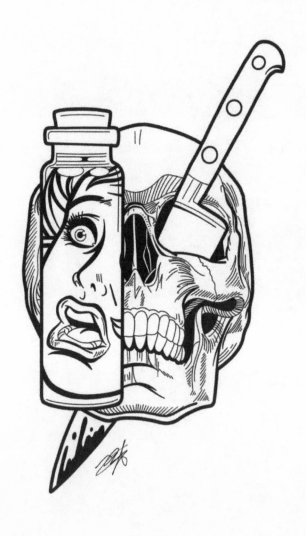

FUNNY LITTLE GAMES

Please allow me to introduce myself: I'm a man of the theatre, a man of the arts. Call me Chapman. I stand before you this fine September eve, happy and glorious with a spring in my step and a story to tell, but, before we start, I must first ask you a question: are you paying attention? Good, for I shall require every last penny of it, and – let me assure you – there will be no change.

Let us begin...

Several days ago – never mind how many exactly – I stood beneath the great Clock Tower at dusk, and decided it was time. I'd been planning it for a while; my walk on the wild side, my evening of devilish iniquity, my funny little games. What can I say? I felt buoyant, I felt frivolous, I felt ready – my white hot passion for mischief burned every bit as bright as the shining night of theatrics ahead, for *it... was... time*. The Red Fiend of Whitechapel had lit a fire in my belly and, I must confess, ever since the third whore's carcass was found carved up like a plump Christmas turkey – giblets and all – inspiration had caught ablaze. Her name was Chapman too, funnily enough. Anyway, let us just say that *this* night – for whatever reason – was *the* night. I could feel it in the pit of my stomach, in the marrow of my bones. Whitechapel was crying out like a bastard child on the cool, autumn breeze, and yours truly heard the call loud and clear.

It was an hour's walk to Whitechapel – give or take – and though the prospect of the Underground was tempting, I wanted to savour every last drop of the evening's festivities. I wanted to drink it in for as long as humanly possible and – looking back – I suppose I wanted to stir the melting pot of expectation in my stomach that little bit more, so that when the show finally started, the spectacle would taste that little bit sweeter.

Leaning back on my ebony walking cane, I put a gloved hand to my beaver-skin top hat and checked the immense clock: five minutes to six. The Great Bell would soon toll, signalling the end of another afternoon, and the beginning of game night – oh yes, it was *definitely* time. I shifted my gaze from the hands of the enormous dial to the setting, pale orange sun. It was quite lovely. I jerked the lapels of my black cashmere overcoat up around my neck, picked up my cane, and headed north along the Victoria Embankment. Heaven forbid I should be late for my…important date.

It was a fine evening.

The crushed velvet sky was a delightful blend of

reddish pinks and ripe, juicy oranges, with irregular – yet somehow deliberate – strokes of powdery lilacs brushed across a cloud-stained horizon. It was stunning. Inspiring. The silhouettes of a thousand pointed arches and rolling brick chimney tops adorned the sharply focused panorama like black desert dunes in the dying light, and I was overcome with a sense of awe. London was beautiful, just *beautiful* this time of day, this time of year. Believe me when I say that not even Grimshaw himself could have painted such a vivid urban landscape. In a way, it was a terrible shame to be leaving such pleasantries for the dregs of the East-End but, thankfully, the night's entertainment promised to quash any hint of melancholy that threatened to dampen my spirits. As I strolled along the cobbled walkway, the gold and sickly-smelling river to my right, the sinking sun at my back, I fingered the serrated knife and two glass phials in my coat pocket, and I mulled over the night's itinerary one last time.

Now, I know what you're thinking: "For God's sake, Chapman, enough with all this scene-setting nonsense, just get on with it already." Well, I'll say to you what a dear friend once said to me – let's call him Dodgson. He said: "Druitt, my dear boy, good things come to those who wait."

He also favoured a curious little phrase about the devil's being in the detail, and that one should never let the truth get in the way of a good story – or maybe that was someone else. I digress.

*

As I trailed from the embankment heading east onto White Lion Hill, dusk had turned to twilight, and a kaleidoscope of vivacious butterflies had hatched into life in my stomach. The first stop on my tour was close. My eyes gleamed with great expectation. My heart fluttered in my chest. My right hand still twirling away in the silk-lined pocket of my coat, I ran my thumb along the cutting edge of the jagged blade and smiled. *By the pricking of my thumbs…*

White Lion Hill became Queen Street. Queen Street became Lombard Street, and as I neared Whitechapel High Street, edging deeper and deeper into the gutter of London, the last of the streetlamps that lined the dirty, teeming pavements were being lit. Thick coils of pallid smoke rose from below, swirling up and around, then evaporating. I had been scouting the smog-choked slum for some time so, in retrospect, it shouldn't have come as a surprise that the streets were still crawling with vermin. I saw hundreds – maybe thousands – of fat, pale faces bobbing past me, dirty white balloons with human features. The population of the rotten crucible had exploded in recent years, and it never failed to shock or disgust when eyes, ears and nose were laid upon their awful existence. I loathe the degenerate, destitute bastards with a passion like no other; their smell, their essence, their mere being – the East-End is but a smudge of bloody excrement on our noble Queen's shoe and Whitechapel… Whitechapel is nothing but a greasy plump cunt asking for the knife. And I am that knife.

As I neared The White Hart Pub, the fluttering in my stomach seemed to grow, smothering any feelings of rage or discomfort that had crept to the forefront of my racing mind. The last thing I needed now was one of those blasted headaches. I needed to keep my composure, my focus. I stopped. I drew a deep and purposeful breath from the fetid air, and stood for a moment just outside the public house. I listened to the dull growl of the ghetto and the din beyond the doors. I shifted my cane to the other hand and stared into the purple and green diamonds of the mucky, stained glass window. Suddenly, a cough. I glanced to my right. An old, mangled woman lay on the ground in a river of her own urine. She sat up. Her yellow eyes staring deep into my own.

"Spare any change, mister?"

I smiled. I put an eager hand in my trouser pocket, then spat into the woman's chipped face.

"Not for you," I hissed as she put a set of blackened fingers to her wet chin. I turned to face the door of the establishment, put a gloved hand on the rusty brass handle, and pulled.

Let the games begin.

I'll spare you the finer details, but I will say this: the inside of this grotesque pub was every bit as vile as one might expect. Hot, hazy, loud; everything seemed to be a foul shade of beige and the thick, smoky air was filled with the horrible sound of laughter and the smell of cheap gin. *Disgusting*, I thought, as I carefully made my way through the throng of peasants to the bar, *bloody disgusting.*

"What can I get ya?" an ugly redhead with a face full of freckles shrieked from behind the bar.

"Glass of sherry."

"You wot?"

"A glass… of… sher-ry!"

"Glass of sherry," she repeated, wheeling away.

I fought back the urge to leap across the grimy bar and rake my knife down the whore's back. I turned to face the crowd. I was looking for two things: one – a place to sit, preferably against a wall; and two – an unattended drink. At first, my eyes struggled to penetrate the dense, stomach-churning concoction of white-grey smoke and dirty brown flat caps. I squinted, honing my gaze as I panned and scanned the room for a decent spot. Suddenly I clocked a vacant chair in the left-hand corner of the room, beneath a faded painting of an old warship. *Splendid.* Now for the drink. Most of the glasses seemed to be either empty or stuck to a grubby hand. I couldn't see anything that took my fancy. I grew perturbed. Worried. The lack of prospects began to settle on my mood like an anxious cloud. I was practically on the verge of tears, when I glimpsed what appeared to be a half-consumed glass of red wine on a table maybe ten paces from my desired seat. *Perfect.* I put my hand in my right coat pocket to confirm the special phials were still in my possession. They were. *Game on.*

"That'll be a thrup'ny bit please, sir," the whore screeched from behind me.

I turned, paid the bitch, then made for the vacant chair. As I approached, I tucked my cane under my left armpit, shifted my glass into my left hand and fumbled for the smaller of the two phials with my right. Nobody was looking. Not as far as my eager eyes could tell, at least. I was maybe six paces – give or take – from the lonely glass when I concealed the phial in the sleeve of my coat, popping the cork and breaking into a graceful skip as I closed in on my target. I removed my right hand from my pocket and added a dash of my homemade blend into the now-poisoned chalice. I could barely contain my excitement. I placed my refreshment on the dark brown table, and ushered myself into my front row seat with aplomb. I took a deep breath of the rancid, stale air. It was abhorrent. Sickly. But it was all part of the game. I paid it no mind, for the show was about to start.

So often it is the case with the finest productions that one can expect to be sat for an eternity before the players – or in this case, *player* – finally take to the stage. So imagine my surprise when, no sooner than I had sat down, the young female lead emerged with a pork pie of some sort in one hand, reaching for the glass of claret with the other. I nearly fell off my chair.

She was a pretty thing: long black hair, milky white skin, a sharp yet petite nose that lit up her innocent face. If I had to hazard a guess, I would have put her at – say – nineteen or twenty years of age. Twenty-one at the most.

"*Frailty, thy name is woman*," I muttered into the musty din, inching towards the edge of my seat, a dryness in my throat. I swallowed. At that moment, I perhaps felt something in the way of regret or guilt, but it was soon replaced with mind-bending excitement as the little bitch raised the glass to her still chewing mouth. *Drink me.*

I sat up.

She took a sip.

I leant forward. She took another. Then another, and in the blink of an eye, she had consumed the whole glass and my poor, poor heart was doing somersaults in my chest. I thought I was going to faint.

What was in the phial, you ask? Oh, nothing much. Just a playful little mix of strychnine and rat poison. It goes terribly well with pork and red wine, I'm told. Anyway, where was I? Ah yes, the prelude. The young actress stood for a moment, her thirst quenched, chewing away with one hand on her hip, looking about the sea of brown and beige. I checked my timepiece. Twenty past seven. She had five minutes – give or take. The supporting cast would be along soon. *Ladies and Gentlemen of the show, this is your five-minute call. Five minutes, please.*

I took a sip of my poor excuse for a sherry, and sat with my elbows leant atop the table, stroking my beard with my right forefinger and thumb.

Watching.

Waiting.

If all went to plan, I wouldn't have to endure the stench of the dreadful place for much longer. Looking back, it was nothing short of a miracle that I was able to summon enough courage to even touch a damn thing in that cesspit. Thank God for my black leather gloves.

I checked my pocket watch again – twenty-four minutes past seven. My eyes widened. *This is your beginners' call for act one. Beginners to the stage please.* A fat woman approached our leading lady.

I listened.

"You want another drink, luv?"

"Nah, I'm alright thanks Jules. Best be…" she paused, "…off home to me Mum in a bit…"

She coughed.

I stirred in my seat.

She coughed again, and again.

I put a fist to my mouth so's to hide the grin that had besmirched my knowing face.

She put a hand to her mouth also.

"Bloody 'ell, you all right girl?" The fat woman asked.

The leading lady shook her head, her eyes glassy and panicked. She stuck out her left arm and grabbed the fat pig by the shoulder, coughing violently now.

"Easy Pen, the pies ain't that bad."

I sniggered through my gloved fist.

Her stirring rhapsody of coughs and grunts and gasps intensified.

"Jesus, Penny!" the fat woman squealed, panic rattling her voice for the first time as she vigorously thumped and thwacked the protagonist's back. A river of thick blue veins pulsed and writhed on the side of the leading lady's neck. Her face had turned a curious shade of purple. She removed the hand from her twisted mouth and began to claw and grab at her swollen throat.

"Jesus Christ, she's choking!" the fat bitch bellowed. "Somebody 'elp! She's fuckin' choking!"

A few patrons turned and frowned, but most were oblivious to the unfolding drama.

"Somebody fuckin' 'elp! She's bloody choking! Penny! Please!"

A handful of extras scrambled to the stage.

"*The lady doth protest too much, methinks,*" I said mockingly into the dank room. Nobody heard. Nobody noticed. They were far too invested in the scene now, and who could blame them?

The "choking" woman batted away her co-star, spewing blood and bile and small chunks of pork and pastry as she fell to her knees, her eyes bloodshot, wet and bulging with terror and confusion. There were a few gasps. A few screams. The fat lady started to bawl as the fallen woman slumped – face first – to the sticky hardwood floor and began to convulse. More blood and phosphorous oozed from her stupid, gurgling mouth like frothy cranberry sauce as she flopped around on the ground like a fish. The pain must've been excruciating.

I took a sip of sherry.

There was bedlam. Complete and utter bedlam as the audience descended into divine chaos. They swarmed on the shaking woman, clutching their heads and faces, crying out in incredulous horror and confusion as she lay dying, dying, dying.

Dead.

A smothering stillness fell over the room.

The fat woman sank to her knees and howled.

Bravo.

End scene.

*

Now, I enjoy the theatre as much as the next man, but you must believe me when I say that young Penny's performance truly belonged under the bright lights of The Globe Theatre. It was worthy of rapturous applause – a standing ovation, even – but I resisted the urge. I raised a glass to our dearly departed. A bittersweet refreshment. I finished my drink, checked my timepiece, and made for the exit.

The first act had gone swimmingly, but the night was still young, and I was merely warming up.

The games were afoot.

Full dark now, and Commercial Road was surprisingly quiet for a Saturday night. The moon, pale, pink and full, hung just above the tip of the great cathedral. It was quite lovely. Off somewhere, a large dog could be heard barking on the light breeze. Its angry cries faded, then ceased. I chuckled. Coincidentally, I was on my way to see a man about a dog.

As I turned from Commercial Road onto Back Church Lane, I spied a late night barbershop across the grimy cobblestones and debated a quick shave so's to alter my appearance. I decided against it. In hindsight, I probably should have lost the beard there and then, but the thought of what lay waiting for me less than five minutes hence clouded my better judgement. For my next trick, I had something far more, shall we say, *intimate* up my sleeve.

*

As I neared the end of the barren, stony lane, and the second stop on my Whitechapel tour, I looked about the empty path. Puddles of waste and general rubbish lined the gutters. Two large rats fought and screeched over a scrap of soggy bread, then scurried off. The lane, as always, was poorly lit.

I reached the alleyway I was after and stopped, peering down into its gloom. And there they were: the vagrant and his dog. I picked up my cane, and approached.

"Good evening," I said, bearing down on the pathetic wretch and his mutt, both lying on a mess of shit-stained blankets and old newspaper. I think it was *The Daily Star*. Anyway, I leant over the man and said:

"Please allow me to introduce myself. Maybrick's the name. What's yours?"

"M-Mister?"

"Mister? Mister what?"

"Oh. J-John. My name's John."

"Pleased to meet you, Mr. John," I said. My attempt at humour fell on deaf ears. "Do you like Shakespeare?" I asked, wedging my cane under my left armpit, sliding my hands into my coat pockets.

"Mister?"

"Shakespeare. William Shakespeare. The Bard."

"Oh, uhh, I- I dunno. I guess so."

I cringed. "I can't attest to being a huge admirer of his poetry. I'm more of a Wordsworth man myself. But his plays. My Lord, his *plays*."

The tramp bore the expression of a dog that's just been shown a card trick.

"*Othello*, *Macbeth*, *King Lear*... and the insatiable *As You Like It* are all top-notch but – if pressed – I'd have to say *Hamlet* is my personal favourite. What's yours?

"I dunno Mister. C-can ya spare any change please?"

"Oh. Very well. Pick a hand."

"Mister?" The tramp was confused, so I knelt down to his level to elaborate. The pungent stench of stale piss and vomit all but sent me sprawling.

"Right," I composed myself, "in each of my pockets, I have a hand. A left hand and a right hand. One of these hands contains a ten-pound note, the other contains something far better."

"Ten-ten pounds?" The stuttering tramp could hardly believe his luck.

"Yes. Ten *whole* pounds. But which hand is it in, John?"

"Oh uhh-"

"You take a moment to think it over. Maybe your little friend here can help you decide. What's his name?" I asked, shifting my gaze to the scruffy dog.

"Ch-Charlie."

"Charlie. How lovely. Well, like I said, you two mull it over. This is a big decision. But whilst you do, let us converse with one another a little about *Hamlet*, shall we?"

I returned to my feet.

"Not only is it Shakespeare's longest play, but it's also his most engaging."

John actually looked as if he might be paying attention.

"In *Hamlet*, we see The Bard revisit several weighty subjects like death, betrayal, revenge, madness and, of course, love – or lack thereof, to be precise. But it's the *way* in which he tackles these big-ticket themes in his 1602 opus that makes *Hamlet* such a joy to behold. Have you made a decision, John?"

"Umm…" He had not.

I pressed on.

"Through *Hamlet*, the Prince of Denmark, whom many consider to be Shakespeare's finest ever character given up to fiction, the preeminent playwright portrays just what happens to a man when he feels as if the entire world has turned against him. Something I'm sure you can relate to, John?"

John said nothing.

"I first saw it at The Globe many years ago. Johnston Forbes-Robertson played the lead and, let me assure you, there'll never be a finer portrayal in our lifetime."

John still looked as if he needed a few more moments. I knelt back down to his stinking level, gripping the handle of the serrated knife in my right pocket.

"It's hard to pick a favourite among so many exceptional lines but – knife to my throat – I think I would have to go for a particularly stirring verse from act three, scene four. Have you come to a decision, John?"

"Yes, Mister."

"Splendid. Left or right? What's it going to be?"

"Left."

"Left it is," I said, removing my left hand from my coat pocket and, with it, a crisp ten-pound note.

"Here you go," I held out the money, checking both ends of the narrow alleyway.

John seemed lost in a world of incredulity.

"Oh, John, I wasn't codding, dear old boy. Take the money. You've earned it."

"Oh, oh, th-thank you M-Mister," John was most pleased, "you're-you're a good man Mister, you're a good man." He was practically sobbing into the precious piece of paper. Poor chap.

"*I must be cruel only to be kind*," I hissed into the tramp's blistered face as I slowly removed the knife from my right pocket, "*thus bad begins, and worse remains behind!*"

I drove the jagged blade up and under his bearded chin, through the floor of his mouth and into his tongue. He didn't scream. He didn't do much of anything. He must've gone into immediate shock, for his eyes had rolled into the back of his skull and his arms lay limp at his sides. There was no resistance. Just a deep, animalistic moan as I yanked the knife down and returned it to the same spot over and over again in a kind of frantic sawing motion. Blood and phlegm and strings of tissue poured from his mouth and neck like hot tar, spilling onto my glove and sleeve. I didn't mind. It was all part of the show. Little Charlie yipped and yapped, visibly distressed by the nature of the scene, but the mutt seemed reluctant to come to his owner's rescue.

Good dog. I turned my attention to the tramp's midriff, stabbing and hacking away. John's legs were spasming violently now. He tried to clutch his leaking stomach but I continued my attack. I sliced and slashed at the backs of his grimy hands and fingers and then I noticed something that gave me real fits. He was still clutching the ten-pound note! *That wasn't in the script.* He fell to his side in the foetal position, and I responded with some improvisation of my own. I leapt to my feet and proceeded to stomp on his skull repeatedly. It took some doing but I eventually landed the all-important *coup de grâce*, splitting the vagrant's head wide open like a watermelon. I was almost surprised to see that he did in fact possess *some* brains. They spilled out onto the ground in a steaming pile of red-grey pulp.

Satisfied that poor old John's race was run, I took a well-earnt breather. I knelt to retrieve my money and was just about to exit stage right when I remembered little Charlie. I turned my gaze to the stinking mutt, grabbing it by the scruff of the neck, and… well, let's just say I'm not much of a dog person.

Are you still with me? Marvellous. It's quite a story thus far, wouldn't you agree? We've not much further to go now, though, I promise. I can see your interest is fading, but fear not, for after this short interlude, it's onto the final act and the most stupendous of finales that you will not want to miss.

Let us conclude…

*

Several hours had passed since my thrilling encounter with Messrs. John and Charlie, yet my pulse was still racing. I'd found a nearby park and taken the opportunity to clean myself up with a number of handkerchiefs I'd tucked away in my breast pocket just in case things got a little messy. I wanted to look my best for the big finish, you see.

The park was largely deserted, save for a few stray dogs and a couple of drunks. I debated casting them as extras, but I'd had enough ad-libbing for the time being, plus it wouldn't really offer up much in the way of variety now would it? No, I'd already seen to the homeless and the hairy, and what I had in store for the final act was far more befitting of a man of my stature, I can assure you. I checked my trusty right pocket for the larger glass phial. You hadn't forgotten about that one, had you? I certainly hope not.

I'd taken up refuge on a cast iron bench that overlooked a series of ferns and shrubberies and rustling trees. The low growl of Greater London could still be heard rumbling on the late night breeze. The moon, still pale and pink yet clear-edged, hung a little higher in the black sky. At various points, cauldrons of large brown bats could be seen flapping and scrapping above the skeletons of moonlit oaks and birch. It was spectacularly macabre. Not even Poe himself could've written such a scene of gothic splendour.

Sufficiently rested, I got to my feet, dusted myself off, and was just about to head for the south-side exit when suddenly a white rabbit ran close by me.

Oh, don't worry, it wasn't wearing a little waistcoat and getting all worked up over the time – that would be absurd – no, it merely hopped and hopped along, zigging and zagging up the long and winding path towards the far exit before vanishing into the street. Needless to say, a certain curiosity washed over me, and I couldn't help but think this was a sign that perhaps I should mix things up a little. Now, I'm not exactly in the habit of chasing rabbits, you understand, but I deemed it, shall we say, *appropriate* to follow the white thing's trail. What if it was merely showing me the way?

I made for the northern exit.

I was striding north on an unfamiliar street – Berner Street, I believe it was called – when, lo and behold, something caught my eye. A rather fanciful two-wheeled horse and carriage that looked somewhat out of place in these detestable, run-down parts. It was parked maybe fifty paces up ahead, on the left-hand side of the otherwise secluded street. I couldn't tell you why, exactly, but I sensed a certain darkness about the carriage; a blackness. Something cold and sinister that lurked in the shadows and black images began to form and congeal in my mind like warm glue. And I liked it. Burning with curiosity, I approached.

Two dashing black horses stood at the front of the glistening carriage. One with a white stripe down its forehead and the other blacker than a moonless night. The coachman sat just behind the two black beauties, motionless, his arms resting in his lap. I was maybe thirty paces from the carriage when, suddenly, there was a high-pitched scream. The coachman jolted. He shouted something to his right that I couldn't quite make out and, with that, a cloaked shadow burst from the large gap between the two brick buildings and disappeared into the back of the carriage. *How bizarre*, I thought, as the coachman gave the order and the horse and carriage soon hurtled past. *How bizarre indeed.* Naturally, I proceeded to the location from which the shadow had emerged to satisfy my curiosity.

Between the two large buildings was a dark and derelict asphalt yard of some sort. Shreds of rubbish and hunks of dirt and rubble filled the vacant lot, and there was something large and black towards the back end of the space. It was moving. It was writhing. It scuffled its frame against the rocky ground in some distress. Evidently, I wasn't the only one playing games this fine September eve. *Could that be?* I turned to face the black carriage, but it had long since vanished. *Could that be the man of the hour?*

I smiled, I turned, I approached.

Curiouser and curiouser.

And then I saw it.

"He-hel-hel," an ugly woman lay squirming in a pool of dark blood and tears. She was clutching her flopping maroon throat, looking up into my watchful eyes.

"Hel-hel-hel," she gurgled through a mouthful of the red stuff.

"Hello," I said, "please allow me to introduce myself. Gull's the name, what's yours?"

"Hel-hel," she continued. *How rude.* For the life of me I couldn't work out what she was trying to say.

"Helen? Helena? Hell? Oh, oh of course *Hell*. Yes, you'll be there in about, let me see…" I removed my timepiece from my breast pocket, "…oh, about two minutes I'd say. I wouldn't worry your pretty little head though, my dear. *Hell is empty, for all the devils are here.*"

I knelt down to examine the dying whore. Her throat had been expertly cut but there were no signs of mutilation that I could see. Maybe this wasn't our man, after all. But, then again, maybe he was in a dreadful hurry, or had merely been interrupted by yours truly. I removed my serrated knife, still damp with the blood of the man and his mutt.

"Hold still," I whispered into the woman's long, bloody face as I leant forward and sliced the lobe of her left ear clean off, pocketing it for safekeeping. I returned to my feet with a grunt, yawned, then pushed off on my cane. All of a sudden, I felt rather spent. Jaded. Alas, I headed home. A smile on my face. The inaugural evening of games, though technically unfinished, was every bit as majestic and fulfilling as one could have possibly dreamed. The first of many to come, I'm sure.

So, there you have it. My glorious night of funny little games was cut short at the death – no pun intended – by none other than the *Red Fiend* himself. What are the chances? Well, let us be honest here, there's a possibility this shadow might've been somebody else, but based on the fatal wound and the *modus operandi*, I really do suspect it was the man of the hour. Although, I can't say I'm much of a fan of the *Red Fiend* or *Leather Apron* nicknames the editorials have bestowed upon him, are you? No, I have a feeling they'll be calling him something a little more *saucy* in due course. Anyway, two questions before we call it a night. One – what did you think of the story? And two – how was the wine?

The woman lay half-naked and paralysed on the double bed, her watery eyes wide with panic and something far beyond terror.

She couldn't move.

She couldn't scream.

She could barely even breathe.

The only thing she had been able to do for the past half-hour was watch and listen in absolute horror to the bearded man's ramblings.

His mouth pulled back into a malicious grin, Chapman or Druitt or Maybrick or Gull approached the deathbed with a spring in his step and a knife in his hand.

The woman tried to scream with all her might but she just couldn't. She just *couldn't*. The only thing she could muster was a series of breathy grunts.

"Ch-Ch-Cha-Chap–"

"Oh please, my fair lady," the knife-wielding fiend broke in, "you and I are well met, are we not? Let's not stand on ceremony. Call me… George."

Tears crawled down the woman's temples in inky black tendrils.

"The vast majority of my story was true, you know. Well, except for the part about my night of funny little games being a few days ago. No, I must confess, that was a little white lie. Just a *little* one. You see, that all happened this evening… and you, my dear Alice, *you* were always the final act. Although, after that run-in with the man of the hour – let's call him *Jack* – you're more of an encore now, I suppose."

She looked about the room for help, but nobody was coming.

"Now, before we close, let me put your mind at ease. You've probably figured it all out by now but, just to clarify – you've ingested a rather powerful sedative but fear not," he gently caressed her bare, throbbing stomach with the serrated knife, "you won't feel a thing."

A whimper.

"You've good reason not to believe me, of course, but really, would I lie to you? We're on first name terms now after all. Doesn't that make us friends?"

The woman closed her eyes.

The man raised the knife.

"These violent delights have violent ends…"

SAUCY JACKY

The following postcard was received by the Central News Agency at their premises in the city of London on 1st October, 1888. The night before, 44-year-old Elizabeth Stride and 46-year-old Catherine Eddowes were both murdered less than forty-five minutes apart.

The true origin and authenticity of the postcard are debated to this day.

I was not codding dear old Boss when I gave you the tip, you'll hear about Saucy Jacky's work tomorrow double event this time number one squealed a bit couldn't finish straight off. Had not time to get ears off for police thanks for keeping last letter back till I got to work again.

Jack the Ripper

LUSK LETTER

He was in his early fifties and was living, then, in a large semi-detached house on Alderney Road with his three little girls. It had been a hard year. A dark year. A hard, dark year that George Lusk couldn't wait to see the back of. After falling into a diabetic coma, his poor wife, Susannah, had died from suspected kidney failure in February, leaving George to raise Maud, Selina and Lily alone, their four older children having already flown the nest.

George worked in construction and was an interior decorator by trade. He was a firm, yet peaceful, man. A good man; an active, well-liked and respected member of the community who regularly volunteered at the local church and had been a member of the revered Freemasons for a number of years.

In the city of London, serious wealth and abject poverty had been bitter neighbours for generations, and people like George were caught somewhere in the middle. Wedged between a golden rock and a very, very hard place; not quite rich, not quite poor – middle class, you could say, although, if anything, George was slightly closer to the working-class end of the spectrum – someone industrious yet cultivated who had the common touch.

He had recently been elected Chairman of the newly founded *Whitechapel Vigilance Committee*, a small council of local business owners who had come together to form a neighbourhood watch outfit in response to the recent slew of brutal murders in the district. The general feeling around Whitechapel was that the police just weren't doing enough to protect the locals and, as a result, businesses were starting to suffer.

Some would say this appointment made George something of an important man. Others would say he was in over his head. Some would even go as far to say he was now a marked man. Whatever you thought, there could be little doubt that – in this moment – George Lusk was something of a celebrity in the East-End of London. A celebrity whose star was about to shine that little bit brighter.

The days were getting shorter. The nights, longer. Dusks and twilights had both begun to loiter, and the sudden dip in temperature brought with it a chill of bad memories that George wished he didn't have. He missed her. He would always miss her. The cold, the dark, the biting winds; these elemental things all reminded him of the day Susannah was taken from him. From them.

George sat in his father's old rocking chair, staring into the newspaper, listening to the crackling of the open coal fire that soothed an ache that refused to leave him. Susannah had been gone for a little over eight months now but, in truth, the coma had snatched her away a long time ago. But that didn't make it any easier. He missed her. He would always miss her.

It was a cold and blustery October evening and the streets of Mile End were blanketed with crispy yellow and orange leaves that appeared brown in the gloom of the pale moonlight. It was the first cold air to have touched London since February. Since Susannah's death. It wasn't the kind of weather that called for thick coats and woolly scarves, but it was just about cold enough for the first coal fire of the season. It was a slippery slope to winter from here.

George had just finished tucking his three girls into bed with mild resistance. It had actually taken less than twenty minutes this evening, a personal best. He was getting good at it now. He figured it was merely a matter of routine. A splash of perseverance, perhaps. Some strictness, maybe a few cups of patience – large cups. But George didn't mind. They were good girls. Sensible. Caring. A tad mischievous at times, but he didn't mind that either. Not really. And when all else failed, he always had the trusty words of Lewis Carroll to fall back on. If the girls were in a particularly excitable, restless mood, he knew he could always break out *Alice's Adventures in Wonderland* for a bedtime story, and the three little rascals would soon settle down.

George had been pouring over the politics and current affairs sections of the *Telegraph* with forced interest. It had been the better part of two weeks since that grisly night in late September which saw a total of five innocent souls ripped from the gutters of Whitechapel, and yet, it was all the papers could talk about. Was it the work of one man? Or was there something else afoot? Nobody knew. Was the poisoning of the young girl in the White Hart Pub linked to that of the brutal stabbings on Berner Street and Mitre Square? Nobody knew. And what about the tramp found beaten to death in an alley by Church Lane and the woman found drugged and skinned alive over on Montague Street? How did they fit in? Did they fit in? Or were they just grotesque coincidences? Everybody had an opinion but nobody knew, and the whole ordeal and lack of police action made George Lusk feel sick to the pit of his stomach. He was considering a small glass of whiskey, or perhaps even a cigar or two to calm his nerves and lighten his grim and heavy reading. He took a deep breath, and sighed. It had been a long day. All the days had been long since Susannah's death, but he had to admit they were slowly getting easier. Slowly.

By his own admission, he'd done a damn fine job of keeping up appearances these past few months which, in truth, wasn't too difficult considering how busy he'd been with work, and the girls, and the church, the Masons, and now the committee. Every now and then, though, his mind would wander and he'd think of his wife; her chocolate-brown curls, that pinkish mole on the left side of her collarbone, her insatiable laugh. Then he'd get to thinking about all the good times they shared; the evening walks along the Thames, the trips to Bottom Wood with the kids, that weekend in Portsmouth…

Sometimes, try as he might, George was powerless to hold back the tide of memories that came crashing like waves upon the lonely shore of his conscious mind. He let out another sigh, and turned the page.

George stared at smudged blocks of black ink on the thin white sheets, trying his best to engage his brain, but he just wasn't in the mood for reading. Not tonight. The thought of the cigars and the whiskey – especially the whiskey – was far more appealing. *Darling,* his wife's voice spoke up in his head, *just try and finish this last article, then you can treat yourself to a few drinks in front of the fire, all right?*

He nodded.

He was a few paragraphs from the end when he heard a scuffle above, followed by a chorus of muffled giggles.

"Girls," he said aloud into his enormous paper, refusing to tear his eyes from his place in the article, "back into bed, please."

Soft and distant cries of "Sorry" and "Daddy" echoed through the house, followed by more whispers and giggling. George faintly smiled to himself, and carried on reading.

He was just about finished with the article when there was a loud knock at the door. He tore his eyes from the paper and checked the old grandfather clock from across the room. He frowned. Quarter-past eight?

Who the bloody hell could this be at this hour?

Susannah's voice again.

George folded his paper with a harsh *scrunch* and rocked forward and up onto his feet with a groan. He headed for the front door.

"Evenin' Mr. Lusk." A short, plump man stood shivering on his doorstep, his nose, cheeks and ears all pink from the biting winds. "Got a parcel for ya sir."

"A parcel?" George frowned, his voice high with a blend of confusion and mild outrage, "at this hour?"

"S-sir?"

"Oh, oh good Lord, where are my manners? Sorry, Henry, sorry," George slid to the side, "come in, come in, I'm away with the bloody fairies tonight. Of course; evening post, isn't it?"

"Right you are sir," the postman said, chuckling, "you're my las' one of the night as it 'appens."

"Good stuff, Henry, good stuff," George smiled, glancing down at the small brown package in the postman's hands.

"'Ere you go," the postman said, offering him the parcel.

"Much obliged," he took the parcel, "uh, won't-won't you come in for a quick cup of tea? A nightcap, perhaps?"

"That's alright sir, thank you sir. I bes' be off home to the old dear."

"No problem Henry, no problem. You have a safe trip home, all right?"

"Right-o, Sir. You 'av a nice evenin'."

"And you, old boy, and you. Bye bye now," George

closed the door.

*

He was on his way back towards the comfort of his living room when something caught his eye. He stopped. He listened. He slowly lifted his gaze towards the top of the stairs.

"Girrrllls," louder this time, "what did I say?"

Nothing.

Nothing but the ticking of the old grandfather clock, and the not-so-distant cracking of the open fire.

"Little pigs, little pigs, don't make me come up there little pigs…" his playful threat was met with a series of faint shuffles and giggles followed by the creaking of now-occupied beds. George rolled his eyes, shook his head, then made for the warmth of the living room.

He placed the parcel on his small oak desk and stood staring at it for a while; his back to the hissing fire, his left arm cupping his right elbow, his right forefinger and thumb slowly twizzling the corner of his thick, brown moustache as if he were contemplating his next move.

Don't open it, George.

He expelled a short blast of air from his nostrils in amusement. A gesture that caused his shoulders to jerk and the hairs of his well-oiled moustache to quiver ever so slightly. *Well, this is different,* he thought, reaching for his letter opener, *it's usually bloody letters but a full-blown parcel, and at this time of day, how should I get so lucky?*

George had a good idea what it might be or – at least – what it might be in reference to. The frequency of these prank letters was getting a little absurd now. For the past month, the weird and demented post he'd received from an army of sick minds claiming to be the perpetrator of the brutal murders accounted for around a third of his mail. At first – like anyone – he was alarmed, but over the past few weeks they'd actually started to amuse him. His favourite one so far had been the surreal crayon drawing of what appeared to be a bloodied corpse surrounded by a bunch of cats with the words iT WOz Me? scrawled underneath in red. *Bloody fools.* He shook his head, a wry smirk on his lips as he ripped the letter opener along the top of the parcel – *ccccrrrrrrrrrrrckk.*

In spite of his disgust at the callousness of these idiots, George wasn't really surprised he'd received such correspondence. It was, he figured, to be expected considering how many flyers were plastered about town with his name on. All it took was some degenerate with half a brain to consult the city directory, and they'd have his address. It wasn't anything he couldn't handle, and he was always sure to turn them over to Scotland Yard – minus the child's drawing of the cats, of course. He didn't quite fancy getting laughed out of the building by Inspector Abberline and his men.

George put his letter opener to the side of the parcel, and began to pick and tear at the thick paper wrapping. He wasn't quite like a child at Christmas, but the anticipation burning in his stomach coupled with the snap, crackle and hiss of the coal fire certainly made it feel like the big day had come early. *A parcel*, he thought, *not a letter – a parcel. A package. A present. And in the evening post? Usually they come first thing in the morning.*

George removed the last of the brown paper, scrunching and balling it in his large rough hands. He tossed it into the fire. The flames ignited the ball and briefly lit up the dim room with brilliant shades of gold and amber. His eyes caught the light and blazed into life. He pried the box open with his thick fingers.

"Good Lord!" he coughed, putting a hand to his twisted mouth and recoiling, the stench of stale piss and vinegar hitting him in the face like a splash of ice water. The pungent, eye-watering miasma seemed to fill the room in an instant. He gagged. He coughed a few more times, blew a sharp blast of air into the foul-smelling room and then, slowly, tentatively, George Lusk peered inside the box.

At first, he wasn't sure what he was looking at. The object didn't quite register in his brain. It didn't make any sense. A slice of meat? A hunk of flesh? An organ of some kind? He didn't know. He wasn't a medical man. And yet, what lay before him certainly seemed to resemble what he'd always imagined a kidney would, perhaps, look like; brownish red with a thin, shiny coating; palm-sized and curved in the middle, almost like a… kidney bean. It couldn't be human. Could it? No, it was too small but, then again, what did he know? He was just a builder.

There was no blood. No stains or splatterings on the inside of the box, just the… whatever *it* was, perched atop a few shreds of scrap paper. George moved an unsteady hand back towards his letter opener. *What on earth are you doing, George?*

"It's all right," he said under his breath as he gripped the blunt knife, "it's fine." He prodded the meaty thing in the box – it was quite firm. Rubbery.

"Bloody hoax," he spat into the stuffy room, "rotten bastards have gone too far this time." He slammed the letter opener back on the desk, and was just about to close the flaps of the heinous box when he noticed something poking out from underneath the thin shreds of brown paper. George put his hand in, careful not to get anywhere near the meaty thing. He pinched the side of the partially hidden object with his forefinger and thumb. He removed it from the box. It was a small piece of yellow paper. Folded. George frowned. He unfolded it and the opening two words caused his bare arms to break out in gooseflesh. His lungs tightened as a pair of wraithlike hands crawled up his chest and wrapped their long, cold fingers around his throat. The letter said:

From Hell

Mr Lusk,
Sor,
I send you half the Kidne I took from one
women prasarved it for you tother piece I
fried and ate it was very nise. I may send
you the bloody knife that took it out if you
only wate a while longer.

> *Signed*
> *Catch me when you can*
> *Mishter Lusk*

"…catch me when you can Mishter Lusk –"

"Daddy?"

George jumped out of his crawling skin.

"OH! Good *Lord* Lily, you-you scared me half to death!"

"Daddy, there's a man outside my room. Can I have a glass of water?"

"Wh-what? What? A man?" his heart hammering in his chest, "Where? *Where*? Show me. Show me!"

"Can I have a glass of water?"

"In a minute darling, s-s-stay there," George folded the flaps of the box shut, slammed the letter down on the desk, and rushed to the front door.

There was nobody there. Nobody at all. George stepped out onto the pavement, his eyes wide with alarm, looking left then right then left again. The street was completely empty.

Nothing. Nothing.

If it wasn't for the low hum of the unwinding city, and the howling winds that tossed fallen leaves along the old cobbled ground beneath the dark moon, Alderney Road would've been completely dead. *Go to the police, George.* Sussanah's voice. He shook his head incredulously and closed the door.

"Daddy?" Lily was standing in the hallway now, rubbing her eyes.

"Lily," he went to her, "Lily, are you sure you saw a man out there?"

"I-I don't know. Daddy, can I have a glass of water

now please?"

"Y-yes of course sweetheart, come on," George scooped his youngest daughter up and headed for the kitchen.

"A beard?" George asked, tucking little Lily back into bed, her thirst quenched.

"I think so," she yawned, "I don't know."

He didn't want to press her for any more details. He didn't want to scare her. Maude and Selina were also miraculously asleep, and George couldn't risk waking them at this hour – God help him.

"Daddy?"

"Yes, sweetheart?"

"Do you still miss Mummy?"

"Every day," George sighed, tears threatening to flood his eyes.

"I miss Mummy."

"I know sweetheart, I know. And she misses you too, I'm sure of it."

She smiled.

He gave her a peck on her tiny, cool forehead, and wished her goodnight. He took one last look out of the bedroom window, then hastily made for the living room.

"From Hell," George croaked into the fire, gripping his tumbler of whiskey with a firm yet shaky hand as he read the contents of the awful letter over and over again. He had made himself that drink after all. It was less a reward for making it to the end of his article, and more a necessity to take the edge off what lay atop his living room desk. What lay in his quivering right hand.

"From Hell." The words raked across his nerves like a fistful of jagged fingernails on a dusty blackboard: a terrible, soul-shredding scrape from an infernal nightmare.

From Hell.

He shuddered.

What are you getting so worked up for? he cursed himself. *It's just a stupid hoax. A stupid, vile hoax.* He took a sip of his drink.

But what if it's not, George? Susannah.

He took another sip.

What if it's from him? Her voice in his head was as loud and as clear as he had ever heard. *What if it's from Jack?*

Despairing, he sank the rest of his drink, then poured another.

George was back at his desk now. Adrenaline was still coursing through his veins, hot blood pounding in his ears but he felt a little calmer. He had wrapped the so-called kidney or "Kidne" in an old cotton cloth and stowed it in his bottom desk drawer. He had placed his drink and the letter on the wooden top, and was sifting through a stack of dusty papers.

Go to the police, George. George shook his head, his fingers flicking through the thick wad at a frantic pace. *George, please.*

"Found it," he hissed, removing a copy of the

Telegraph dated October 5ₜₕ.

He thumbed through the newspaper, searching for the facsimile of the "Dear Boss" letter that had been made public by Scotland Yard a few weeks back. They, like Lusk, had received dozens of letters from all kinds of fools professing to be the murderer terrorising Whitechapel, but this particular letter was considered to be the real thing.

George, please.

He found it. He flipped the paper in half and placed the printing of the "Dear Boss" letter alongside his own, shifting his eyes between the two – back and forth, back and forth, back and forth. The crackling fire had died down to a seething pile of lurid red coals, but the large grandfather clock could still be heard loud and clear, its pendulum swinging back and forth, back and forth, back and forth.

In the ticking silence, George eventually came to a half-hearted conclusion: they were different. The letters were different. The language was different, the spelling, the grammar, the font, the style – it was all different. He breathed a sigh of relief into the warm, musty air, and reached for his glass.

But what if your letter is the real one, George?

He shook his head.

Go the police, George. Think of the girls. Please.

He folded the letter in half, and then he stowed it away in his top drawer.

"It's just a hoax," he snarled into the empty room as he slumped into the old rocking chair, "just a stupid, bloody hoax." He took a big gulp of his drink. Sank it. Set it down.

But what if it's not, George? What if it's not?

George stared into the smouldering redness of the open fire, his throat dry. He swallowed hard. The gravity of the situation had settled on his incredulity in a dismal haze. *But what if it's real?* He shook his head, rocking back and forth in the old rocking chair. It creaked, it squeaked and almost seemed to speak to the old grandfather clock. Their conversation ticked back and forth, back and forth, back and forth.

Martha Tabram.

Mary Ann Nichols.

Annie Chapman.

Elizabeth Stride.

Catherine Eddowes.

Five. Five innocent women murdered. Mutilated. Cut down, cut up, and left for dead on the filthy streets of London.

"Just a hoax," he muttered under his shaking, sour breath, "just a stupid *fucking* hoax."

But what if it's not, George?
What if it's not?

What if it really is...

...from Hell –

Suddenly an ear-splitting scream echoed shrilly from above and filled the world, prickling the hairs on the back of George Lusk's neck and stirring his stomach.

"DADDY COME QUICK! COME QUICK! HE'S BACK!"

THE PHANTOM ROSE

It was a crisp autumn night in the largest city in the world, and the air was still from the chill of the evening's frost. The shops were closing, and the gaslit streets were dark and secluded. To the west, a large clock struck eight and in the murky twilight gutters, giant rats shrieked and scurried into nearby drains as if summoned by some malignant force.

The air was so cold it almost had a copper-like taste to it, and a thick ethereal fog hung over the dank metropolis like a veil of ominous secrecy. From the distant east, a crescent moon rose slowly, clawing its way into the sky- a shrouded, ivory eye casting its scornful gaze on the misty world below.

The fog cared little for the pale moon's stare, allowing next to nothing in the way of light to pierce the gloom it had conjured. Coupled with the foulness of the city smog, it was as if the entire capital had been imprisoned under an enormous cloud dome. It was blinding. Unnerving. Maddening.

All sounds were muffled, all shapes were blurred –

anything and everything seemed hopelessly grey and damp and, save for the low roar of the seething city, all was deafeningly quiet.

In spite of its corruption and hideous poverty, many still thought of London as the beating heart of progress – the epicentre of the new world and a mighty place of great importance that was shaping the very fabric of the century; yet for the past three months, none of that had mattered. The stone and brick cesspool had been in the clutches of fear, and but a hairsbreadth from the mouth of madness.

Things had changed.

Blood had been spilt.

A rank, polluted essence filled the sour air, and in this dismal slice of London, in this smog-choked purgatory, a killer was at large.

Rose Clarke stepped out of darkness and into darkness. She crossed the grazed, dirty cobbles and headed south on Crispin Street. Her flat and lightly freckled nose was powdered, her wiry auburn hair tied tight, and her tattered scarlet dress, like everything, appeared black in this sinister light. She was on her way to pour pints at The White Hart and, understandably, the part-time barmaid was a rustling bag of nerves.

Ever since Annie Chapman's body had been found, a shadow of violent death and manic trepidation loomed large and monstrous over the East-End of London. Everybody felt it – especially the women – and much like the ominous, sulphurous fog that had swallowed the district whole this ghostly October eve – All Hallow's Eve, to be precise – the smell of fear seemed to be everywhere; creeping in and out of every alleyway, doorway and courtyard, crawling up and under the cracked nostrils of anyone brave (or stupid) enough to stay out after dark.

It was the worst of times.

It was the epoch of incredulity.

It was the season of darkness.

Just imagine – over a million pairs of eyes all scanning the shadows for just one man, and finding... nothing.

At first, the punters didn't seem too bothered, but then came the letters to the papers, and business slowed. A few days later, the fourth and fifth victims turned up within minutes of each other – one with her throat slashed and the other mutilated beyond comprehension. That very same night, Rose had watched on in horror from behind the bar as a young girl choked to death on the floor of the pub. It turned out she had been poisoned. The police were quick to rule out any connection between her death and those of the other unfortunate women, but after that night, things had all but ground to a bitter halt. There was something in the air: a dread; a madness. You could feel it. It was palpable. Like a cold, rattling breath on the back of your neck. Even some of the regulars had turned tail and gone crawling back to their miserable wives and children, but it had been nearly a month now since the phantom had struck, and the sinners were slowly emerging from their pathetic caves once again to wet their whistles.

"Come on girl," she whispered to herself as she started down the grimy, cobbled street.

Put it outta your mind, she thought.

It's been ages since anything's 'appened.

It'll be all right, you'll see.

It won't.

The bastard's probably moved on by now, anyway.

He hasn't.

Move your arse, come on.

She walked.

It was the same speech she'd given herself almost every night for the past six weeks, but she never truly believed it. Not really. She wanted to, of course, but the fiend was still out there somewhere.

Watching. Waiting.

Rose could feel it stirring way down in the pit of her empty stomach, but she walked on anyway.

Ain't gonna let that evil sod stop me from earnin' a livin', she raged, listening to her leather boots on the jagged cobbles.

Why should us girls down tools when he's the one who needs bangin' up?

All of a sudden, she stopped.

She listened.

Nothing. Silence.

The street was completely empty.

Rose knew this part of town like the back of her hand and yet, she did not. At least, that is to say, not tonight. Something was terribly wrong with Crispin Street. It was a lot quieter than it used to be, sure, but what of it?

That was to be expected, all things considered. The weather wasn't exactly peachy, either. No, there was something else. The street felt different, smelt different, looked, somehow, different, and that fog – she'd never seen anything like it. It was unholy and dense and diseased and just... well, bizzare.

The fog, she thought, just the stupid fog.

Her legs slowly started to carry her towards the sanctuary of the pub.

Then something caught her eye.

"What? What the bloody hell is that?" she spat into the mist.

That ain't always been there, has it?

Rose stopped, wheeling right to face a monstrous stone wall. It must have been at least twelve feet high and ran parallel to the curvature of the street, bending off to the right before disappearing into the eternal fog.

She took a cautious step towards the wall for closer inspection.

Scarce yet strategically placed streetlamps cast an irregular pattern of light and shadow on its rugged texture. The shadows shifted and bent as she inched closer. The lamps illuminated the towering – almost surreal – structure and somehow made the wall appear even taller.

Strange.

She couldn't have been more than ten feet from the base of the monolithic thing when her attention was drawn back the way she came.

"No... what...? Tha-that ain't right?"

The wall stretched back as far as the eye could see before curving left and off into that damned fog. A mirror image, almost, of what lay ahead of her to the south.

She didn't like it.

She hitched up her filmy skirts in an act of defiance, turned and proceeded south towards the Thames as planned.

Nonsense. Load of old nonsense, she thought.

Must've worked their bollocks off to get that 'orrible thing up 'past few days, she figured.

Can't even remember what was on that side of the road anyhow. Just a load of old lamps and tramps and benches and shit –

And that was when she heard the sobbing from beyond the wall.

She froze.

A woman's cry? She couldn't be sure. It was soft and snuffly at first. A pitiful concerto of moans and groans that intrigued Rose more than anything.

"…'Ello?" she prodded.

The crying continued.

"Are-are you all right? Where are you?"

The crying intensified.

She shuffled towards the wall.

What the bloody hell are you doin', you fool?

I have to see if they're all right.

The sobs grew louder and deeper, now laced with sickening despair.

"Where are you, luv? I can't see you. What's the matter?"

She was at the base of the wall now.

Leave it, you fool!

Tentatively, she reached out as if to comfort the wall

itself.

"What's going o–"

The sobs suddenly sharpened; began to sound almost like a hound or a wolf or a –

Rose snatched her hand from the wall and recoiled. "Jesus. Wha-whatever's the matter, luv?"

Such pain, such anguish. Rose was no stranger to grief, and had shed her fair share of tears over the years – the tragic death of her little brother Tim, then the loss of both Mum and Dad to cholera no less than a year later. Then that bastard ripped Annie to pieces. Oh yes, Rose Clarke could cry with the best of them, but this wailing was something else entirely.

"Wh-wh-wh…" the words escaped her.

She quickly turned from the wall for help, or answers, or God only knew what, and laid eyes on something even more chilling than the sounds coming from the mysterious wall.

"I… what… no."

Fear prickled her spine.

Where a tall and gnarled line of brick buildings had once lined the street, now stood another wall – grey and ugly and faintly illuminated by a string of amber gas lamps which stretched on forever and into the fog – identical, almost, to the wall she had just touched. Shadows on top of shadows. Black on grey, orange on black.

She was hemmed in on either side.

The feral crying escalated and could now be heard all around.

She stumbled into the middle of the maze, her face a twisted mask of palid horror, clutching her cheeks with quivering hands, her heart thundering a staccato tune of terror in her ears.

She tried, and failed, to steady herself.

What the hell is this? What the *hell* is this?

Make it stop, she thought, God please make it bloody stop!

Then, no sooner than the insane cries had started, they ceased. Vanished.

Rose slowly removed her pink hands and listened.

Nothing. Nothing.

Absolute silence.

"Bloody hell," she breathed.

Everything was frozen in time – it was almost as if the abandoned street was listening to her.

What in God's name is going on 'ere? she thought. I must be goin' mad.

She quickly took note of her surroundings; the ugly twin walls were still standing and the fog had cleared a little. She could now see a little further down a warped and eerie Crispin Street that she no longer recognised.

She took a nervous step.

There was an echo.

She took another step. Another echo.

"Come on", she pleaded with herself, "only a ten-minute walk from 'ere, if that. Wait 'till they hear about this down The White Hart. Come on."

She moved quickly now. Her boots slapping on the cobbles as she ran. She blotted everything out except the necessity of putting her left foot before her right, her right foot before her left.

Quicker.

Quicker.

Rose devoured the ground beneath her feet like a woman possessed.

Should be comin' up to White's Row soon, she reassured herself, thoughts racing. Pulse pounding. Sod the backstreets. I'll cut down onto Commercial Street and follow the road down to the pub from there. Should've never come this way to begin with.

Up ahead, she heard the faint yet familiar sound of a horse and carriage, and breathed a half-hearted sigh of relief.

Her thundering heartbeats began to ease.

The *clip* and *clop* of heavy hooves and rattling wooden wheels on unsteady cobbles was music to her ringing ears; its sweet symphony rose and fell, rose and fell, rose and fell.

She chuckled.

"Stupid cow," she teased herself, "what are you bloody like?"

With that, she veered left in anticipation of the turn onto White's Row.

The second wall stood firm.

Must be a little further up, she figured.

Turn back.

No, it should be just up 'ere. This ain't a long road.

It's not the same road.

She picked up the pace, her legs moving almost independently from her body.

Then she froze again. The once soothing toll of horse and cart ahead now seemed to be coming from behind.

Clip clop, clip clop, clip clop.

Getting louder.

Clip clop, clip clop, clip clop.

To the left now – beyond the wall.

Clip clop, clip clop, clip clop.

Getting louder, still.

CLIP CLOP, CLIP CLOP, CLIP CLOP.

To the right.

CLIP   CLOP,   CLIP
CLIPCLOPCLIPCLOPCLIPCLOPCLIPCLIP–

She thrust her hands to her face and covered her bulging brown eyes.

"Ohhh God! Please!" Her desperate screams were lost in the relentless cacophony of the unseen horses. Rose had never heard anything so loud or demented and, in a strange way, as this maddening surge of noise pummelled every last fibre of her terrified being, she realised she couldn't even remember how she'd found herself on Crispin Street this hideous night.

"STOP! PLEASE! GOD! PLEASE!"

A thousand wild horses screamed in agony.

"PLEASE!"

Silence.

Stillness.

Nothing.

Rose stood with her eyes clamped shut in the middle of the empty, endless street. Her throat was bone dry. Her breathing was heavy, her arms heavier and her whole body shook like a helpless spider's web caught in a swirling wind. The silence was immense and unbelievable and – for a second – Rose felt as if she might have lost her hearing altogether.

She opened her eyes and stared into the vile, yellow

haze of the hellish fog.

Rose had company.

RUN!

She couldn't run. She couldn't move. All she could do was watch in paralysed incredulity and grim-faced horror as the dark and distorted shape darted from the cloud of smoke some sixty feet ahead.

"Oh my god!" she cried.

The ghostly silhouette was heading right for her.

"Oh god! No please!"

Draped in a silvery, almost translucent robe, the phantom appeared to be floating, cruising, careering towards her at a blistering pace that defied all logic.

Rose tried, again, to turn and run, but she couldn't. She just *couldn't*.

"GOD! HELP! SOMEBODY HELP ME!" she cried. Inky black tears of fear and frustration streamed down her face.

"I CAN'T MOVE!"

The cloaked spectre was now thirty feet from where she stood rooted.

It's got a knife.

It's him!

It's the phantom!

She screamed.

Twenty feet.

"HELP! SOMEBODY!"

Twelve feet.

She stood stone-like beneath the luminous half moon, starring wide-eyed into its sharp, stone-white face. A wafer-thin layer of acrid flesh stretched across its bones – its bulging, bloodshot eyes were an impossible shade of white and almost sunk back into its toothless skull.

Was it… smiling?

Six feet.

She screamed again.

Three.

I don't wanna die!

An explosion of internal fireworks filled Rose's head as her heart hammered in her chest. She slammed her eyes shut and threw up her arms in one last act of defiance or defence, or both.

This is it!

But nothing happened.

Nothing happened.

Rose's blood-curdling screams soon gave way to a melody of soft cries and whimpers as she winced and strained and called upon every last ounce of courage she had left. Slowly, agonisingly, she peered through her trembling fingers.

"Morning Missssss."

Her eyes shot open and she howled into the phantom's alabaster face as it grabbed a handful of her reddish hair with one hand and plunged a rusty blade deep into her abdomen with the other.

Rose's whole body began to jerk and spasm as the demonic thing thrust the blade upwards, tearing through her viscera, slicing through her intestines like a hot knife through butter. Blood poured out of her midriff as the phantom frantically worked the knife up and up through her small intestines then her colon; her stomach then liver until it reached the base of her sternum and would go no higher. Crimson bile began to ooze from Rose's quivering mouth as she stared dumbly into the lifeless eyes of the murderous ghoul.

As she slipped into shock and darkness, the pale thing yanked the blade from the gaping wound and hurled it to the side. It clattered against the stone wall and fell to the ground.

The phantom dropped its evil eyes down as if to marvel at its pulsing creation before driving an icy hand into her torso. And then it began to root around in her innards like a blind hand searching for something of the utmost importance – tugging and ripping out handfuls of guts and entrails like some kind of deranged butcher from hell.

Rose's dying body convulsed wildly.

The fetid smell of hot and salty blood and faecal matter filled the air as she stood shaking in a pool of scarlet gore.

She opened her bloodied mouth to bellow one last gurgling cry –

And awoke in her single room in the early hours of Wednesday morning.

"Uh-uh-uh," she couldn't scream.

She wanted to scream more than anything in this bastard world but she *couldn't scream.*

She couldn't move.

I'm dead, she thought, oh God, I'm bloody dead.

You're not dead.

I can't move. I can't breathe.

You can.

Lying flat on her back, her forehead teeming with beads of icy sweat that glistened in the flickering candlelight, Rose shifted her confused eyes down and stared at her hands, they were gripping a damp – but intact – belly.

Move, her brain ordered her fingers.

Move!

They refused.

Her eyes darted back to the ceiling.

Rose had company.

She screamed.

And, with that, her paralysis broke.

The phantom's curse had been lifted, its demented spell reversed.

The nightmare was over.

Rose sat bolt upright in her soaking, narrow bed and cradled her shivering body. She wept.

"You're all right," she said through choked and salty tears that clung to the back of her throat like leeches.

"You're all right. Just a dream. Just a stupid bloody dream."

She drew several deep breaths of the cold and dusty air and looked about her sparsely furnished room.

Then she cried some more.

32-year-old Rose Clarke of 19 Robson Court did not sleep the rest of that cold October night. Instead, she pottered about her tiny quarters in an anxious, meandering daze – peering through the solitary window of her grimy, ground-floor room every now and then to watch the passers-by and seeing her fate in every shrouded face and shadow.

By dawn, she was still shaking, but nevertheless ready to face the outside world. As warming shades of orange and pink brightened her dullen room, Rose began to dust herself down and fix herself up.

"Some of that fresh London air will do you good," she tried to joke with herself. "Clear your head, girl. Come on."

She blew out her withered bedside candle, took a deep breath, and then she made for the front door.

Rose Clarke stepped out of the darkness and into the light and walked among the people of Whitechapel, her feet slowly carrying her along the stained and lumpy cobbles and away from the depths of her haunted room. It would take days, maybe weeks, to shake the horrors of her vivid Halloween nightmare.

As she walked, she could hear the faint hum of the busy shipyards floating in on the gentle morning breeze. She sensed, too, the low growl of a thousand firing furnaces and textile mills as a new day broke and Greater London came to life.

Rose headed south on Crispin Street, her footsteps lost in a hundred others, her spirits gradually lifting as she came back to reality.

There was no fog. No weeping walls. No screaming horses. No knife-wielding phantom.

Well, that last part wasn't entirely true – five innocent women including Rose's good friend Annie *had* been brutally murdered by a crazed lunatic, and the whole of Whitechapel *was* still teetering on the edge of the abyss.

That much was real.

That much was true.

Did he float on thin air and have a sunken, skeletal face? Probably not.

Although, you never really knew these days, what with all the travelling shows and elephant men that came limping through the East-End.

No, thought Rose, he's just a man. Just a stinkin', rotten man.

He was still out there, though.

Watching. Waiting.

The Phantom; The Fiend; the one the papers now called *Jack*.

Rose slipped out of the foul-smelling crowd and made a beeline for a public bench to her right.

She sat.

She slumped.

She sighed.

"All right, Rose?" a sweet, confident voice called out.

Rose shook herself awake and sat up.

A young, fair-haired woman in a ruffled navy-blue dress approached.

"Oh. Oh, 'ello Mare. You alright?" Rose replied listlessly.

"Yeah not bad luv, not bad. Just off home. You workin' down the Hart t'night?"

"Uhh, yeah, yeah I'm on. I think."

"Here, you sure you're alright? Look like you've seen a bloody ghost or summit."

"Nah, I'm all right, darlin'. I'm all right. Just a rough night is all."

"Yeah, you 'n' me both Rosie, you 'n' me both. Anyway, just thought I'd say 'ello. Best be off home. Stay safe, yeah?"

"Yeah, you too luv, you too. Catch ya later."

The fair-haired woman wheeled away.

Nice girl that Mary Jane, Rose thought, relaxing her posture. Proper good egg. Hope she didn't think I was being rude or nuffin'.

She melted into the cast iron bench, and a forlorn expression washed over her tired face as she craned her head and watched Mary Jane Kelly disappear into the swarming crowd.

A few moments later, a stiff breeze rose and whistled down a chilly yet sun-kissed Crispin Street. Something off-white and flimsy brushed against Rose's left leg and clung to the hem of her skirts – a torn piece of paper. She frowned and lent forward to retrieve it. Blank.

She flipped it over and her heart sank. She gasped. She gasped for air as every last hair on the back of her arms and neck stood up.

It was *him*.

It was The Phantom – a hideously dark, sharply-etched drawing of The Phantom from some kind of newspaper. Haunting. Grotesque. Rose didn't know why but it instantly brought to mind a series of eerie cartoons she'd once seen in a book as a child. The title escaped her, but it didn't matter. It was *him*. There could be no doubt. She'd never forget that twisted, malignant face for as long as she walked this wicked earth.

Those bulging eyes.

That taut, chipped skin.

That gaping mouth.

The knife.

Her right hand went to her stomach.

"Ohh… ohhh God…"

She slowly tore her gaze from the nerve-shredding image to the caption beneath:

> *"There floats a phantom on the slum's foul air.*
> *Shaping, to eyes which have the gift of seeing,*
> *Into the spectre of that loathly lair.*
> *Face it – for vain is fleeing.*
> *Red-handed, ruthless, furtive, un-erect,*
> *'Tis murderous crime, the nemesis of neglect."*

Rose's heart froze in her chest. She didn't know what half the words meant and yet, she understood enough. As she sat clutching the scrap of torn paper like some stone-carved statue of despair, she felt a looming, cloaked shadow slither up beside her.

112

Rose had company.
"Morning Miss."

THE BARBER

The old man stood perfectly still with the straight razor to the young man's throat. He was staring up into the beads and tendrils of water that blurred the conveyor belt of shoes streaking past his basement window.

"Ray?"

It had been a long afternoon of rain, wind, and flickering yellow streetlamps on grey. It was the fifth of November, a date to remember, and the whole of Whitechapel seemed to be rushing about in anticipation of *Bonfire Night* – God knew they could use a distraction – but, in this small, musty room, in this quiet corner of the world, time stood still.

"Ray?"

It was almost dark, and the shops and parlours that lined Commercial Road were either closed or closing, but not this one. Not yet.

"Ray?"

The proprietor of the small barbershop beneath the florist on the corner of Commercial and Weyhill was a man by the name of Raymond Tandey, and he was a little over halfway through his last wet shave of the day when his fractured mind had stumbled off into the dark rooms again.

"Oi Ray, you all right, mate?" the young man with a faceful of thick soap asked, a tad perturbed by the cut-throat razor that had been pressed against his Adam's apple for some thirty seconds now.

"Oh," the barber jolted from his daze, nicking the youngster's neck with a *ffft*, "oh bloody 'ell George, I'm-I'm sorry mate," Ray said, embarrassed, swooping a small towel down from over his shoulder and dabbing the bloody wound.

"That's all right, Ray," George chuckled, reassuring his barber of ten years, "I've had worse. 'Ere, maybe we should change your name to Sweeney Todd after all?"

The barber, still tending to the cut, glanced into the young man's eyes through the large mirror. He forced a smile. Ray had been in this game for over forty years and had endured enough Sweeney Todd quips to last a lifetime – he supposed it was the same for all London barbers, and God help the ones on Fleet Street – but maybe George had a point. Up until this autumn, September 29ᵗʰ to be exact, Ray could probably count on one hand the times his trusty blades had seen red. But things had changed. They were gone. They were both gone, and he couldn't stop thinking about it. About them. About *him*.

First there were the tears. Then denial, then anger. Something resembling a light at the end of a long, cold tunnel could be seen, and then his poor wife, Eve, did what she did, and his whole world turned black. His drive, his meaning, his concentration and deftness with the blade were all blasted out of existence, and even though the 64-year-old barber wasn't exactly slicing customer's heads off and handing them to some madwoman to fill her dodgy pies with, Ray Tandey had probably drawn more blood in the last five weeks than all the barbers in London combined. It wasn't intentional. There was no malice involved. No, the problem was with his heart. The crippling bouts of arthritis he could handle – for now – but his heart just hadn't been in his work since his beautiful daughter and wife were ripped from him.

"Maybe you're right," Ray croaked into the stained mirror, his voice rusty with fatigue, "maybe I should change the sign above the door to *Todd's*. You sure you trust me enough to finish?"

"Yeah, course Ray, course," George said, "I-I was only jokin'. How-how you doin' anyway mate?"

"I'm all right," Ray lied, flicking the bloodstained towel back over his shoulder and forcing another rueful smile. He was about as far from "all right" as a man had ever been, but he appreciated the concern. George wasn't the first to tentatively approach the elephant in the room, and he wouldn't be the last. Ray held the razor to the young man's neck with an unsteady hand, and began to brush upwards in smooth, small strokes.

Ray accepted the young man's tip, handing him a small paper towel along with another apology.

"Don't worry about it, seriously," George said, slowly making his way towards the door, the old barber trailing. "See if you can get yourself down to St. Mary's Park t'night for the bonfire, yeah? Shame about the rain and that, but it should still be a good'un."

Ray nodded, "Yeah, I might do son, I might do." He

had no intention of going, but he didn't want to be rude. "You have a good one alright?"

"See ya soon," George opened the door, sending the mounted bell just above the frame into song. A blast of wet and noisy air filled the room, then vanished with a bang.

Ray Tandey was all alone.

As the old man tidied up his shop, sweeping short strands of damp hair into neat piles, his mind began to drift again.

You need help, Ray. His wife's voice echoed through the chasms of his head. She had been nagging him for years about getting a hand around the place, an apprentice or maybe even another barber, but Ray was a proud man who had always thrived on running things himself. He enjoyed the craft, the hustle, the bustle; the general chit-chat with the punters. It was all he knew and, until recently, his shop had always served as a kind of "hang-out" for the local gents. It was more than just a barbershop, and they came from all over the Borough not just for a shave or a quick trim, but to catch up on current events and have a chat with him or whoever else might be hanging around the basement that day. They didn't come as much now. He didn't know why exactly, but he figured it was probably for a number of reasons; he'd become distant, erratic, wrought up and, above all, unpredictable with the blade. Maybe it *was* time to give up the ghost, after all.

On the one hand, you could say the little barbershop was all Ray Tandey had left, but – in this moment – he didn't really care for it. He didn't really care for much of anything anymore. Maybe he *should* finally listen to Eve and bring someone else in or, better yet, hand the business over to someone who actually gave a toss.

Ray shook his head. He looked down at his cracked and trembling forearms as he retrieved the dustpan and brush from the chipped, walnut cupboard. His hands were on their way out. He knew it, and he wasn't sure how much longer he could keep things up – or if he even wanted to. And then there was what had happened just now with young George. Was there more to it? Tonight had been an accident, sure, but what about the other times?

On his first day back after Eve's funeral, one of his regulars had made a remark to another customer about all the victims of the brutal murders being "good-for-nothing whores", and that it "wasn't the end of the world". Ray was overcome with a sudden sense of fury. He instinctively angled his razor mid-stroke, and took a two inch chunk from the man's soft neck. There was a lot of blood. Ray apologised and blamed the razor, but deep down he'd known what he was doing. He didn't know *why* he did it. He knew the man wasn't talking about his wife or daughter. He knew people didn't share his beliefs about the madman being responsible for their deaths. Maybe he was just sick of hearing about the fucking bastard every damn day. Since the back end of the summer, it was all anybody seemed to want to talk about and he was sick to death of it. The Ripper was like a cancer eating away at the district one cell at a time. One soul at a time. And what did it matter what these girls did or didn't do for money? *Who are we to judge?*

Times are hard. They weren't hurting anybody. They were good women. They had children, parents, and families.

Ray sighed, kneeling down with the dustpan and brush to collect the clumps of hair. His mind was all over the place which meant it was only a matter of time before he got to thinking about Penny.

He dumped the mound of hair into the bin, hurled the dustpan to the side and made for his workstation.

He had no son to hand the store down to, no siblings, no family to really speak of at all anymore. He and Eve were both in their early forties by the time their only child came into the world. But she was worth the wait. Tears threatened to fill his glassy eyes as he placed both palms on the worktop, and heaved a deep and dejected sigh into the room. He glared into his reflection, his sad eyes tracing one of the larger lines that adorned his cracked, sad face. He bowed his head.

"Oh Penny," he whispered into the empty basement, his mind wandering into that dark room he wished he was strong enough to slam the door on, "I'm so sorry, love."

The police insisted there was no reason to suspect that Penny's death was related to the other three killings that fateful night. Inspectors Abberline and Dew told Ray and Eve that, as far as they could tell, only two of the four murders were connected; a woman named Elizabeth Stride who had her throat cut on Berner Street, and another called Catherine Eddowes who suffered a similar fate less than half a mile away in

Mitre Square. Abberline said that Eddowes had experienced a number of other "hideous" wounds which he wasn't willing to share, but that the cause of death was the same as Miss Stride's – massive blood loss due to severance of the left carotid artery. He also said the two bodies were found within forty-five minutes of each other in the early hours of the morning, which would put the time of deaths between six and eight hours after Penny was poisoned in the White Hart Inn. The other victim that night was a homeless man who was found stabbed and beaten to death the following morning near Back Church Lane – only a five-minute walk from Ray's shop. Abberline said the type of weapon that caused the man's wounds wasn't consistent with that inflicted on the two women. He also said the murderer had killed what they believed to be the vagrant's dog.

Ray didn't understand. He'd lived in Whitechapel all his life and was under no illusions – he knew it was a dangerous place – but four murders in one night? He was no lawman but surely something was wrong there. Abberline agreed it was "highly irregular," but poisoning just wasn't this man's style.

"As far as we know, Mr. and Mrs. Tandey," Abberline said, "this man's killed five women so far. But we don't believe your daughter was one of them. As a matter of fact, we're beginning to suspect it may have been four women, based on a pattern that's starting to emerge with the severing of the main artery." Eve, sobbing, tried to calm Ray down – he'd always had a bit of a temper – but the old barber wasn't convinced by any of this.

"Either it's the same man or the bastard had an accomplice – or maybe even some kind of sick admirer or something," Ray knew he wasn't making any sense, but he couldn't help himself, "and who's to say he didn't have more than one knife? You fuckin' find this bastard, Inspector. You find him!"

Ray didn't know what he was saying. He was just a barber, but – for some reason – he believed that the same man was in some way responsible for all of this evil. And even if he was wrong, the harsh and Earth-shattering fact still remained. She was gone. His beautiful Penny was gone and she'd never hurt no one. She was a good girl. Not a prostitute like these bastards in the papers were trying to make out. And so what if those other poor girls were involved in that sort of stuff from time to time? Who were they to judge? *Who* are *we to judge?* Times were hard. They weren't hurting anyone. They didn't deserve what happened to them.

"Bastard," Ray spat into the mirror, his hands gripping the worktop as tightly as his withering joints would allow, "fucking bastard."

His thoughts racing, Ray flung open the door to dark room number two and paid his poor wife a visit.

When they learned of their 19-year-old daughter's death by apparent choking, Eve couldn't accept it. She was perplexed, and borderline despondent. She didn't even cry. Ray had done enough of that for both of them, and in the coming days, he stayed home and did his best to hold together his broken family. But when Abberline showed up on their door with the post-mortem papers concluding that their little Penny had been poisoned, Eve became hysterical. A few days after the funeral, Ray returned to work, leaving his wife in the double bed she seldom left. He thought she'd be all right; he thought she was getting better.

When he came home later that day, he found her hanging from the bedroom ceiling.

Between the moment he clutched her swaying, limp body and her funeral a few days later, Ray couldn't remember much. In the days and weeks following her burial, he would dream dark dreams and wake up in the middle of night to the creaking of the taut rope. Sometimes he saw her legs dangling at the foot of the bed. Sometimes he heard her weeping. Some nights he woke up screaming, but it was just a dream. He knew he should've done more to help her, but he didn't know *how* to. It was just a dream. Just a dream.

A cold, dark chill ran the length of Ray's spine. He grimaced. He wiped away the tears with the sleeve of his shirt, grabbed a handkerchief from the stack next to his shaving brush, and blew his nose.

"You closed?"

Ray spun to face the deep, crisp voice, his hands still clasping the cloth to his scaly, pink nose. He didn't even hear the bell.

"Oh, oh bloody hell," Ray said, removing the damp handkerchief from his wet face, "I thought I'd flipped the sign on the door around. Sorry mate."

A tall, dark man with a stern, sharply-etched face and a thick, black moustache stood oddly erect just in front of the closed door. He wore a low, black top hat and a heavy-looking cashmere coat, also black. It was streaked with beads of rain.

How long has he been standing there?

The dark man shifted his gaze to the inward-facing "closed" sign on the door. He slowly flipped it around.

"But, I've – uhhh – I've got time for one more," Ray, flustered and embarrassed, tossed the tissue into the nearby bin.

"Yes," the dark man said, craning his head back towards the barber with a peculiar, almost disgusted look on his face, "I know you do."

The dark man slowly removed his drenched coat and top hat, revealing a headful of shaggy black hair that was streaked with strands of white. He hung his belongings on the ancient wooden coat stand to the right of the entrance. His eyes locked on the barber as he slowly made his way across the scuffed, ceramic floor. The sound of his wooden soles on the tiles was unsettling. Deafening. He sat in the cracked leather chair with a nerve-shredding *rrreeeacchhhk.*

Ray, still gathering his tools, noticed that the man was wearing a blue signet ring of some sort on his little finger. He scoured his mind for a time he might've seen the man in here before, but he couldn't place him. He frowned. The light in his shop wasn't particularly bright, just a few amber wall lamps, but the dark man's face was not the sort you'd forget. His wide-set, almost reptilian eyes looked as if they were sunken back into their sockets. There was something dancing in them that

Ray didn't like. They gleamed with baleful contempt and an icy intelligence. With arrogance. With hostility and power. Ray stiffened.

"What… what can I do you for then, sir?" he asked.

The dark man, glaring deep into Ray's eyes through the mirror, said nothing. *Maybe he didn't hear me. Maybe he's got a hearing problem.* Ray was about to ask again when the man responded in a deep, flat croak:

"A little off the top, and then a shave."

"Right you are –"

"Dry."

"Excuse me sir?"

"No soap."

"Oh – fair enough," Ray murmured, "might be a little uncomfortable and a bit irritable and that, though, sir. Just a word of warning."

"I'll live."

Ray nodded, grabbing a small spray bottle from his workstation. *Strange bloke.* He removed a small comb from his breast pocket and began to wet the dark man's hair.

"So, you from round here?" Ray asked, removing his shears from his toolbelt, doing his best to keep his concentration this time.

"No."

"Oh. What brings you through 'ere on Bonfire Night then? Got a party to go to or summit?"

"I'm not sure that's any of your business, barber."

Ray stopped.

He slowly raised his face from the back of the man's

skull in a look of confused incredulity. He looked into the mirror. The dark man's sharp face almost seemed to be carved into the glass itself. It wasn't even a face. Not really. It was more like a mask. An unearthly mask full of cunning. Full of scorn. And those eyes: they were like a pair of black opals that shimmered in the half-light: glistening with austere malice. *Has he even blinked yet?*

"Sorry, I'm – jus' makin' conversation, mate," Ray said, "I didn't mean to pry or nuffin."

"Jus' makin' conversation, mate," the dark man repeated back, mocking his cockney accent.

Ray was stumped. He'd come across all sorts of strange and rude customers over the years, foul-mouthed degenerates with chips on their shoulders and bad attitudes, but never someone as insolent or threatening as this. Most men enjoyed a bit of a chinwag. There were those who didn't always fancy a chat, sure, but they always seemed perfectly happy to just sit and listen to him prattle away out of politeness. Then there were those who wouldn't shut up, like this chap who came in every now and again and rambled on about Shakespeare.

"You can take it or leave it mate," Ray said, trying to ease the bizarre and unexpected tension, "I didn't mean to cause offence."

The man's eyes somehow seemed to widen. Scolding. Pinning the barber to the spot. Were they black? *No, people don't have black eyes. Must be a dark shade of blue or green.*

"Proceed," the dark man said, his mouth stretching back into a wicked smirk.

Ray swallowed hard. He tentatively lowered his puzzled gaze back to the man's head, pinching a tuft of thick, damp hair between his index and middle finger, and began to trim.

Ray continued to cut and snip in absolute silence, checking every now and then to see if the dark man's dark eyes were still on him. They were.

He was just about done with the cut when the man in the chair suddenly spoke up.

"So tell me, barber," there was no life in his monotone voice, "what do *you* make of The Ripper's handiwork?"

"Handiwork?" Ray frowned.

"That's what I said."

"Well, I – I wouldn't call it handiwork."

"What would you call it?"

"He's murdering innocent women, mate. Nothing handy about that, is there?"

"Well you know what the French say; *ne saurait faire d'omelette sans casser des œufs.*"

"Sorry, I don't speak French," Ray's initial confusion was bubbling into annoyance.

The dark man let out a throaty chuckle. "You can't make an omelette without breaking a few eggs, barber."

"Oh. Well, I ain't sure what you're really getting at, mate, but they were innocent women. End of story."

"Innocent?" the dark man sniggered, then broke off, "Oh barber, please. Are you trying to tell me those filthy sows didn't have it coming?"

Ray gripped his shears a little tighter; he could feel

his face simmering as annoyance turned to anger. He continued to cut.

"Are you listening, barber?"

"What are you trying to say, mate?"

"There's no such thing as an innocent whore, do be serious."

Ray frowned "Times are hard, mate. People gotta earn a crust somehow."

"Oh, so you'd condone thievery then, would you?"

"It's not the same thing."

"Isn't it?"

"Look," Ray lowered his shears and eyes down into the reflection of the man's malevolent mask, "I've heard it all in here the past two months, all right? And there's bugger all to say any of them girls were prostitutes by trade other than the bollocks they're printing in the papers. I coughed once and it sounded like a bark, does that make me a bloody dog?"

The dark man put his head back, cackled, then said: "Oh barber, please, there's no need to get angry. Besides, if you tell a big enough lie and tell it frequently enough, it will be believed. Allow me to enlighten –"

"No, you're all right," Ray snarled, "I don't wanna hear it and to be honest, I couldn't give a toss what you or anybody else has to say, all right?" He was gesticulating wildly with his shears, losing his composure, "And besides, who are you to judge unless you've been there, and been them?"

"Oh barber, never compare yourself to others. If you do, you are insulting yourself."

Ray screwed up his face, utterly perplexed by the man's ramblings.

"I seem to have struck a nerve, barber. My sincere apologies," his voice showed a glimmer of compassion, though it was clearly exaggerated. The dark man gleamed mockingly at him through the mirror.

"I'm just – I'm just sick of hearing about it is all," Ray said, trying to cool his temper.

"Well, I was only *making conversation, mate.*"

"Very funny. Look, we're nearly done here and I've had a gutful today, all right?"

"Such passion, barber, such passion. Tell me, do you think he's singling them out *because* they're whores or is it merely coincidental?"

"Look, I said I don't want to talk about it, didn't I?"

"Why?"

"Why? What do you bloody mean *why*? Because I don't want to. Because it's evil!"

"Ahh yes barber. Yes. See *that* we can agree on. It is evil. *Necessary* evil."

"Mate, I ain't in the mood for games or that sorta bloody talk. Some of those women had kids. So either put a sock in it or we're done 'ere, all right?"

The dark man smiled.

"As you wish."

A few awkward minutes passed. If it wasn't for the snipping and shuffling of the old barber and the incessant dripping of the busted gutter just outside the shop window, the basement would've been deathly silent. Ray could still feel bubbles of anger simmering in his chest, but he was slowly calming down. Slowly. He had absolutely no idea what this man's problem was, and he had to admit he was a little unnerved by his watchful, knowing eyes. Ray took a deep breath.

"Look, I'm sorry mate. It's been a rough day, all right?"

"No need to explain, barber," he crooned, "no need to explain. Every man is entitled to his opinion."

"I suppose you're right."

"I always am, barber."

Ray forced a half-smile as he put the finishing touches on the man's haircut. He grabbed the small hand mirror from his workstation and angled it behind the dark man's skull to show him *his* handiwork.

"Splendid," he said, not even looking into the mirror. Ray shuffled to his workstation, placed the mirror on the ledge, and reached for his shaving brush and soap.

"What did I say, barber?"

"What? Oh. Sorry. Dry shave."

"Tsk tsk tsk," the dark man sucked his teeth, shook his head, "So tell me, any thoughts on who the man of the hour might be?"

"Oh for God's sake, are we still on this?"

"The Jews are the men that will not be blamed for nothing."

"What?"

"The Jews are the men that will not be blamed for nothing."

"Jews? Mate, I've absolutely no idea what you're talkin about –"

"I have it on good authority that a message – a graffito, if you will – was scrawled upon a wall above one of the harlots who met their maker on that glorious September night."

130

Ray felt a rage burn through him, a tremor of hatred he'd felt in fits and spurts these terrible few weeks. But never this strong. This fierce. *This bloke isn't gonna shut up. Just grab the razor and get this over with so we can go home.*

Ray removed the cut-throat razor from his toolbelt with an unsteady hand.

"It's an odd sentence, really. There's a double negative in there, you see. But if we translate it into proper English, I believe we get: *The Jews will not take responsibility for anything.*"

"Right," Ray said absently, placing his left hand on the man's right temple.

"So you agree?"

"What?"

"About the Jews."

"Whatever mate. Look, let's get you shaved, I best be closing."

"But you're already closed, barber."

"You know what I mean."

"What do you mean?"

Ray removed his hand and took a step back, "That I'll be finished for the day once I'm done with you."

"Done with me, yes," a vile smirk crawled across his thin lips.

Ray shook his head and took a step forward. He cocked the man's head back with a little more force than was his custom, and began to brush his bristly right cheek with quick, short strokes.

"I reckon our man has it in for them, you know – the Jews, the whores. He's punishing them. Do you own this place, barber?"

"Yes"

"Just you?"

"Yes"

"You live alone?"

"Yes. No. I mean, yes."

"Well which is it?"

"Look, it's probably best you don't talk while I've got this bloody razor right next to your eye."

"You've no idea what you're talking about, do you, barber?"

Ray had never felt so provoked. He ignored the man and continued to shave.

As he finished up the right cheek and worked his way around the chin, turning his attention to the left side, a mad thought began to take shape in the back of his mind: *what if it's him?* The hairs on the back of Ray's unsteady arms stood up. Everything seemed to slow and come into focus. He tentatively glanced up at the man's impossibly dark eyes. They were angled in his direction.

Watching.

What if it's him?

Watching.

What if it's The Ripper?

Watching.

Awful questions tore through his brain; *What if it's actually him? What if it's the bastard what took Penny? And Eve? And all those poor girls? We could put an end to this right now!*

A bead of sweat trickled down the side of Ray's face. He struggled to keep the razor steady in his quivering hand as he finished up on the man's left cheek.

"What we doin' with the whiskers?" Ray tapped the man's moustache with the handle of his razor.

"They stay, barber."

Ray nodded, tilting the man's head back, putting the blade to his gruff neck.

Do it.

"Do you think they'll ever catch him, barber?"

Do it, Ray.

"Bloody hope so," Ray sneered.

"Ahh, so you do want to talk about it?"

"No."

"Tell me, do you think he's behind these other slayings about the rookery? I believe Scotland Yard officially have him up to five, but I reckon it might be more. Don't you?"

Ray ignored the question.

There was a moment of smothering silence. Deafening, palpable silence. Mind-bending silence.

"Are you still with me, old man?"

"Fuckin' look," Ray shifted his furious gaze to the dark man's black eyes once more, "I've got this bloody razor right next to your throat. If you keep flapping your gums I might accidentally nick you – or worse."

"Or worse," the man chuckled then broke off. "Calm down, barber, calm down. A little blood never hurt anybody."

Ray was visibly shaking now, but the dark man didn't seem to notice – or care. *Bastard.* The old barber had never felt so enraged. *Fucking bastard.* There was no fear. Perhaps there should have been. Perhaps he should have been afraid of this vile man and his vile words, but there was nothing he could give or take from

Ray Tandey that he hadn't already sustained or lost.

Do it Ray!

He put the straight razor back to the man's neck.

Fucking do it!

His heart was thundering a fiery beat in his chest, he could almost feel the vibrations burning his fingertips.

Do it!

He gripped the handle of the blade tight, pushed down on the man's soft flesh, and continued to brush his neck in short, upward strokes.

Ray was maybe a minute from the end of the most testing shave of his career when the dark man started up yet again.

"I can see you're at the end of your tether, barber, so I'll just say one more thing then I'll leave you in peace," he paused for dramatic effect.

"I don't care," Ray sighed. He was sweating profusely now.

"Sure you do. See, I believe this master craftsman of ours is something of an educated man, a protected man, why, maybe even an important man."

Ray said nothing.

"Whoever he may be, you can't deny he's had a peculiar effect on the capital. Why, I think it's clear for all to see that a certain kind of mass neurosis has enveloped the East-End, no?"

Ray said nothing.

"Yes, Barber, yes. Enveloped. Consumed. An irresistible wave of madness has undoubtedly washed over the borough. Embalming the populous in a kind of blinding red mist. Oh, I believe his work will be dissected for centuries to come."

"You sound like you admire him." Ray sneered.

"Ha, yes – I suppose I do, don't I, barber? Then again, how do you know I'm *not* him?"

END HIM!

Ray didn't rise to the dark man's taunt, no matter how loud the voices in his head had begun to scream.

"I'm obviously joking. I wouldn't hurt a fly," he grinned, "although, if I was going to – shall we say – *do the deed,* then I like to think I would employ a far less barbaric method of… extermination."

The old man's blood was boiling in his veins. His pulse was racing at an impossible speed. Rage. Fury. Hatred. Murderous hatred.

We've nothing to lose, just do it!

"Take that incident in the public house over on the High Street the other month."

Ray gripped his straight razor a little tighter.

DO IT!

"I read in the papers there was no blood or gore, which is far more to my taste – but, then again, we're all different. Aren't we, old man?"

Their eyes locked for the last time as Ray ceased his strokes with the cut-throat razor. He pressed the silver blade against the dark man's left carotid artery.

"You know what they say, barber – *one man's meat is another man's poison.*"

Ray Tandey took a deep breath, and finished the job.

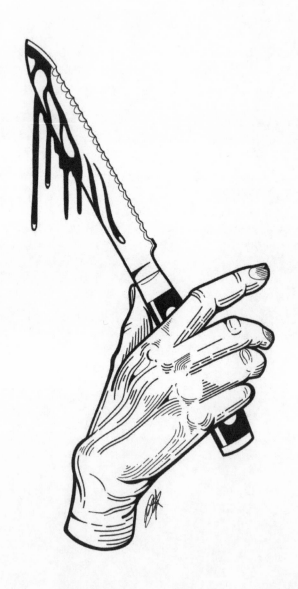

NIGHT TERROR

You are a child. You are eight years old. You live in a small, damp room on a dangerous street in a desperate part of town. Lucie is your sister, and she lies fast asleep in the bed beside your own, putting faraway foghorns to shame like she always has, and always will.

It is a cold and blustery November night, and the strong winds, laced with rain, can be heard sobbing down the giant chimney breast that dominates the fourteen-foot-square room. So harsh and tormented are their cries that they somehow manage to drown out the throaty grunts and snores coming from your big sister. Something you would've deemed *impossible* before tonight.

It is late. Extremely late. Impossibly late. That time of night in which you feel as if the whole world is empty, and you're all alone in some strange and non-existent time. A time that belongs to the creatures of the shadows, and the wandering, sinstorous demons who prowl the depths of wicked dreams and nightmares. You look towards the old brass clock atop the cast iron fireplace and it looks as if it reads half past two – you think – but it's pretty hard to tell in this black light.

You are worried. You are scared. The cold and

uninviting city outside your dusty, ground floor window tosses and turns in its sleep, but not you – not tonight. You are tired, you are weary and yet, you dare not close your eyes.

Despite being tucked up in the so-called comfort and safety of your own bed, you are on the verge of tears. Your eyes, bloodshot, bleary and wide with terror, dart about the blue-black room in search of the one thing in this world that would put these feelings to bed, but you cannot find it. You cannot see it. You cannot, to be precise, see *her*. You cannot see Mum.

You want your mum. You *need* your mum. You need her now more than you've ever needed anything in your short, fatherless life, but she isn't here. She isn't home. *Where is she?*

Your face is prickling with a hundred pins and needles, your ears buzzing with a thousand angry wasps, and your heart, your heart is drumming the unsteady beat of a million drums in your frail, pale chest, and you *want* your mum. *Where is she?*

You have no business being up this late and if Mum caught you, you'd be sure to get one of her infamous tongue lashings but, in this moment, in the doom and gloom of the mouldy room, you do not care. You'd take the lashings. You'd welcome them with open arms if it meant you got to see her face just for a second.

You have just woken from a nightmare. A terrible, recurring nightmare. The one about The Man; The Man who smiles, The Man who points, The Man with the rotten yellow teeth, The Man with the big red knife. He haunts you. Stalks you. He follows you up and out of the shadows of your dark, vivid dreams and into the even blacker world of this year 1888. Mum says he isn't real. Mum says it's just a dream. Mum says you have a wild imagination, and that the horrible man's no different to the ghost of Jacob Marley or the Demon Barber of Fleet Street. But what does she know? She wasn't there. She didn't see. He *is* real. You *have* seen him, for that is why you dream of his evil face over and over again. You've seen him up close and far too personal. So close you could smell his hot and sour breath. So personal you could taste the dried blood on the end of his rusty blade.

It was eight weeks ago. The day of the big storm, the day they found Miss Nichols behind the old slaughterhouse. Mum had been crying all afternoon, insisting you and your sister let her "grieve in peace". You are only eight years old. You know little of death and grief, but you did as you were told, heading out into the lanes in search of something, anything, to pass the time.

The late afternoon sky was a peculiar colour you'd rarely seen – greyish red with strokes of luminous green. A few drops of rain hung on the sticky, dirt-smelling air, and you could almost feel the long and angry vibrations of thunder on the warm winds.

Lucie wanted to go look through the market stalls over on Brick Lane before the storm hit, and you were more than happy to tag along. You had a feeling the Bird Fair might be in town which meant you might just see some budgies or canaries or maybe even a funny grey parrot. If you were *really* lucky, you might just catch a glimpse of a rainbow lorikeet. At the very least, there were always the horses. You love birds, but horses are your favourite and, more often than not, Brick Lane was absolutely teeming with brown and black beauties.

"I c-c-can't see the B-B-Bird Fair," you said to your sister, leaning, stretching, practically bouncing on the tips of your brittle toes. Brick lane, as always, was beyond crowded.

"I c-can't see them, Lucie –"

"They're probably over on Sclater Street ain't they, you little ratbag," she snapped, "just stop going on about it, all right?"

"C-can we go? P-please?"

"No."

"P-p-please Lucie?"

"No."

"J-just for a l-little b-bit."

"Oh for God's sake," she conceded, "right, you know where Sclater Street is, don't you?"

You nodded.

"Where then?"

"Up th-there," you said, pointing excitedly, "to th-the right. Past the b-bakery –"

"Right, you've got half an hour, all right? But don't tell mum I let you go off on your tod!"

"I w-w-won't,"

"Jake!"

"I won't, I p-promise."

"Good. Right, there's clocks all through here. Just meet me back here at half five, yeah?"

You nodded.

"And don't talk to anyone."

You nodded.
"All right, go on then. Go."
You ran.

By the time you got to Sclater Street, it was too late. The storm clouds were circling, and most of the bird merchants had already packed up and left. You looked around, but there wasn't much to see. Just a few pigeons, some doves and a couple of chickens. No budgies, no canaries, no parrots. No parakeets. You were disappointed, annoyed. You sighed. You were about to turn back towards the lane when a massive fork of lightning tore across the angry sky – *kkkkrrrrrrrrccccctttcchhh*. You threw your hands to your ears in horror, scrunching your eyes as tight as they would shut, ducking for cover. You could hear the thunderous echoes over the hammering of your heart. You hated thunder and lightning. You hated storms.

You remained crouched for a few seconds before you found the courage to peel your eyes open, and then you saw it. A sea, an ocean, an entire universe of black birds all swooping and looping, and diving and parting and joining in perfect unison against the grey red sky. *Wow*. You had never seen such a sight. There must've been at least a thousand. You stood up. *Is anybody else seeing this?* You blinked in glorious disbelief, but the enormous flock of birds were still dancing their graceful dance. *Is this real?* If it were, you were sure this congregation, this dance, this dazzling display of harmony *had* to have a name of some kind but – in this moment – you did not care. It was breath-taking.

As you watched on, your mouth in your hands, the flock began to twirl across the sky in a westerly direction. It was getting smaller. *Where are they going?* Your feet shuffled in spite of yourself. *Are they scared of the storm like me?*

Before long, you were running and skipping across the grazed, dirty cobbles – your head in the clouds – ducking and diving and laughing through the lanes and throngs of city dwellers with a grace that would've impressed the starlings you were so eager to catch. Time flies when you're having fun. The chase was on.

Try as you might, there was just no way you could keep up with the flock's swiftness. They were getting away from you but, every now and then, the giant silhouette seemed to swarm closer – only to swing back, up and away from the blackbrick chimneys and pointed arches of the East-End, up into the red west. You were just about to give up the chase when a sudden blast of thunder rocked the entire world, snapping you from your reverie, stopping you dead in your tracks. The black birds dissipated.

You looked around.

Where am I? You were lost.

What time is it? You were late.

Your eyes darted about the brick walls and houses that lined the road in search of a clue as to your whereabouts.

Nothing. Nobody.

Oh no.

You started to panic.

Oh no, oh no, oh no.

Despairing, you turned on your heels, heading back

the way you came in a desperate attempt to retrace your steps, but it was no use. The monstrous maze had chewed you up, swallowed you whole. *Oh no, oh no, oh no.*

You ran.

You ran, and you ran, and you ran, darting in and out of darkened alleyways and back passages, thoughts racing, sounds amplified, jagged shards of lightning cracking open the charred sky every other minute and then – hope. A street sign.

"Th-Thrawl Street," you rasped, looking up at the stained sign through misty eyes. It rang a bell. The street itself didn't look familiar but the name definitely struck a distant chord. "Thrawl Street," you said again, edging towards the sign. *Thrawl Street* – and then it came to you – *Miss Nichols, this is where Miss Nichols used to live. Wasn't it? I've been here before with Mum and- and didn't we come down Brick Lane to get here? Maybe. Maybe.*

Something lukewarm and wet tapped the nape of your neck. You lifted your gaze from the sign, looking skywards. Rain. It was here. The storm was here. The sky had darkened into midnight. You stuck out your palm, and another fat bead of rain splashed down on your tiny pink fingertips. You rubbed it with your thumb. Another bolt of lightning. Another crash of thunder. You ran.

You ran, and you ran, and you ran down the neverending street, your tiny feet slapping against the dirty pavement in blind hope your hunch might be true, that Brick Lane lay just ahead beyond the sheet of smog you were fast approaching. Out of the corner of your eye, a large cat eyeballed you as you tore down the street like a tiny locomotive. Usually, you would stop to say "Hello," but – in this frantic moment – you had far more important things to worry about. *I'm late! Lucie's gonna kill me! I'm late! Lucie's gonna kill me! I'm late!*

As you neared the wall of smoke, you heard the reassuring *clipclopclipclop* of a horse and cart over the babbling hum of what had to be (*had to be*) the Brick Lane market. You put your head down and dug deep, a warming sense of relief beginning to wash over the shore of your racing mind as you neared the sanctuary of the crowd, and – you hoped – your big sister.

And then it happened.

The Man who would haunt your dreams for years to come burst out of the smog like a bat out of hell, wheeling a janky old handcart you were powerless to avoid. You crashed into it with a terrible bang –

"'ERE, MIND WHERE YOU'RE GOIN' YOU FUCKIN' LITTLE BASTARD!" the Man roared.

"S-sorry m-mister," you said, "I… I… d-d-didn't see ya. I'm s-s-s–"

"Didn't see me?!" the Man croaked, his face twisted in something beyond rage, beyond hate. "Didn't fuckin' see me?! You're havin' a FUCKIN' laugh, int cha?!"

You stood wide-eyed and stunned, your eyes locked on the boiling man's red right hand.

He had a knife.

"You hear what I bloody said, boy? Or you FUCKIN' deaf as well as d-d-d-dumb?!"

"Uh-uh-uh," you couldn't speak. It was hard enough to get the words out at the best of times but you *couldn't* speak, you couldn't move. Something warm and wet in the crotch of your trousers. *Oh, oh no. I'm sorry. Oh no, please.* Your bottom lip began to tremble. Your eyes, still misty from before, began to sting and fill with salty tears. *Mum.* Your knees felt as if they could buckle at any second. *Help.* You couldn't take your eyes off the rusty knife.

The Man looked at the blade.

Please help me.

Then he looked at you.

He's-he's going to get me!

The Man's evil eyes went back to the knife once more. He slowly raised it, pointing the tip of the dark red knife right between your glassy brown eyes. *Mummy, Lucie, somebody.* It was the biggest knife you'd ever seen, and it was now but a whisker away from your wet, pink nose.

The Man slowly lowered his gaunt face to your level, looking you square in the eye. His eyes were piss-yellow, unblinking. His ashen skin was the colour of milky tea. He looked ill. He looked dead. And then he smiled a hideous smile you would never forget.

"If I ever see your stinkin' face again, boy," he growled, "I'll cut your fuckin' nose off 'n' feed it to the dogs. Now… *FUCK… OFF*!"

You don't know how or where you found the strength, but you bolted into the smoke, tears streaming down your face. *Oh god, oh god, oh god, please let this be Brick Lane, please let this be Brick Lane, please, oh please, oh please…*

It was.

*

By the time you found your way back to the agreed meeting point, the rain was coming down in tonnes and avalanches, and Lucie was hopping mad. You'd never seen her so angry.

"Where the bloody hell have you been!?" She cried, grabbing you by the shoulders and shaking you profusely, tears in her eyes. "Twenty minutes! Twenty minutes I've been standing here! Twenty *bloody* minutes!"

You said you were sorry. You said you got lost. You tried to tell her about the man and the cart and the knife, but she wouldn't listen.

"Not a bloody word of this to Mum, you hear!?"

You nodded.

"God," she grimaced, looking down, "what the bloody hell have you done to your trousers? You stink!"

You cried.

"Oh, oh Jake, I'm sorry. I-I just got scared," she put an arm around you, "Come on, let's get out of this horrible rain and get you cleaned up."

Over the coming days, you did your best to forget what happened, but you couldn't shake the image of the Man and his bloody knife. It clung to your fragile mind like a thick mess of cobwebs. Then came the dreams. They were nearly always the same: you'd find yourself alone in the middle of Thrawl Street, peering up at the mounted sign and trying to make sense of the words, the world. A single blob of rain would rap the back of your neck. You'd wipe it away then hang out a hand in hope – or fear – of catching the next drop. Sometimes it was regular old rain. Sometimes it was red. Sometimes you'd turn and run for the smoke at the end of the road immediately. Sometimes you'd just stare at your crimson-smeared fingertips then a clap of thunder would send you on your way. Sometimes you knew what was coming. Sometimes you did not. Sometimes, when you remembered what lay waiting in the mist, you'd turn and run in the opposite direction but the street was just one big mirror. Whatever happened, the outcome was always the same – he would be there. The Butcher. The Cat's Meat Man. No matter how hard you tried to avoid that janky old cart, you always found it. The Man would roar, your blood would freeze, the knife would appear and the scene would repeat itself over and over again. When you woke, it was often to the sounds of your own cries, although, sometimes, you'd lay dormant, frozen, unable to move a muscle, unable make a sound. And then, in the corner of the dark room or sometimes on the ceiling, you would see the Man's alabaster face. Sometimes you'd scream. Sometimes you'd wet the bed. Sometimes Mum would come. Sometimes – like this cold and blustery November night – she would not.

Where is she?

Lucie still doesn't believe you, and she made you promise – made you swear – not to tell Mum what happened that day. So, you have to lie and pretend it's just a figment of your imagination and nothing more, and you hate your sister for it. She keeps saying that you're stupid, that he doesn't exist, that he's not the one you should be worried about, because there is another, far more evil man who stalks the streets of London after dark, and he *is* real. For some reason, your Mum and Lucie argue about him a lot. You don't understand why they fight and shout. You think it's something about Mum's job, but you're not sure – you don't even know what she does for a living. She tells Lucie she is scared, and tired, but someone's "gotta put food on the bloody table". Lucie says she should give it all up and do something else and if it's so important then why doesn't she just take her with her to help. And that's when Mum gets *really* angry. You are an eight-year-old child; you know nothing of these things.

"Lucie," you hiss, "Lucie."

Nothing.

"Lucie, w-wake up."

"Huh?" she groans, twisting her head towards you, half asleep, "what? what's up?"

"It's Th-Th-The Ca-Cat's Meat M-Man again."

"Oh… go… just go back to sleep."

"I can't. I w-won't."

"Mmmmgh."

"Wh-where's M-Mum? Sh-she sh-should be back by n-now, right?"

No answer.

She snores.

You sigh inwardly.

Where is she?

The howling winds continue their assault on Dorset Street, hurling thick sheets of rain and sleet into the brick façade of your tiny, narrow home. The single dusty window that looks out onto the empty street seems almost willing to absorb the brunt of the blows, taking everything the wet gusts have to offer, protecting the dingy room and your trembling body from the cold, hard rains as they thrash the small glass pane and trickle down. *Where is she? She can't be out in this weather, can she? Can she? Come home, Mum. Please, come home.*

And then it stops. The wind, the rain, the moaning and groaning of the chimney breast; the empty fireplace; even Lucie falls silent. Everything just... stops. Even the ticking of the old brass clock. The world has ground to a halt and every last hair on your trembling body rises up in response to the inexplicable and immense stillness.

You listen.

You pull the thin cotton sheet up to your chin, glancing at your sister to check she's still in the room, still in the world. Suddenly, off somewhere, a sound. A dog. A big, angry dog barking and snarling and howling at something or someone –

"I'll cut your FUCKIN' nose off 'n' feed it to the DOGSSS," the Man's gruff, blazing voice rips through your soul, and a sharp gust of wind tears down the chimney, its cry – its dreadful essence – filling the dark blue room like an evil spirit. You yank the bedsheet up and over your tiny head, slamming it down onto the hard mattress in terror. *Oh no, oh no, oh no.*

Something is going to happen.

But there is only silence, again – nothing, again.

The din that preceded the ghostly interlude slowly comes back into focus: the rain, the wind, the ticking of the clock, Lucie's snoring – they are all back and the roars and barks of the man and his dog are no more. You hesitantly peel the cover off your prickly face. Everything is as it was before. The lashing winds and rain have eased to a kind of low, static fizz that soothes your jangling nerves. If it wasn't for Lucie, the room would feel quite peaceful. Pleasant, even, but the harsh and worrying fact remains – Mum still isn't home.

"Where is she?" you whisper into the murky room, your hands clasped together in prayer. "God, I'll n-never talk about th-the m-man with the kn-kn-knife again if you p-please send Mum through the d-d-door, I swear."

The wet winds rise up, rattling the front door and window almost in response to your prayers, but nobody was listening. Not now, not tonight, not ever. *Where are you? Where are you, Mum?*

Clipclopclipclopclipclopclipclop–

You bolt upright.

Clipclopclipclopclipclopclipclop–

You listen closely.

Clipclopclipclopclipclopclipclop–

The clangs are distant and muffled by the weather but you'd recognise that sound anywhere. "Horsies," you mutter under your breath to nobody in particular, your eyes brightening for the first time this awful, long night. "They're coming," you whisper, flinging and kicking the sheet from your body, rolling onto your side in one swift movement. Your feet are a centimetre or so from the wooden planks when a terrible thought explodes in your mind (*he's under the bed!*). You hurl your legs back up.

Clipclopclipclopclipclopclipclop–
The horses are getting closer.
Clipclopclipclopclipclopclipclop–
You don't want to miss them.
Clipclopclipclopclipclopclipclop–
You shift your fearful gaze to the window.
Clipclopclipclopclipclopclipclop–
You look at Lucie.
Clipclopclipclopclipclopclipclop–

Gripping the edge of your bed, you peer over the side, grimacing, utterly convinced you will see an icy hand clutching a bloody knife, but there is nothing there- *of course* there is nothing there. *Silly*. Just to be safe, just to be certain, you shuffle your upper body to the very edge of the mattress, leaning and craning your head down and slowly, tentatively, you look under your bed...

Nothing. The coast is clear.
You breathe a sigh of relief.
You swallow and get out of bed.

The floorboards creak and squeak beneath your cold, bare feet as you inch towards the window. *Maybe there'll be more than two horsies. Maybe there'll be different colours and kinds, and maybe there'll be a pale horse. Maybe they'll be pulling a nice, fancy carriage, and maybe it'll stop outside the window and maybe, just maybe, Mum will be inside.*

As you walk the planks with caution, you glance in the direction of the moaning fireplace, then up at the old clock: ten past three. You never knew such a time of night existed. You do now. Shifting your gaze back towards the glass pane, you take a deep breath, hold it tight, and approach the window to the outside world.

You carefully prop your elbows atop the dusty, splintered windowsill, and breathe. *Made it.* You compose yourself for a second – maybe two – before wiping away the foggy moisture from the frigid glass – *eeeuuughheeeeuuughh.*

What do you see?

A ghost? A fiend? A beast?

A man?

Through the small, blurry opening, you look right then left then right again, but you cannot see much of anything – let alone the horses. You can still hear them and they certainly sound as if they are getting closer, but they are nowhere to be seen. *Where are they?* You wipe away a little more moisture in an attempt to widen your scope. You squint. You peer through the looking glass. There are – you think – a string of old lanterns mounted along the endless row of blackbrick buildings opposite, but only two of them look to be alight.To the right, a handful of small windows glow a dull shade of yellow. They are hardly worth mentioning. To the left, there is nothing. Blackness. The only real source of light – if you can call it that – is the full yellow moon that hangs low and to the distant right. It's blotchy. Cracked. Bright. It casts a wide beam of shimmering yellow down upon the rippling puddles that have all but drowned the dreary road. Dorset Street has never looked so dark, so grim. The hairs on the back of your beck prickle as a set of glacial, wraithlike hands wrap around your throat. *Maybe this was a mistake.* Maybe you should go back to bed –

From the right, the silhouettes of two large horses creep into view. Trotting and snorting, clipping and clopping and flicking their long heads to the moon as if to shake the rainwater from their soaking mains. One of the horses lets out a soft neigh and, as they saunter clearer into view, you notice one of them has a large white spot on its forehead. "Patch," you whisper into the damp window, your eyes gleaming. The other horse, as far as you can tell, is completely black. "Shadow," you croak, applying a thin layer of mist to the window. You wipe it away.

You can now see the outline of the coachman's top hat swaying from side to side as he guides Patch and Shadow through the shallow river formerly known as Dorset Street. The large wooden wheels rattle and splash through the dark water, and a warming sense of expectation settles on your mind in a pleasant haze. You have yourself a front row seat to the show. You press your nose to the glass. Warm puffs of air creep from your pink nostrils, causing the corner of the window and your poor line of sight to fill – once again – with steam. You chuckle. You wipe away the fresh white mist, then watch the horse and carriage roll closer.

A sudden, bittersweet pang of realisation punctures your heart, causing it to drop and sink into the pit of your empty stomach- the beautiful dark horses are right in front of your eyes in all their glory, but the carriage isn't stopping; alas, it cannot be carrying Mum. You sigh. It was a long shot, but a shot nonetheless. *Where is she?*

Patch, Shadow, the coachman and the unlit carriage roll by, and you're suddenly overcome with a sense of despair as a terrible, almost unthinkable question begins to form in the back of your mind, a question you've been fighting back all night – *what if I never see her again?* Your bottom lip starts to quiver; a lump takes shape in the centre of your dry, dry throat, and you exhale a shaky breath into the window as the rear of the carriage gradually disappears into the black – suddenly, it stops. *Mum?* Your pulse quickens. Your heart rises back into your chest. You frantically wipe the right-hand side of the window, sliding your feet and pressing the right side of your face almost through the cold, damp glass as you try to find the best angle. It's difficult, really difficult, but you can just about see a vague shadow emerging from the right side of the carriage – two shadows, two shapes. A man and a woman – you think. One looks to be larger than the other – mainly because of the big top hat – but that's about all that really distinguishes the two figures from one another. The black shapes approach the row of houses, pause, then disappear into what can only be a doorway. You think it's Miller's Court. Maybe it's one of Mum's friends. Maybe it's Miss Cox or Miss Kelly. You can't be sure, but... it doesn't matter. *It's not Mum.*

A soft orange square appears in the area of the large brick building the shadows stepped into – a lantern, you presume – and your heart drops with it. *It's not Mum. It's not Mum.*

Patch, Shadow and the big dark carriage soon disappear out of sight, and you stare into oblivion through sore and teary eyes. *Where is she?* And then you get a wild idea- *What if I go and ask Miss Cox or Miss Kelly or whoever went into Miller's Court if they've seen Mum? She's over there all the time. I can put on my coat and my cap and my shoes and sneak out quickly. Lucie would never know.* The orange square suddenly vanishes, no sooner than it had appeared. *Strange.*

You're just about to turn from the window, when you hear a howl or a scream of some kind. A lady? A dog? A dog. *A DOG!* Something across the street catches your eye. Another shadow. Another shape, slight and narrow, swiftly gliding across the pavement from left to right. It moves past the once-orange window, past Miller's Court, gradually coming into some sort of vague focus in the moonlight. And then it stops.

What is it?

The shadow turns towards Miller's Court, and then it slowly turns towards you. *What?*

It steps into the road.

It puts a hand into its robe or pocket or whatever, and slowly removes something. Something long and pointy. *No.* Your blood turns cold. *No.* Your heart begins to freeze. The shadow stops again. *No.* It tilts its hooded head to the side, taking another step towards you, and then another. *Oh God, please no.* Every last fibre of your being is screaming at you to turn and run and dive into the "comfort" and "safety" of your own bed, but it's as though someone or something has nailed your bare feet to the hardwood floors. The shadow, still moving, raises its right arm and points the long thing directly at you.

He's found me!

It breaks into a run.

The Man's found me!

The rain crashes into the window, the wind barks down the chimney, and – for some reason – you suddenly become aware of the ticking of the clock behind you. *Time's up, Jake.* You cry out, miraculously breaking free of the imaginary nails, and scramble for Lucie's bed.

"What the –" Lucie bolts up right.

You scream "HE'S COMING!" as you hurl yourself into her lap. *Ccchkchhcchckckhckk* – something clatters into the front door, banging and clawing and scratching at the lock, the doorknob shaking furiously.

"IT'S THE CAT'S MEAT MAN!"

The door flies open.

Every terrible thought, every hellish vision you ever had in your short life comes rushing to the shore of your shattered mind in a crashing red wave. You scream.

The shadow bursts into the room holding a large cast iron key.

"What the bloody hell are you two still doing up!?"

You run to your mum.

NO REST
FOR THE WICKED

The following letter was received by the Central News Agency at their premises in the city of London on 11th November, 1888.

Two days prior, the body of 25-year-old Mary Jane Kelly was found extensively mutilated in her bed. The entire surface of her abdomen and thighs had been removed, and the abdominal cavity emptied of its organs. Her breasts had been cut off, and her arms, neck and face severely mutilated.

The true origin and authenticity of the letter are debated to this day.

Dear Boss

Did you miss me? Its been a little while since Jacky's double event but well worth the wait this last job. I've been tied up with far less exciting work you see but fear not, your old pal is still alive and kicking. What is it they say boss? No rest for the wicked ha ha. I was sad to hear Commissioner Warren left his hole because he couldn't buckle me. This whore was for him. My best work yet I'd say nobody to disturb so I could take my time and do my work in pieces. The lady enjoyed her pretty necklace but her heart just wasn't in it shame about her pretty face. I hear the locals kicked up a fuss. How many is that now boss? I've a terrible memory. Never mind my knives will never fail but I fear I may have peaked so maybe I shall quit ripping for good and look for pastures new but maybe not we shall see.

Yours truly
Jack the Ripper
PS. They say I'm an actor now. ha ha

BEAST OF THE THAMES

The beast moved swiftly along the riverbank with hot blood pouring from its mouth. Some of it belonged to the beast; most of it did not. Some of it gushed from a thick, flat nose, and had combined with the old man's flesh to make a kind of metallic strawberry jam that appeared black in the dim light.

The beast was frightened. The beast was confused. The beast was lost, wild and utterly consumed with a senseless, blood-thirsty rage that it did not understand. It had no concept of these emotions or why it was feeling them. It didn't know what was going on, where it was, how it had gotten here or where it was even going. In this moment, it knew but one thing – and one thing only – it *needed* to kill again.

It was a bitterly cold night in the middle of November, and the only thing blacker than the murky river was the city of London itself. There were no stars, no moon; no electricity, for it would not come to this part of the capital for a few years yet. It was a dark night, in a dark place, at a very dark time.

A man and a woman walked slowly along the side of the river, the warm air from their lungs frosting in the air. They stopped and stood for a moment, staring into the dirty water, inky black with ripples of green, gold and silver toing and froing in a beautiful display of serenity. If it wasn't for the dreadful smell, this gaslit winter scene could almost pass as romantic. Idyllic. The couple shared a quick kiss then shuffled arm in arm towards the steps that led to the old stone bridge. They were both drunk and the man tripped on the top step. The woman giggled, took his hand, and together they staggered along the bridge, laughing and joking.

The lateness of the hour meant few people were inclined to use the poorly-lit bridge, and the cold winds meant that even fewer would feel the need to loiter on its exposed length; but there was another, far more sinister reason for its emptiness this moonless night. There had been another murder. The Ripper had struck again and, according to the papers, the other night's brutal killing of Mary Jane Kelly was the worst yet in what was now becoming a long red line of unthinkable cruelty. The latest victim brought the official death toll up to six, but the bloodhounds in the press were doing their best to stir the bloody pot and bump up those numbers. Just imagine, over a million people all teetering on the precipice, peering over their cold and cynical shoulders every time they heard a sound – strange or otherwise – as the entire East-End of London spiralled deeper and deeper into a winter of despair.

"I can't get over how bloody cold it is," the drunken

man declared to the woman, his speech slurred, "I mean, it's only November but it's already like the fuckin' Arctic through here, know what I mean?"

"Ohhh, you've been up that way before on your travels have ya, love?" The woman replied in a high, facetious tone, "Didn't know ya was an explorer *and* a blacksmith."

"Keep mouthing off like that, woman, and I'll be having my bloody coat back thank ya very much."

The woman jabbed the man's stomach playfully. He let out an exaggerated cry, clutching his gut. They laughed, embraced, and headed south along the secluded bridge.

Several hundred feet ahead, the bloodied beast sensed a sudden change in the atmosphere. It snapped its bulging green eyes to the black, velvet sky. It listened. It heard the sound of the couple's laughter crisply on the biting breeze, but it couldn't see them – not yet. The beast sucked a deep breath from the cold air, twisted its bulging head towards the faraway sounds, and ran.

The couple continued along the old bridge at a leisurely pace, their feet scuffing and scraping against the cobbled ground as they inched towards the centre of the structure and their untimely deaths.

The beast could see them now. It didn't know what it was seeing, exactly, but it could smell and taste the stink and that sent it into a frenzy. The beast unleashed a guttural, blood-chilling scream and accelerated.

"Did you hear that?" the woman stopped, feeling fear for the first time.

"Aye? Oh, oh yeah, probably just one of those bloody tugboats pulling out of the harbour or summit," the man replied, pointing lazily towards the docks.

"No, no, it-it sounded like… like a howl. Like a dog or a wolf or summit."

"A wolf?" the man chuckled, "Seen many of them on *your* travels, have ya love?"

"Shut up Jim, you –"

And then they saw it. Tall, broad, limbs flailing madly; getting bigger and bigger with every millisecond as it hurtled towards them at an impossible speed.

"Bloody hell, have a look at the size of this bastard," the man scoffed, oblivious to the severity of the situation.

"J-J-Jim, let's go back, yeah?" The woman pleaded, trembling.

"Aye? Oh he's probably just being chased by the Old Bill or summit love, don't worry. We'll just stay out of his way and step to the side like –"

Another thunderous, nerve-shredding cry filled the world, plunging them into a stone-cold pool of sobriety.

"Jesus fuck!" The man cried into the wind, grabbing hold of the woman and spinning her to face the way they came.

"Jesus! Okay, run, run, Claire, *run*! RUN!" The man shoved the woman ahead of him.

"JIM, OH MY GOD JIM!"

"GO! NOW! RUN! RUN! *RUN!*"

They ran.

They ran as fast as their unsteady legs would carry them, but they didn't get far.

The beast closed the gap in a roaring heartbeat, leaping on top of the man's shoulders and clamping its teeth down hard on his exposed jugular. There was no initial pain, only a violent jerk on the side of his neck as he fell to the ground with the hulking mass of wild flesh still straddling his back.

"Jesus!" He bellowed as hot blood erupted from his carotid artery like a busted pipe and, with that, pain struck like a fork of lightning. He screamed.

The woman, still running, snapped her head around to face the ear-splitting cacophony and was overcome with a sudden bout of dizziness. She stumbled, froze, and put her hands to her face.

"JIM!" she cried, tears streaming down her red face, her brain refusing to deal with what her eyes were seeing. She wanted to faint, she wanted to look away more than anything, but she couldn't. She was drunk on panic and in the paralysis of her shock and repulsion, the woman tasted hot bile and looked on. She looked on in something far beyond horror as the repugnant scene unfolded before her wide, wet and disbelieving eyes.

The man was fumbling frantically to his feet, clutching at his gushing neck when the beast smothered and pinned him down with its enormous frame, flipping the defenceless, blood-soaked man onto his back with sickening ease, its eyes ablaze, black lips stretching back from scarlet gums and yellow teeth in a hideous growl, and then it began to furiously pound, thump, claw and tear at his face and throat. The man cried out: "OH GOD!" But in the depths of his burning brain he knew his prayers were in vain, he knew that The Almighty had abandoned this shithole a long time ago and, above all, Jim Price knew his number had been called. He felt blood spilling from his throat, pouring from his mouth which was being furiously hacked and lashed and smashed by the grotesque waves of a bloodthirsty storm he could not weather. He felt mind-blowing pain scorching out of the redness of his eyes and it was not his past that flashed before them but a future he would never have. A future with the woman he loved and their unborn child. Hunks and chunks of flesh flew from his wet face in a scarlet mist as he gagged and drowned in a mess of thick blood, phlegm, and pulp – *hergghh heergghh*. After maybe thirty seconds of carnage, the beast ceased its attack and began to scoop large mounds of warm mince, blood and bone from the man's smashed head. It shovelled them into its frothing mouth, crunched then swallowed. Crunched then swallowed. The man's legs shook violently. The woman screamed.

As the beast turned its attention to the helpless woman, Constables Sloan and Tyler broke into a sprint towards the blood-chilling cries. They'd been patrolling the southern embankment when they heard a volley of strange sounds coming from the long stone bridge.

"D'ya reckon it's him, Sloan? D'ya reckon it's The Ripper?"

"Shut the hell up and keep running!"

"He's a bit of a way outside of Whitechapel if it bloody is him –"

"Shut up Tyler, for fuck's sake!"

They were maybe four hundred feet from the

massacre when the woman's paralysis miraculously broke. She scrambled to the side of the bridge, launching herself onto its stony ledge, ready to jump. She didn't have time to consider the height of the drop to the freezing black below. Thirty feet? Forty?

She didn't know.

She didn't care.

She couldn't outrun this thing. She had to get away somehow –

The beast grabbed a handful of her thick black hair and yanked her from the ledge like a rag doll. The fear and panic the woman had felt less than a minute ago now paled in comparison to what was coursing through her veins. She kicked and punched and scratched with everything she had but it was no use. The beast didn't even flinch. The beast would not be denied.

She wailed.

The rampaging beast didn't understand her cries – and yet for a fleeting moment... maybe it did. There was perhaps a shred, a molecule of realisation or recognition – or *something* – as it drew the woman's pulsing head to its evil, elongated face.

(*Eeeeeee*)

(*EeeeEEeee*)

Something in the beast's head – a sound? a noise? a thought? Something.

(*EeeeEEeeel*)

(*EeeeeelLLll*)

The beast didn't understand.

"SOMEBODY HELP ME PLEASE –" the beast sank its bloody teeth into the screaming woman's upper lip and nose, ripping them away from her face like melted cheese before chomping into the crook of her neck and thrashing violently. The nerves in her brain jangled around like fireworks. Her feet slapped against the ground like the fins of a fish out of water. The pain was indescribable. She cried out with one last guttural call for help before the beast wrenched her tiny head back, cracking her neck like a breadstick and ending her life. The beast tossed the limp body to the side, roared, then bolted northwards with a mouthful of wet tendons, its ears ringing profusely.

"Bloody hell," Constable Tyler shouted, reaching for his whistle, still running, "what the hell is it, Sloan? What the bloody hell is it?"

"I dunno lad, keep running!" Sloan spat back.

The weary constables were nearing the bloodbath, blasting sharp puffs of hot air into their whistles, when they began to slow and wilt as the grisly scene came into focus.

Constable Sloan removed the whistle from his lips with a shaky hand, a thick string of spit breaking off six inches from his now gaping mouth.

"Dear God!" he cried, his eyes wide with incredulous, abject horror, his face numb, his throat dry. "St-st-stay back Tyler. Don't get any closer, all right, lad?"

Tyler ignored his partner's request and reluctantly shuffled towards the gory carnage, towards what remained of the man's head- a steaming, lumpy stew of brains and bone on a deathbed of crimson bricks.

"Oh-oh my god," Tyler put a rattling fist to his mouth, "Who? Who? Wh-what?" His knees buckled. He stumbled to the nearby ledge and vomited. Sloan shifted his eyes from the unfathomable gore to his fallen partner and took a step towards him.

"I'm all right, I'm all right," Tyler reassured him, holding out a firm but shaky hand. He wasn't all right, but Sloan nodded, lifting his gaze towards the body of the woman twenty paces ahead. He took a deep breath and approached.

"God almighty," he coughed into the rusty, shit-smelling air, "T-Tyler. You just stay there, mate. You stay there. We'll have more men here soon –"

A deep and thunderous roar from the north singed the cold air.

Both Sloan and Tyler's eyes darted towards the terrible sound. They could just about make out the giant shadow of the beast before it vanished into what could only be the entrance to the Monument Underground.

"Wh-wh-what the bloody hell is it, Sloan? It-it-it can't be him, can it? It can't be The Ripper?" Tyler rasped through a series of shallow burps and grunts, propping himself up against the ledge for support.

"I-I don't know mate, I don't think so," Sloan croaked, his voice rusty with fatigue, powerless to tear his eyes from the end of the bridge, "but whatever it is, we're gonna need all the bloody rifles we can get."

A well-dressed man checked his silver timepiece as the steam train screeched into Whitechapel station. He shook his head and *tsk*ed. *Bloody District Rail*, he thought, *even at this hour the idiots can't get their poxy trains to run on time*. He snapped his pocket watch shut with a sharp *thwap*, seized his tan leather briefcase, and made his way towards the nearest door.

The empty ghost train he was about to disembark was a whole four minutes late as it ground to a halt at the platform, but this wasn't the reason for the reporter's bad mood this late evening. He'd been assigned to the Ripper Case by his local paper – the *Daily Echo* – who thought it "imperative" that he got to Whitechapel *'post-haste'* to interview the locals about the latest murder. He didn't see why he couldn't just get a train the following morning or, better yet, not bother at all.

Whitechapel is the bloody pits, he thought, *who the hell cares what goes on here? Bloody peasants brought it on themselves if you ask me. Why couldn't Jenkins just give the damn assignment to Green or Anderson or someone who gives a toss?*

He stepped off the train, and looked about the dirty, vacant platform. *Shithole.* The iron doors slammed shut behind him. The mechanical leviathan pulled off in the direction it had come, for this was the end of the line. The dark-haired reporter watched the train disappear into the pitch black, then walked to a nearby bench to tie his shoe.

The invisible train omitted a loud, unusual growl that echoed through the tunnel. The man briefly looked up from his laces, frowned, then returned to his shoe.

"Right," he muttered, straightening up, pulling the lapels of his thick, black overcoat up around his neck, "let's get to the inn and get this bloody over with." He picked up his briefcase, turned, and stepped straight into a small puddle of urine.

"Oh, oh… the filthy, rotten bastards," he snarled into

the musty tunnel, vigorously flicking his foot to the beat of his ranting, "bloody filthy, rotten *heathens –*"

Laughter.

A child's laughter?

High, soft giggles came from the near east where the line stopped, and yet there was nothing but a vast black hole.

"Hello?" the reporter said into the void.

Nothing.

"Hello, who's there?"

Nothing.

To the west, the recently departed train was barely audible now, but this unusual sound definitely seemed to have come from the opposite direction.

"Hello?"

Silence.

It's been a long day. You're tired. Get to the blasted inn already so we can knock this day on the head. The man nodded to himself, his brow furrowed. He shot a final dagger in the direction of the odd noise, then took a step towards the exit.

Laughter again.

A tad louder, but far more distinct. A little girl's laughter – he was sure of it. The man stopped in his tracks. He wasn't scared, he wasn't even confused; he was just annoyed.

"Who's there?"

Silence again.

"What the bloody hell is this nonsense? Who's there?"

There was little doubt in the man's mind that the sounds had come from the tunnel to the east, but that just wasn't possible.

"This isn't funny, you know."

Silence.

The laughter he'd heard – or thought he'd heard – didn't sound particularly threatening or ominous. There was no malice in the sounds coming from the shadows; they may have been laced with a hint of playful mischief but – of course – they didn't make any sense, and that was what made the hairs on the back of the man's neck stand on end.

"Why don't you get a bloody life, you little wankers?"

Nothing.

The reporter scowled at the gaping black hole. *See, Jenkins? See what kind of a place this is?!*

He tried, again, for the stairwell.

The beast moved quickly through the underground with warm blood streaming from its ears. They wouldn't stop ringing; they wouldn't stop buzzing, they wouldn't stop screaming their insane, high-pitched whine –

(*EeeeeeEEEeeellll*)

The beast wanted it to stop, clawed and thumped at the sides of its throbbing head in a desperate mix of pain and frustration –

(*iiiiiIIIIiiiiiiiZZZzzzzzzzzz*)

– it was no use. The beast unleashed an outlandish howl that seemed to shake the entire underworld, reverberating up the length of the District Line and into the soul of a certain agitated reporter.

He stopped.

He craned his head away from the stairs and towards the direction of the far-off train. Now he *was* scared.

"H-hello? Who's there?"

Another howl. Louder.

The man squeezed the handle of his briefcase, its contents and latches shaking like an angry rattlesnake's tail – *chktchktchtkch*. He turned his head back, stomping towards the stairs for a third time. *Ridiculous. Bloody ridiculous.*

Another guttural roar filled the stifling, underground air.

He heard footsteps.

And then he ran.

The panic-stricken reporter wasn't the only person to hear the beast's demented cries. Constable Sloan had led a small band of armed policemen into the Monument Underground station; they'd followed the thick trail of blood all the way down to the platform, and were searching the shadows when they heard the distant roars.

"Did-did you hear that? What the bloody hell was that, Sir?" the first constable asked, gripping the butt and forestock of his rifle close to his chest.

"What d'ya think it was, you fool?" the second constable hissed, "It was that bloody train just went by, wasn't it?"

"Sounded like it came from the other direction to me, and it sounded more like a bloody wolf than a train," the third and final officer chimed in.

"A wolf?" the second officer responded, perplexed,

"When the bloody hell have you ever seen or heard a wolf, Tyler?"

"Shut up you lot," Sloan snarled. "Listen…"

They listened.

Another roar echoed through the great tunnel.

Then another.

"Tyler, you're good with these trains. What stops are there to the east?"

"Two, I think: Aldgate East, then the line stops at… Whitechapel."

The men all looked at each other for a brief moment. Not even a bullet from their rifles would be apt to pierce the tension.

"Right, how long until the next train's due?" Sloan asked.

"That westbound one that just went by us is the last, I think."

"Bollocks!" he spat. "Right: Jones, Price – you two get up top, get a message to Abberline and his men and get your arses over to Whitechapel Station. If you go for it, you can be there in twenty minutes. Go!"

"Right!" Jones and Price responded, bolting for the stairs.

"Tyler, grab that lamp over there. You're with me, lad."

"Sloan?"

"Just grab that bloody lamp. Come on!"

The reporter was a third of the way up the dark and endless stairwell when another booming cry reverberated up and almost through the walls. His legs had been pistoning up the narrow steps for what felt like hours and his thighs and calves were practically on fire. *Oh Jesus, when will these bloody stairs end?* He panted furiously, the dry taste of copper filling his mouth. He spat a thick glob of steaming white phlegm against the wall as he cleared another three steps. He was exhausted, but the adrenaline searing through his veins drove him on and up towards the safety of the street. *Come on! Come on boy! It can't be far now! It can't be —*

Another ear-splitting roar from below, followed by a far more terrifying sound – footsteps. Hard, fast and thunderous footsteps smashing against the ground and echoing up and up through the stairwell.

"Oh God! Oh God Jesus!" he cried, pushing his legs even harder up the steps. Three at a time now, blind panic giving him much-needed strength and stamina.

"Oh God please no!"

The beast could taste the heat coming from the scrambling reporter a mile away, and it was now less than forty steps from its prey. Its ears were still ringing profusely, it's temples still throbbing, but the scent of yet another kill rushed over the beast in an awesome wave, and despite its waning strength and appetite, it had to have it.

Thirty steps.

The man was losing ground.

Twenty steps.

He could practically feel the thing breathing down his neck.

Ten steps.

He dropped his briefcase.

Five.

The beast's wild growls and snarls and clawing nails against the walls and steps filled the entire world.

"OH MY GOD FUCKING GOD PLEASE NO –"

The reporter was maybe thirty seconds from the world above when he felt a jolt. A violent, heart-stopping jolt on his right ankle which tore a plethora of ligaments from his Achilles right up to his knee, sending him into shock. He went down in a twisted heap and cried out like a wounded animal. The beast almost seemed to answer by screaming its terrible, thunderous scream as it clambered up and over the man's convulsing body. The ringing in its ear drums intensified into a shrieking

(*EEELZzzzbeeeEEEEeeeEEEEeteee*)

and the beast went crazy, slamming a giant fist down on the man's sternum, splintering three ribs into his thumping right lung – puncturing it. He gasped, he wheezed, he looked to the heavens for salvation – but there was nobody home, not today. *Damn you Jenkins.* The reporter's bulging eyes rolled into the back of his head and his world went red. The beast hacked and pummelled his jowl and jaw into a slimy, crimson mess before thrusting its giant fingers into the man's shattered mouth and slowly tearing his quivering jawbone from his head like a fortune cookie. The beast didn't seem to possess the same raw power it had on the bridge, but it was still formidable. The incessant ringing in its ears, though, was getting worse. Much worse. It was as though someone or something had sliced off the top of its thick skull and filled it with a thousand angry wasps.

(*eeeeZZZzzlllBBBBBbbbZZZZZzzzzzzzz*)

The beast wailed.

Constables Sloan and Tyler followed the blood-curdling cries like an invisible beacon of terror as they trudged along the underground track. They'd long passed the Aldgate East platform, and could just about see the flickering amber glow of what had to be Whitechapel station up ahead.

"Come on Tyler," Sloan panted, "nearly there lad, nearly there."

"No offence Sloan, but I think I'd rather stay in these shitty tunnels." Tyler laughed nervously.

"I know lad, I know. But we've got guns all right, and this bloody thing ain't got nothing. We'll be fine."

"If you say so –"

Another guttural howl.

They picked up the pace, their running footsteps crunching on the loose shingle as they neared the last platform on the District Line. If not for the rattling paraffin lamp in Tyler's hand and the proverbial light at the end of the tunnel, the men would've been in total darkness.

Yet another howl.

They pressed on.

"...and then, get this right, get this – it turns out that Dr. Jekyll and Mr. Hyde were the same bloke all along!" the young boy revealed to a small chorus of jeers and gasps.

"No way!" said Joe.

"Nooooooo!" bellowed Gordie.

"Oh piss off, Bill," cried Fred.

"Swear down," insisted Bill, holding out both his palms in protest, leaning back on a stained wooden crate, "swear on me mum's life, me gran's life, and even *your* stinkin' life, Freddy boy."

"Now I know you're pullin' our legs," said Fred, springing from the cobbled ground, lunging for Bill, "you little fibber. Come here!" He wrestled the storyteller into a playful headlock. Bill's little arms and legs flailed madly as he choked through a wall of phlegm and laughter.

"S-s-swear down!" he pleaded.

"Swear down?" Fred asked, laughing just as hard as Bill and the other two boys who proceeded to join in the wrestling match by throwing fake punches and kicks to Bill's belly and thighs.

"I-I-I swear," Bill was laughing hysterically now, "I swear."

"Be careful with his legs boys," Fred warned his tag-team partners, "his bloody pants are on fire." They all burst into a rapture of howls and cries as Fred released Bill and they all began to push and shove and pat each other on the back, laughing. They sounded more like a pack of hyenas than a group of twelve-year-old scamps.

"Ssshhh, ssshhh. Quiet l-lads," said Joe, "q-q-quiet." He was trying his utmost not to laugh. "If anybody hears us we're bloody dead."

"Yeah," Gordie chuckled, "k-keep it down boys, keep it down. Think I'd rather run into The Ripper himself than be caught by my old lady."

They all scoffed, trying their best to hold back their

hysterics, but that only made it worse. It was a whole five seconds before they were at it again, flooding the alleyway with the sound of their raucous laughter.

Ever since the body of Polly Nichols had been found on the eve of the big storm, the four friends had been sneaking out after dark once a week. Other than the thrill of insubordination, there was no particular reason for their mischief on the gaslit streets of Whitechapel. This cold and soon to be memorable night was no different. They had no plan, no grand scheme, only naive delusions of grandeur that by bonding together, they might just catch the madman terrorising the streets of their hometown – they were the self-proclaimed *Fab' Four of the East-End*. Bill was utterly convinced they'd see The Ripper at some point, and although the others did not share his morbid optimism, they were definitely up for a laugh and a giggle, and a few scary stories.

"S-seriously though Bill, seriously, is that true? Is that actually how it ends?" asked Gordie, all four boys beginning to simmer down.

"Yep," said Bill, "swear down. It's a new one, but it's the best Penny Dreadful my old man's ever read me by far. He prefers those new detective ones but this one took the biscuit for me."

"That's mad," said Joe.

"Mad," agreed Gordie.

"It's definitely better than that one you told us about the fuckin' barber, I'll give you that." Fred said, triggering another bout of juvenile laughter.

"I still reckon that old barber over on Commercial

Road might be The Ripper, you know," said Bill.

The boos and jeers returned.

"A new one, a new suspect," said Fred, "I don't know what's more outrageous: that story you just told or some of your bloody Ripper theories."

Bill administered the finger.

"So, what now?" asked Gordie, checking his imaginary wristwatch.

"It's bloody freezing. Maybe we should call it a night?" said Joe.

"I know, I know – how about we head on over to the underground?" Fred raised his right eyebrow.

"Nooooooooo," the others said together, kicking and booing the tall boy.

"What?" Fred protested, "What?"

"I ain't bloody going down there after what happened last time," said Joe.

"Nothing happened last time," Fred dismissed, an impish grin on his face.

"Bollocks, you heard them creepy little girls laughing as well as I did and don't pretend you didn't," Joe was deadly serious now.

"Well," said Fred, "we did tell you not to go for a piss down there mate. They were only reacting to what they saw."

Bill and Gordie gawked and high-fived Fred, who was quite pleased with his razor-sharp joke. Joe was not amused.

"Fine, fine. But it must be gone midnight by now. Surely they would've closed off the entrance already, right?" he said.

"They leave it open half the bloody time. You know

184

this, you chicken," said Fred.

"I ain't no chicken, you lanky dickhead. If you like it down there so much then why don't you go work there?"

"Well, maybe I will someday," said Fred, his arms spread, "but until then, let's go have a butcher's shall we ladies?"

"Oh for Pete's sake," Gordie said, "let's just go have a quick look, yeah? It's only five minutes away and it'll keep Freddy Long Legs here quiet for a bit."

Fred nodded triumphantly.

"Come on then," said Bill, slapping his pink hands against his thighs and pushing off into a standing position, "let's go have a butcher's."

The *Fab' Four* assembled, and headed for the underground.

The beast moved frantically up the stairwell with hot blood and vomit dripping from its mouth. Something was wrong. Something was very, very wrong. It felt smaller, weaker, sick to its bulging stomach. Gone was the abominable lust for blood and destruction it had in abundance no less than five minutes before. Gone was the blind rage. Gone was the demonic speed and strength it once possessed. Everything was fading, fast.

It had been unable to devour the flesh and tendons of the reporter with its usual vigour, cutting its feast short to regurgitate half-digested organs and meat in frothy, shredded chunks.

Something was wrong; something was... resisting.

The beast's eyes were watering. Its muscles were

burning. Its bones ached.

It needed to get away from this place, this scene – it *had* to get away.

It needed air.

It needed rest.

The beast still felt anger, but it was more distress than anything. The incessant ringing in its ears had dulled somewhat but it was still audible, and the beast could now hear other sounds too. A jumble of mumbles, grunts and vibrations- static white noise searing through its head that was beyond its comprehension –

(*hhhttzzzzzzbbbbbblllllzzzzzbbbttthhhheeeeeeeetttt*)

It made no sense.

Everything was a blur. Everything was a mess. The beast stumbled up the dark and narrow stairway towards Whitechapel proper, crying out into the night.

"What the bloody hell was that?" said Joe, grabbing a hold of Bill's jacket.

"'Scuse me boys," said Fred, patting his stomach.

"No seriously, what the hell was that?"

"Sounded like a wolf," said Bill.

"A WOLF!?" Joe cried in disbelief.

"A bloody wolf in London? You've been reading too many of those Penny Dreadfuls, Billy boy," teased Fred, still tapping his midriff.

"Probably just a dog," said Gordie reassuringly.

Joe wasn't convinced.

"Or Mr. Hyde," said Bill.

"Shut up Bill," they hissed in unison.

"No, seriously," Joe jumped in, "I don't see any

bloody dogs. It's dead quiet along here, even for this time of night. Let's just call it a night and head home yeah?"

Joe's plea was met with a flock of clucks and chucks from his three so-called best friends. He rolled his eyes.

They walked on.

They were approaching the secluded Durward Street junction – the entrance to the station in sight – when another blood-chilling cry crackled on the midnight wind, stopping the boys in their tracks.

"What the fuck?" rasped Gordie.

"All right, I'll hold my hands up. Wasn't my guts that time, chaps," said Fred, and his confession was met with forced, nervous laughter, briefly lightening the mood.

Bill pointed towards the station. "Look!"

A hundred feet or so ahead, a giant shadow emerged from the poorly-lit entrance of the underground.

"What the fucking hell is that? It's-it's huge!" said Joe.

"It's just a big fat geezer, stop exaggerating," said Fred.

"Big fat geezer my arse, he's – it's – it's massive."

Fred took a step forward.

"Let's go get a closer look, come on."

Bill took a step forward. "Yeah, come on, it might be one of those curiosity freaks from the travelling circus or something. Like one of those strongmen –"

"Or a bearded lady," said Gordie.

The boys all sniggered under their breaths. Gordie

took a step forward, and a reluctant Joe followed.

*

The boys moved stealthily along the pavement, negotiating the usually busy crossroads with an exaggerated guile that would have put even the most accomplished of sleuths to shame. They could see the enormous shadow a little clearer now, but it was heading away from them, retaining its air of mystery. The boys were closing the gap, but the thing moved fast, dipping in and out of their sight, passing under the sparsely placed streetlamps and into blackness, then back into the flickering light once more. They were still a fair distance from their target, but they could hear the slapping and scuffing of its feet on the stony ground. It was big and strange, and heading south along Fulbourne Street towards the Royal London Hospital.

"Where is he – where is *it* going?" asked Joe.

"Beats me. Looks as if it's slowing down though – look," said Fred.

"Maybe it's going to the hospital. Maybe it's the Elephant Man –"

"Shut up, Bill!"

All of a sudden, the shadow stopped. The boys seized their opportunity and closed the gap. They were maybe fifty feet from the shadow as they took refuge behind a large cast-iron bench across the street. They huddled together and watched.

"What's it doing?!" Joe.

"What *is* it?!" Gordie.

"Look at the size of its head... its legs!" Bill.

The silhouette turned towards them.

"Shit." They all gasped, ducking.

Fred peered through the bars of the bench just in time to see the shadow disappear into a pitch black alleyway.

"It's gone."

"It's gone?!"

"Yeah, down the alleyway between Gilbert's and the greengrocers."

"Isn't that a dead end?" asked Gordie.

They all looked at each other. Fred nodded.

"No!" hissed Joe.

Fred's mischievous eyes gleamed bright and eager in the gloom of the gaslight.

"Come on!" he said.

"No, for fuck's sake, no." Joe was adamant this time. This little escapade of Fred and Bill's had gone far enough. He'd had it.

Fred, Bill and Gordie all scrambled over to the other side of the street where the large shadow had loomed no less than twenty seconds earlier. Joe stayed crouched behind the bench.

"You're all bloody mad," he sneered.

Fred looked over and shook a limp fist in Joe's direction – a well-known gesture in England, reserved only for the biggest of idiots. Bill and Gordie waved him over. Joe groaned aloud, the warm air from his burning lungs becoming visible as the cold air cooled it with aplomb.

He joined his friends.

*

The beast moved wearily along the dark and narrow alleyway with warm blood streaming from its eyes. It was scared, lost and utterly bewildered. Fear and panic had collided in its jangled head to create a perfect storm, the resulting rains filling its black world to the absolute brim.

(*zzZzztTtthHhhlllLiiiBblllelIzEetzzzzllliEelzAeeetttz zzzz*)

Something was watching it. Stopping it, driving it, controlling it, pulling it back. The coarse, black hair that had once covered its hulking frame had all but dissolved, its veiny, sweat-slicked skin shifted and cracked and writhed like a pale blue river. The beast's knees buckled, and it sank to the ground with a terrible groan.

"What now then, Sherlock?" asked Joe sourly.

The four boys stood peering into the black alleyway. They had divided themselves into two tactical units – Fred and Bill on the corner of the greengrocers, Gordie and Joe just opposite on the side of Gilbert's Sweet Shop. They berated one another in harsh whispers from across the void.

"Uhh, well," Fred was thinking, "we go have a look, don't we?"

"Oh brilliant," said Joe, "bloody brilliant idea, Fred. Look, I'm being deadly serious now all right, I'm being deadly serious, what if it's him? What if it's the fuckin' Ripper?"

"It's not the bloody Ripper."

"You don't know that."

"All right, say it *is* Jack –"

"Or Jill," Gordie grinned.

"Shut up Gord," Fred was trying not to laugh, "look, there's four of us and one of *him,* right*?* We can take him. We'd be world-famous heroes. Might even get in one of Bill's books."

"You're bloody mad," Gordie sniggered. Joe didn't see what was so funny.

"I'm joking, I'm joking. Look, if it goes tits up, we'll just run. We caught up to it fine, didn't we? Looked as if it was struggling anyway."

"Good point," whispered Bill.

"Look, I'll go first, you chickens just fall in behind."

They all stared at Fred. Joe was shaking his head.

"Just grow a pair of bollocks, will you? Come on."

"I ain't going nowhere," hissed Joe, his arms crossed.

"Fine. You can be our lookout. But if it *is* The Ripper and *we* catch him, you ain't making it into the book, chicken boy." Bill and Gordie scoffed and giggled. Fred shot Joe a cheeky wink, and slid into the alleyway.

Joe watched on in bewilderment as his three friends disappeared into the pitch black. He shook his head, rubbing his arms and shuffling his feet anxiously.

"Just hurry up boys, yeah?"

Nothing.

"Boys?"

Nothing.

"Boys?"

Silence.

"Bloody wankers," he spat into the alleyway, his eyes drifting down towards his nervous feet.

"It's bloody freezing tonight it is –"

Something caught his eye. Something dark and wet, something shimmering in the gaslight.

"What the hell is that?" he said, squinting.

His heart froze.

"Oh-oh-oh my god," he croaked, "what? What the hell?" He slowly knelt to touch the icy pavement. Something warm, wet and laced with hair. Something sticky. Something, something –

"Oh-oh fuck. Oh fucking fuck," Joe drew his shaking hand to his horrified eyes.

"Ohh. Ohhh," he slowly tore his eyes from his bloody fingers to the cobbled ground that led into the alleyway, and his world came tumbling down.

The narrow alleyway was barely wide enough to fit all three boys side by side, so Bill and Gordie funnelled in just behind their leader to form a kind of human pyramid. As they inched further and further into the abyss, the pyramid seemed to tighten, and Bill and Gordie's shoulders scraped against the old bricks walls as Fred – their shield – spearheaded their stupid stab in the dark.

"How long is this bloody alley?" muttered Gordie.

"Wish we had a lamp," rasped Bill.

"Ssshhh," Fred was in no mood for jokes – not anymore. This was his time. This was his moment. He'd always played the role of tough guy well, but he was beginning to feel something he'd seldom experienced in his short life: fear. Simmering, bubbling fear that sloshed in the pit of his empty stomach. Most boys would turn tail and run, but not Fred Peters. If he could face this, he could face anything. This was his time. This was his moment.

Take whatever fear Fred was feeling, multiply it by a hundred and you still wouldn't be close to what was coursing through both Bill and Gordie's veins. If it wasn't for their protector, their shield and conqueror of bullies, they certainly wouldn't be shuffling down this grimy alleyway right now. But they had to see. They had to know.

Bill Talbot had held a penchant for the macabre since he was eight years old and his dad had told him the tale of Dr. Frankenstein and his tragic Monster. As much as the recent events in Whitechapel had rattled his nerves and bones, Bill was fascinated – obsessed – by what had been going down, and this could well be the man of the hour. His reason for being in this murky alley was simple: he was curious. He had to see. He had to know.

Gordie Cooper, however, just wanted to fit in. He was curious, sure, but not in the same way as Bill. He wanted to act the tough guy too, sure, but not to the same degree as Fred. Gordie was just along for the ride, and would relish telling his side of the story once the dust had settled. Plus, he'd never miss a chance to tease Joe.

They were about three quarters of the way down the narrow stretch of black when they heard something hissing and gurgling just ahead – *eeellllliiiiizzzziishshshhiissssgggh.*

They stopped.

They listened.

A soft, steady wind howled through the alleyway.

The strange sounds stopped.

"Hello?" Fred said into the dark.

Nothing.

They shuffled forward.

"Hello?" Fred called out again as the trio inched towards the end of the alley.

"Are-are you all right? We saw you –"

A torrent of guttural growls and screeches filled the cold, claustrophobic air, rattling their bones and freezing their blood.

They all stopped dead.

The hideous sounds were unnerving enough on their own, but combined with the blackness of the night and the tightness of the foul-smelling alleyway, flat-out confusion swam around the boys and drowned them.

"He-hello?" Bill's shaky voice this time.

Movement.

Fred took a step back, forcing Bill and Gordie to do the same.

Another growl.

They shuffled back a few more steps, and then they saw it.

A writhing, crackling thing, dripping in blood and creamy pus, emerged from the shadows. Its skin was split, its jowl was bulging and bubbling and its demented features seemed to slide around its face grotesquely. In a way, it looked like some sort of –

"Eeeelllllliiiiiztthtzzzhtssh!" it screeched.

"Oh… my… my… my… my…" Fred couldn't find the word.

"GOD!" Joe screamed, clattering into the back of the three frozen boys.

The thing howled a nerve-shredding cry, thrust its gangly arms against the brick walls, and clambered towards them.

"RUN!" Fred screamed, turning and pushing the group of shaking boys. "FUCKING RUN!"

They ran.

They ran faster and harder than anybody in London had run that cold November night. The screaming beast was hot on their heels as they bellowed and bolted and bundled out of the blackness and into the gloom of the old stone street. First Joe, then Gordie, then Bill and finally Fred –

The beast launched itself on the tall boy's back, and they both went down in a sickening heap as they emerged from the alleyway.

"NO! OH MY GOD NO!" he cried, trying with all his strength to wriggle from beneath the beast's hulking, slimy frame, "HELP! HELP ME!"

The boys spun and stopped in horror, rushing to the aid of their fallen friend.

The beast snarled and reared its hideous body over the squirming boy, raising its arms high above its head ready to bring the hammer down on yet another life.

(*sssss*)

The beast glared at the boy.

(*ssssst*)

The beast screamed at the boy.

(*SSSSTOP!*)

And then it stopped.

"FIRE!"

A barrage of gunshots exploded through the street, and the beast went down.

Constables Sloan and Tyler sprinted to the steaming, squirming heap as Fred scrambled free on his hands and knees.

"Don't you move! Don't you bloody move!" Sloan shouted at the floundering beast, pointing his shaking rifle. He'd seen some terrible things this year – this night – but the image of what lay before him now would follow him to his grave.

"Dear-Dear Lord," he rasped, his mind unable to register what his eyes were showing him. The beast was writhing and crackling; dissolving, shrinking, transforming into something that looked like a man. A bloodied, beaten and hideously disfigured man, but a man all the same.

"Sloan, Sloan, it-it-it's a m– it's a m–" Tyler couldn't bring himself to say the word. "How? How is this – who?"

"Mr. Hyde," a tall, traumatised boy named Fred said aloud to the stunned crowd that had gathered around the dying man.

"I… I… think it's more like Dr. Jekyll," said Bill.

"Eh-eh-eh-be…"

"It's-he's – he's trying to speak," said Joe.

They all shuffled closer.

"Eh-li-be…"

Sloan lowered his rifle.

"Eh-li-*zbe*."

Dr. Edward Kessler of the Royal London Hospital lay flat on his back with cold tears streaming down his temples. He stared up at the starless sky, his mouth agape, the light slowly fading from his pale green eyes as he struggled for the right word.

"Elizabeth."

THE GREAT PUZZLE

The following letter was received by the Central News Agency at their premises in the city of London on 21· July, 1889. Four days prior, the body of Alice McKenzie was found murdered on Castle Alley. Her left carotid artery had been severed.

The true origin and authenticity of the letter are debated to this day.

Dear Boss

Where am I? Who am I? Ah, that's the great puzzle. It's been too long but was that really your old friend Saucy Jacky the other night or was it just an imposter. Who knows. I still laugh when I read about me being caught or killed or thrown into the madhouse. I read Mr. Carroll remains a suspect ha ha. Oh boss. How I laughed at the irony. I suspect the lady Alice squealed before tumbling down the rabbit hole but who am I to say. I've missed you boss. Forget me not my knives are always nice and sharp and ready when needed. I shall always be down on whores. Anniversary coming up maybe I shall have to mark the occasion. Maybe not.

Yours truly
Jack the Ripper
PS. Dont be a stranger

DISMEMBER

The following sonnet was received by the Central News Agency at their premises in the city of London on 13ᵗ September, 1889. Three days prior, the decomposing headless and legless torso of an unidentified woman was discovered beneath a railway arch on Pinchin Street. What remained of the woman's body was heavily mutilated.

The true origin and authenticity of the sonnet are debated to this day.

Dismember

Dismember, remember that splendid September,
T'were a season of carnage,
T'were an hour of splendour.
Doth thou recall the cries of the four beasts?
"Come and See"
And thou saw;
All hope was abandoned,

No whore could ignore.
The man and his knife sure inspired fine deeds,
Four rose from the ashes on a herd of pale steeds;
A butcher, a poet, a dark man, a beast,
We commit to the ground this body;
Unknown,
Decreased.

UNDERGROUND

Arthur Gladstone stood stone-like amidst a sheet of fine, grey drizzle, staring in utter disbelief at the notice pinned to the wall of the rundown station. *This is too good to be true*, he thought, ripping the golden ticket from the wet bricks for closer inspection.

WANTED
NIGHT WATCHMAN
NOV. 9TH – 13TH
(STATION TO BE SEALED
OFF ON 14TH)
£8 FOR 5 NIGHTS (6PM –
6AM)
FOOD, DRINK, QUARTERS
PROVIDED
ENQUIRE WITHIN

Eight pounds for five nights' work? Arthur was struggling to do the math, and who could blame him? Eight pounds was more money than the average man earnt in six weeks. Eight pounds was certainly more money than the nineteen-year-old drifter from Portsmouth had pulled in the past three months, which was saying something considering he'd put in some serious shifts across some of the south coast's biggest shipyards.

"Eight – bloody – pounds," he said to nobody in particular, his ears ringing with excitement, his mouth watering. This was exactly the sort of reason he'd packed up his duffle bag and come to London. It was a bit of a gamble, sure, but work had dried up in his hometown's dockyard in recent weeks and he wasn't prepared to hang about any longer. He snuck aboard the first train he could to Waterloo Station. That was Friday, and Arthur had been sleeping rough the past few nights as he bounced around the Thames looking for work. He figured there would be more opportunities in the capital, but in the three days he'd been here, he'd found absolutely nothing. So, he rolled the dice again; abandoned the river, and drifted into the East-End in hope of crossing paths with Lady Luck – and here she was.

What's the catch? There has to be a catch. Today is the 9th, but why would they want a watchman if the tunnel's getting sealed off?

He took a step back, scanning the dirty, dreary street for a clock. A large cloud of steam rose from below, billowed up in the wet air, then vanished. It was getting dark. Arthur leant back and found the large clock above the haggard, brown brick entrance to the station: Four-fifty. *I bet it's gone already and they forgot to take the bloody sign down*, he thought, pocketing the soggy flyer. *Only one way to find out.*

He took a step towards the entrance and peered inside the grazed, filthy archway. A single yellow bulb flickered in the gloom, illuminating a mess of debris, stains, smashed glass bottles, and spatters of fresh, chunky vomit, the smell of which lingered on the sour air and was laced with the unmistakable odour of stale piss. He'd seen and smelt worse. To the far left was a rusty folding shutter gate to what looked like a downbound stairway and to the right, a short corridor with a dark red door at the end.

"Eight – bloody – pounds," Arthur Gladstone whispered into the foul-smelling air, his stomach rumbling as he pulled the lapels on his torn tweed jacket up around his unkempt neck and stepped into Whitechapel Underground Station.

The man across the desk must've stood at least six-four, and when Arthur knocked on the office door, tentatively opening it at the same time with the soggy job advert back in his hand, the tall man seemed surprised. Apprehensive. Arthur held up the flyer, asking if the job was still available. The tall man raised his eyebrows, said it was, and stuck out a large hand.

"The name's Peters. Fred Peters," a lit cigarette wiggled in the corner of his mouth.

"Arthur Gladstone."

They shook.

"Have a seat Arthur, please," Peters said, motioning towards the dark brown chair beside the desk, removing his cigarette and blowing a thick blast of stone-grey smoke into the dingy room, "you mind if I call you Arthur?"

"Course not mate. Uh, I mean, sir –"

"Oh no, don't give me any of that *sir* crap – just call me Fred."

"Ha, all right Fred. No problem," Arthur liked this man already.

He removed his duffle bag and took a seat as Fred slowly made his way around the other side of the desk, a brown file in his hand. The file went into a large filing cabinet. Arthur couldn't be sure but, if he had to hazard a guess, he would've put the man at maybe ten to fifteen years older than himself. Early- to mid-thirties, maybe. Fred took a seat and – to Arthur's surprise – came right out with it: "I bet eight quid for five nights' work seems like a bit of a wind-up, doesn't it?"

The drifter was caught off-guard a little and didn't quite know how to respond. *Is this some sort of test?*

"Oh, well, yeah I'll be honest, it does seem a bit too good to be true, yeah." *Honesty is the best policy*, his late mum always used to say.

"Yeah, you're not wrong mate, you're not wrong. I bet you're also wonderin' why the bloody hell we're asking for a watchman when the station is closed and due to be filled in in a few days, right?"

It was as if the tall man could read his mind.

"Uhh, yeah, it does seem a bit strange, but I didn't realise the station was actually closed. So now it seems even stranger, I guess," he chuckled.

Fred briefly lowered his eyes to the desk, tapping his cigarette on the corner of an ashtray.

Bollocks, he didn't like that.

"You're right, it does," he seemed nervous, "you're not from round here, are you Arthur?"

"No, Mr Peters –"

"Fred, please."

"Oh, sorry. No, Fred. Born and raised in Portsmouth. Sixty miles or so down the road."

"And what brings you through here?"

"Worked in the docks on and off the past few years," Arthur explained, trying his best to qualm his excitement, "but things dried up lately and that, so I thought I'd try my hand in good old London."

"I see. Any family at all? Wife? Kids?"

"No, 'fraid not. Struggle to support myself half the time, so not quite ready for those things yet if you know what I mean?" he chuckled.

Shouldn't have bloody said that either. Idiot.

"No, I get you mate. I get you," Fred actually seemed to understand, "what about parents or siblings?"

"Uhh, no. Well, Mum passed a few years back and I never knew my old man. Got a brother somewhere but haven't seen him in years." *Honesty is the best policy.*

"I'm sorry to hear that mate," Fred seemed almost guilty for asking as he flicked another small clump of ash into the brown china tray, "well, I put that flyer up first thing this morning, and you're the first person to come through that door asking about the job, and seeing as I really wasn't expecting anyone to be interested at all, I suppose I'm just gonna have to go ahead and offer it to you, ain't I?"

Arthur was stunned, pleased – ecstatic, even – but his overriding emotion was that of confusion. *How the bloody hell could the promise of £8 be up there all day and nobody come knockin'? And he ain't even asked if I have any experience yet or nothing.*

"I can see you're in a bit of shock," Fred continued,

tapping into Arthur's psyche once more, "so before you make a decision, I'm gonna have to give you a bit of a – how can I say this – *history lesson* on this place." A rueful smile stretched across his lips as he slowly brought his dying cigarette up to them. Inhaled. Smoke tunnelled through his lungs and crawled from his nostrils in a thick haze, settling in a swirling cloud on the low ceiling. Arthur swept his eyes up and over the swirling grey mass.

"Did you want a smoke, Arthur?"

"Oh, no, no, I'm fine thanks."

"You sure?"

"Yeah, yeah – I'm good. Thanks."

"All right, well, first things first: the entrance to the stairwell and both ends of the platform are in the process of being sealed off, and the lads reckon they'll have it done by the end of the week. They've already bricked up the west side of the tunnel which ran from here to Aldgate East, and they'll be moving on to the east side in the coming days, then finishing with the stairs and entrance itself after."

"Right," Arthur said, pretending he knew what the hell the tall man was talking about.

"Reason for it is pretty simple. Well, simple enough," he paused. "Up until a few decades or so ago, the district line used to end here, but when they tried to tunnel through towards the east they ran into some problems. Took 'em months to finally get it all dug out. A few workmen died in the process, and when electricity came to this part of the line it was all over the place and never really worked properly."

The dim bulb that lit the smoky room flickered ever-so-slightly.

Fred rose a finger to the ceiling. "See?"

They both laughed.

Fred took another drag of his cigarette and continued.

"The engineers call it a "black spot", and we've basically had nothing but aggro' with this bloody platform and the 250-yard stretch of line that runs through it for decades."

"That's pretty weird," Arthur was doing his best to sound at least half-knowledgeable.

"It is. They've had problems on and off with this section of the line going back – gawd..." Fred paused to think, "...gotta be at least thirty years."

Arthur tilted his head slightly, raising his eyebrows. *I wonder when he's gonna tell me about the free food and bed mentioned on the flyer.*

"Anyway, a couple of years ago, the bigwigs at District Rail finally had enough and gave the go-ahead to tunnel round this area and link Aldgate East to a new platform quarter of a mile north of here, and then link that to Stepney Green from there," he stubbed out his cigarette, "don't worry Arthur mate, I know this is boring as fuck – but it's all important, trust me."

Arthur tried to stifle a laugh behind his lips but it would not be denied. It burst from his mouth in a sharp, guttural blast.

Fred smiled, removing a pack of cigarettes and a box of matches from his desk drawer. He offered the pack to Arthur.

"Oh no, honestly, I'm fine thanks."

Fred recoiled and lit another cigarette.

"Anyway, that new tunnel is virtually done now, and this one below has been out of action for just over a month. We've had a salvaging crew and what-not down there for the past few weeks ripping up the tracks, tiles, bits of metal and pipes and all sorts of materials and what-have-you, and they started sealing things up just last week. They work during the day and leave their gear overnight, but this is a bit of a dodgy area Arthur, and despite padlocking the entrance and stairway up, we've had a few break-ins and quite a few things have been nicked."

"Oh, bloody hell," Arthur said.

"Yep. I'm guessing you saw all that sick and shit on your way in?"

Arthur nodded, grimacing.

"Bloody tramps. You see this typewriter here?" Fred pointed to an empty spot on the desk.

Arthur followed his finger, confused. "Uhh, no."

"That's 'coz some bastard took it the other night. What the bloody hell a tramp wants with a typewriter I don't know."

Arthur shook his head in disgust and said, "Have you gone to the police?"

Fred burst out laughing, nearly choking on his cigarette fumes.

"Oh, bloody hell. Good one Arthur," he tapped his cigarette into the ashtray again, trying to compose himself. "No," he coughed, "no, they wouldn't give a toss, trust me. We gotta handle this sorta crap in-house. So yeah, fellas at the union and my bosses at District said I should get a sign knocked up, get someone in for a few nights on bloody good pay. Sort out food and a bed and what not, and here you are mate," Fred opened his hands in a welcoming gesture.

"That makes sense actually," Arthur nodded, "but how come nobody broke your arm off as soon as you stuck that sign up this morning?"

Silence.

Fred seemed nervous again as he slumped back in his chair, deep in thought like a serious chess player considering his next move. He wrapped his fingers on the desk, took another long drag of his cigarette, then leant forward.

"Are you a superstitious man, Arthur?"

Didn't see that coming.

"Uhhh, oh no. I mean, no, not really," he smirked, "Why? Are you?"

Shouldn't have asked that. Stupid.

"No. Well, let's just say I'm undecided."

"What's this all about?" Arthur frowned, genuinely curious now.

"People's imaginations have a tendency to run a little wild around here. Can't say I blame them. Not after what happened back in '88."

Arthur scoured his shallow memory bank. *'88...? '88...? '88 –*

"Oh. You're talking about Jack the Ripper?"

Fred winced, taking the longest drag from his cigarette yet. "Yeah," he shuffled uncomfortably in his chair, "among other things. How much do you know about what went on around here?"

"Bits and pieces. Only what I've heard from my mum and my mates and that, I suppose."

Fred nodded. "You probably got the gist – but take it

from someone who grew up around here, it was a bloody strange time."

"I bet," Arthur said, shaking his head.

For the past twenty years, children all over the country had grown up traumatised by the old wives' tales of the faceless fiend who walks and stalks the streets at night to claim the souls of naughty children.

"You best behave yourself Arthur or Jack'll bloody get ya!" his mum's voice ran through his head. Up until the age of ten, he'd been absolutely terrified of the knife-wielding Ripper and utterly convinced he would come for him in his dreams. He wasn't alone. Jack was Britain's undisputed boogeyman. It was only when Arthur got a little older that he realised he was actually real, and that the police had never caught him.

For people outside of London and in the eyes and minds of millions, The Ripper's notoriety had grown into something resembling urban legend. It no longer seemed as if such a man, such a monster, could have existed, but to the people of Whitechapel, and especially to those who lived through his reign of terror, his looming presence was still felt on every dark lane and every cobbled street.

"They never caught the bloke, did they?" Arthur asked, trying to shake Fred from the bottomless daze he'd seemingly fallen headfirst into.

"No," Fred said, coming up for air, "well, maybe they did, but it was never proven. Nobody was ever charged or anything. There were quite a few suspects, and a number of them were either thrown in the madhouse or turned up dead within a few years of the last known murder."

"Really?" Arthur didn't know that.

"Yeah. Some young doctor washed up on The Thames a month after Mary Jane Kelly's murder; this physician died of old age couple of years after; some geezer called *Chapman* moved to Brighton and was hanged five or six years ago for poisoning three women. I fancy him for it, personally. Then there was the woman."

"The woman?"

"Yeah, Pearcey her name was. Mary Pearcey. She was hung back in the early nineties for cutting her lover's wife's head off and smothering her eighteen-month-old baby."

"Jesus."

"Yeah, I know. There are those who fancy her for The Ripper, seeing as she was living round these parts at the time of the killings. Can't see it personally. It was Jack, not Jill."

"Jill the Ripper?" Arthur tried to hold back another snigger, but couldn't. "Sorry Fred, sorry," he put a hand to his mouth, embarrassed.

"Nah, it's all right to laugh mate," he forced a smile, "about all you can do sometimes." He leant back in his chair. "I guess it coulda been any one of them, really. Or none of them. Everyone 'round here has an opinion or a theory or something."

"What do you think?

Fred shifted his gaze to the door, then back to Arthur.

"I dunno. There are so many theories you could end up bloody lost in them. But like I said, I fancy that geezer who moved to Brighton after the Ripper murders and poisoned those poor women. Some young girl was poisoned in my local around the same time of the murders so there might have been something in that you know, but I ain't no detective," he sniffed, sat up, and began to fiddle with the box of matches on the desk.

"They banged quite a few nutters up in the local loony bins around the time of the murders as well and quite a lot of sickos were hanged, including this mad butcher what killed a bunch of other people that autumn of '88. I won't get into that, but he wasn't The Ripper," he coughed, leant back. "The papers liked this one fella *Cutbush* who got chucked into Broadmoor for stabbing a few women in the early nineties. There was also an old bloke, a local barber, the father of the girl who was poisoned in the pub as it happens. Anyway, he off'd himself the day after the killing of Mary Jane Kelly. Story goes they found the body of some Freemason in his shop who'd had his throat cut but regardless of what some people 'round here say, I don't think the old barber was The Ripper. Funnily enough, a lot of people liked this other barber called *Kosminski* for the murders, so maybe it was him. But who the hell knows?" Fred paused. "Add to all this madness the deaths of some of the other suspects and the fact the murders and the weird letters all stopped around '91... I guess they must've got to him somehow."

"Or her?" Arthur grinned.

Fred forced another smile.

"Yeah, throw enough shit and some of it's bound to stick, right?" he took another drag and began his next sentence through a cloud of smoke. "They reckon he only killed five women now, but I honestly think it might've been more. That said, I reckon a lot of those letters the papers claim to be real are probably bloody fakes."

"Yeah?"

"Yeah. Just a theory. An old mate of mine reckons some of them might've been sent in by some nutcase wanting to take credit for the killings, but I've always thought it was probably just the bastards at the papers trying to boost their sales. But who knows. I reckon that one what got sent to Mr. Lusk might've been real, but I'll guess we'll never know for sure."

Arthur had no idea who Lusk was, but he didn't want to interrupt Fred mid-flow again.

"Anyway, this mate of mine was convinced the whole thing was some sort of cover-up by the Freemasons and that some upper-class fella – maybe even royalty – was going round with a licence to kill and he was protected by the Old Bill."

Arthur raised his eyebrows, a look of horrified incredulity on his face.

"I know, right," Fred said, rolling his eyes, "he read far too many books, that boy. You think I know a lot about all this stuff, you should talk to him," he chuckled, "although he was right about this one nutter we had round here back then. Anyway, from the summer of '88 to the winter of '91, there were a bunch of nasty killings round here that could easily have been tied to The Ripper, the worst of which was more than likely Mary Jane – twenty years ago this very night, as it happens," he lowered his eyes to the ashtray in thought. He took another puff of his cigarette. "So much of what happened back then went unsolved, you know. The Old Bill had so many suspects, hardly any good ones. Story goes they were even looking at the bloke who wrote bloody Alice in Wonderland at one point. Then you had the papers making The Ripper out to be some kind of phantom or what not, and we got all these authors now who write about monsters and vampires and ghosts and ghouls and pictures of men that don't age and shit."

What's all this gotta do with this underground station? Arthur thought.

"I bet you're wondering what any of this has to do with this bloody station, right?"

How the hell does he keep doing that?

"Well," Fred leant back in his chair, "there were other things going on around here at the time of the murders as well. Strange things. *Stranger things*, in many respects. Things you probably didn't hear from your old dear or mates or pick up in the papers," he glanced at the door. "Hard to explain, really. It was a dark time Arthur, and I guess you could say this station had a part to play in it all."

"How so?" Arthur leant forward. He was beginning to think that *he* should be paying *Fred* for this history lesson.

"Well, you're gonna laugh, but one of the wilder theories is that The Ripper was a vagrant of some kind who lived in these tunnels, and would *rise from the depths of hell to slit the throats of lustful women.*"

Arthur contorted his face in disbelief.

"Ridiculous, I know. I bet you were always told the victims were all full-time prostitutes as well, weren't you?"

Arthur nodded.

"They weren't. And anyway, why should it matter if they were? You think times are rough now, you shoulda seen this place twenty years ago," Fred looked down at his ashtray, rapping his fingers on the desk again.

Arthur sensed that a large part of him didn't want to be reliving these memories, but that another part *needed* to.

"They were good women. Some had fallen on hard times, sure, but they didn't deserve what happened to them. Mary Jane Kelly used to live round the corner from me when I was a boy. I was only twelve or so but take it from me, she was a lovely girl. Beautiful, she was. Me and my mates fancied the pants off her, and that evil bastard tore her face up so bad that when they brought in her poor fella to identify her, he was only able to recognise her by her fuckin' eyes," he coughed, and held out an apologetic hand, "'scuse my French, Arthur."

Arthur shook his head. He could feel the hairs crawling on the back of his neck.

"Anyway. The Ripper rising from the underworld is obviously a load of old tosh, but there is one thing – well, two things I guess – you should know about the underground, and they're probably the reasons nobody else has come through that door today."

Here it comes, Arthur thought, *here comes the catch*. He shuffled forward in his seat, his elbows on his thighs.

"I'm gonna level with you mate; a couple of nights after Mary Jane was killed, a man – a reporter – was brutally murdered on that stairway you passed on your way in."

"By The Ripper?"

"No, a scientist," Fred scratched his neck, and took another puff on his cigarette. His skin had turned the colour of milky tea, "I won't get into it. Point is, the poor bloke was beaten to death on them stairs, and over the years people have claimed to have heard things late at night."

Arthur was intrigued.

"What sorta things?"

"Growls, screams, footsteps, all sorts of horrible stuff. Coulda sworn I heard a few things myself down there when I was a nipper, but I can't say I hang around here too much after dark since I grew hairs on my chest," he chuckled nervously, "maybe I am a superstitious bastard after all."

Arthur smiled.

Fred continued. "Truth is, I do most of my work around the other stations along the District and Jubilee lines, and I'm only here out of a favour to an old pal – look where that's bloody got me," he flicked his head to the empty part of the desk where his typewriter once lived.

Arthur stifled another laugh. "What was the other thing?" he asked.

"The pits," Fred stubbed out his second cigarette, immediately reaching for a third.

"The pits?"

"Legend has it that when you walk down that stairway towards the platform below you're basically passing through a space that was once occupied by a large plague pit."

"Plague? *The* Plague? The Black Death?"

"Yeah. 1666. Took out nearly a quarter of London, they say. The East-End got hit pretty bad, with Whitechapel bearing the brunt of the impact. Always the bloody way. Anyway, there are these mass grave sites all over the city, and apparently when they were building all the tunnels back in the sixties and seventies, they did their best to avoid these known pits, but every now and then someone ballsed it up and they'd end up running right through one of them."

Arthur couldn't believe what he was hearing.

"Honestly, there's just no end to the madness round here," Fred glanced through the closed door, presumably in the direction of the stairwell, "my old man was in one of the crews that helped dig out the tunnels round here, and he said they pulled out over a thousand skeletons from a pit measuring over fifty feet wide. Took 'em bloody weeks."

Arthur felt an icy tremor rattle the length of his spine. "So, people think the station's like, I dunno… haunted or something, then?"

"Something like that," Fred nodded, "nothing much seems to happen during the day down there but at night, we've had all sorts of reports and sightings over the years – and to tell you the truth, I ain't been down there by myself after dark in a very long time."

Fred was shrouded, now, by a small cloud of smoke and seemed to be deep in thought. There was a long, awkward silence as the two men sat staring into nothing.

Suddenly there was a barrage of loud bangs at the

door. Both of them flinched in their seats. A bearded man with a dusty face and helmet opened the door.

"Jesus Christ, Rob," Fred said, standing up, "me and Arthur nearly shit ourselves then."

"Sorry Fred mate," Rob held out a set of keys, grinning, "that's us done for the day, chief."

"Good stuff Rob, good stuff. How'd you get on?"

"Yeah, gettin' there mate. Got a load more of the track out and the brickies made a start on the other wall. Shouldn't be long now," he shuffled across the room, handed the keys to Fred then turned to Arthur, "this the new guard?"

Arthur smiled nervously and looked at Fred.

"Maybe. Just been giving him the rundown on the place."

Rob smiled, slowly making his way back towards the door, still looking down at the out of town drifter.

"Not scaring you too bad, I hope? We need someone down there to stop those thieving bastards."

Arthur shook his head, "Nah I'll be all right. Lots of haunted places and that where I'm from."

"Ha, yeah… I wouldn't say "haunted" but it does get a little weird down there sometimes I'll admit," he paused, "anyway, I've left the lamps lit and that down there. You lads have a good one, I'm off down The White Hart."

The three men said their goodbyes.

Fred returned to his chair.

"So anyway, Arthur, I've been chewing your ear off for nearly an hour now. I know it's a lot to take in, but there you have it: that's the history of Whitechapel in a nutshell," he paused then stuck out an open palm in jest, "that'll be eight pound please."

Arthur laughed, Fred joined him, and together they just about managed to cut the tension in the stuffy room.

Don't do it.

"Listen, Fred, I probably shouldn't ask but... why are you telling me all this?"

You bloody idiot.

"I mean, if they want someone down there so bad for a few nights, why didn't you just, you know, keep me in the dark or whatever? Not that I'm put off or anything – I still want it – but like you said... it's a lot to take in and stuff."

"Yeah, I know," Fred replied, stubbing out his cigarette, "and I honestly don't know why I came clean with you, mate. I guess it just wouldn't feel right sending you down there without telling you all this, you know? Especially with you being from out of town and that."

"Honesty is the best policy," Arthur said.

Fred nodded, starting to his feet and jangling the set of keys.

"Right," he said, "now the workers have packed up, you fancy going down and having a look around? Not that there's much to see with all the machines and tools and that, but I can show you the little room down there and stuff."

"Yeah, sure," Arthur said, reaching for his duffle bag and rising to his feet.

*

The two stood for a moment beneath the flickering bulb

at the top of the stairs as Fred fumbled for the right key. The entrance to the stairwell itself was blocked by an old collapsible gate, and Arthur stood peering through the diamond shaped gaps in the rusty metal – down into the flickering amber gloom of the descent. There wasn't much to see. Just the muck and battered texture of the steep looking steps and the stained walls, poorly lit by an old, wall-mounted lantern. The steps dipped and disappeared sharply around the curve of the dark spiral, down into the depths of the London underground.

"Fuckin' keys," Fred sneered out the corner of his mouth – he had lit yet another cigarette. His hands were shaking.

Arthur glanced at the street behind them. The rain looked as if it had stopped but it was hard to tell. It was dark now.

"Gotcha," Fred said triumphantly, grabbing what looked like a brand-new padlock with one hand, inserting the key with the other. He slid the folding iron gate to the side with an ear-splitting *reeaacchhkkkk*.

"Right, come on then," he said, stepping down onto the first step with a hand still on the collapsed gate. Arthur slid into the stairwell and Fred slammed the gate behind them, bolting the padlock and locking the gate from the inside.

"Here, look," he motioned to Arthur, "see this key here, this is the one for the new padlock and this one, this is for the entrance itself. You can see I've left it open for now 'coz I'll have to pop out and get you some food and stuff in a bit before I leave you for the night."

The mere mention of food nearly made Arthur forget the keys Fred had just showed him.

"Right, got it," he said.

"All right, let's go," Fred turned and led Arthur down into the Underground.

There was just under a minute of silence between the two as they slowly made their way down the winding staircase. The sound of their shoes scuffing on the old stone steps was all that broke the silence, and they were a little over halfway down the smoky stairwell when Fred angled his head slightly towards Arthur and said: "Up until they opened the Covent Garden station a couple years back, this stairwell had the most steps of all the underground stations."

"Really?" Arthur was becoming increasingly fascinated by Fred's nuggets of London trivia.

"Yep. A hundred and seventy-five steps. That new one has a hundred ninety-three, I'm told. You can see why Rob and his boys don't fancy lugging all their gear up and down here every bloody day can't you?" he chuckled.

"Yeah," Arthur agreed, "sod that."

Fred took a drag of his cigarette and coughed.

"Here, remind me not to light another one of these up before I head to the shops to get your bits, yeah. I might not bloody make it back."

They both chuckled, although Arthur was beginning to suspect Fred's apprehension was building with every step and his jokes were maybe a way of lightening the mood. He'd only been in his company for a little over an hour but, he had to admit, any neurosis or superstition Fred bore towards the underground was beginning to rub off on him a little. The fact that Rob had chimed in with a comment suggested that it wasn't just Fred overreacting or playing games. Not that he seemed like the type of bloke to pull stupid pranks.

It does get a little weird down there sometimes, I'll admit.

They continued their descent.

Down, down, down. *Will the stairs never come to an end?*

It was another minute and seventy hard, uneven steps before they finally reached the foot of the stairwell. Fred, seemingly out of breath, shuffled towards a nearby pillar and leant beneath a dim yellow lamp.

"Bloody hell. I'm knackered," he took a long, satisfying draw on his withered cigarette. "How you doing?" he asked through a jet of yellow smoke.

"I'm all right," Arthur chuckled, looking about the dingy platform. There were all sorts of tools and machines, and large piles of debris, bricks, sand and dirt scattered about.

"Take a look around," Fred said, still struggling for his breath.

Arthur inched towards the edge of the platform. The track below was no longer a track at all. Just a long strip of rubble and dirt. Seventy yards or so to the left stood a large brick wall – maybe twelve feet wide and twenty high. He started to walk towards it, careful not to bump into any of the machines or piles of metal lying around.

His footsteps echoed along the tube of the large tunnel as he neared the dark red wall. It had been perfectly fit to the shape of the tube, completely sealing off the western entrance to the platform. He looked about the area. Just as Fred had told him, there really wasn't much to see. Just a series of old cast iron benches, cracked tiles and scatterings of wall-mounted oil lamps and flickering electric bulbs. Most of them looked as if they were out of action. As he made his way back the way he came, the clouds of smoke from Fred's location coming into view, he noticed the beginnings of the other brick wall Rob mentioned earlier. He picked up the pace and approached.

"They'll probably have that end all sealed up tomorrow I reckon," Fred bellowed from behind, making his way towards Arthur. His voice echoed up the tunnel.

Arthur turned from the three-foot wall to the tall man. "Yeah?"

"Yeah," Fred said, his breath all but caught now, "Rob's blokes don't mess about. That down there is where the line stopped for a few years," he said, pointing a long finger behind the new nightwatchman.

Arthur craned his head back to face the waist-high wall and stared into the abyss. He could maybe see ten yards – give or take – beyond the wall, then it was nothing but blackness. He couldn't tell whether the rest of the tunnel dog legged around a corner or just kept going straight.

"What d'ya think then Arthur? Nice place innit?"

Arthur turned to face Fred. The colour had come back into his face, but it was weird seeing him without a smoke in his mouth.

"Yeah, pretty much what I was expecting to be honest."

Fred reached for his shirt pocket but soon realised he'd left his cigarettes upstairs.

Arthur grinned, "You did *tell* me not to let you light up another one before you went back up them stairs."

Fred chuckled, "Yeah, suppose I don't have a bloody choice now do I? Right, let me show you the little room I got the bed set up in, then I'll pop out quickly and get you a loaf of bread and stuff."

Fred started to lead him back towards the stairs when Arthur heard a strange sound from behind him.

He stopped.

What was that?

He twisted his head slightly to the right, peering out the corner of his eyes.

He listened.

Sounded like… giggling?

Nothing.

He twisted his head a little more to face the wall and the black hole beyond. He frowned.

"Strange," he whispered, turning back to follow Fred. Had he seen the tall man's colourless face at that moment, he would've seen a look of stone-cold dread. Fred Peters had heard the laughter too, and a dark wave of bone-chilling memories had come rushing to the shore of his wounded mind.

"Right," the tall and visibly flustered man said over his shoulder as he hurried round the corner towards the internal brick building, "This used to be an office-slash-storage room, but I got the lads down here to clear it all out just in case we did get a watchman in."

The small building was maybe ten yards in from the edge of the platform, and fifty or so from where the tunnel wall was under construction. Fred reached the door, and was foraging through the set of keys again when he dropped them.

"Fuck," he spat, bending down.

Arthur couldn't see Fred as he was just around the corner of the protruding building, but he was taken aback slightly by the venom in his vicious curse.

"Sorry Arthur mate. It's been a long day," he breathed an anxious chuckle into the dusty, oddly humid air.

"That's all right Fred, don't worry about it."

"Right, here we go," Fred clumsily inserted the small key into the lock and swung open the door. Inside was a small, ten-foot-square room with a single bed pressed up against the far wall, no pillow. Next to the bed was a stack of old books atop a low wooden stool, and to the left a chamber pot and a small table with a brass lantern, a box of matches and a pack of playing cards on top. A single chair was pushed under the table and a row of cupboards were mounted just above, presumably containing food and supplies.

"It's not quite The Ritz," Fred said, "but it'll do for a few days and nights, yeah?"

It sure as hell beats sleeping on the streets.

"Fred, mate, this is absolutely fine, trust me. I appreciate you setting this up and stuff."

Fred flicked a light switch on and off several times just inside the doorway, but nothing happened.

"Yeah, none of the bulbs down here seem to take, and you probably saw all the lanterns scattered around."

Arthur nodded.

"There's a lamp on the table there and some matches just in case you need them. Last thing you want down here is *total* darkness." They both laughed nervously for what must've been the hundredth time.

"So, that's your lot Arthur," Fred said, "sorry there's no food in the cupboards and that but like I keep saying, I really didn't expect anyone to come forward. But I'm glad you're here mate; at least the workers can sleep easy knowing their gear is safe and there's a presence down here, you know," he paused.

"Yeah, I appreciate it Fred," Arthur said, moving towards the bed and tossing his duffle bag down, "and if there's ever anything else like this going, I'm always up for it."

"Ha, yeah, we'll see how you feel after a few nights down here mate. You might struggle to get some shut-eye during the day what with the workers and stuff, so if you end up going out and about that's fine by me. But yeah, I'll bear you in mind for future jobs. I know you're probably thinking it's a bit weird I ain't asked whether you have any experience with this sorta thing," he paused, briefly looking over his shoulder. "For all I know, you could be some nutter who's gonna run off with all these tools."

"Up *them* bloody stairs?!" Arthur motioned to the London underground's second longest stairwell, fifty yards or so over Fred's shoulder. "No bloody chance."

Fred smiled.

"I know, I know. Point is, I don't really care, mate. You've saved me a lot of hassle doing this. I appreciate it. Anyway, I've prattled on long enough. Let me run to the shop for you quickly while you get settled in – but just one more thing before I shoot," he took a long, tentative pause, "are you sure about this, Arthur? I know eight pounds is a lot of dough, but if you don't fancy it, you can say. There's no shame."

Arthur Gladstone couldn't deny he felt a little apprehension towards the task at hand now. Certainly after hearing what he'd heard – or at least *thought* he'd heard – coming from the east tunnel; but it would take a little more than that to put him off six weeks' pay, a roof over his head, and some proper food.

"Nah, I'm good Fred, honest," he said with a reassuring smile on his face.

"All right. You're a braver bloke than me. But just in case you do get any of the thieving bastards down here, I put a hammer under the bed," he flicked his head towards Arthur's feet.

Arthur leant forward and put a hand under the bed, removing a long ball peen hammer.

"There's plenty of tools down here of course, but I'd love to see the bastard's faces if you came at them with that thing," Fred chuckled.

Arthur studied the hammer. "Yeah, I bet they'd think I was the Ripper himself, ha."

Fred stopped laughing, turning from the door.

"Right," he said, "I'll be fifteen, twenty minutes. I'll see what they got over the road but I'll probably just pick up a couple loaves of bread, a few pots of jellied eels, a few bottles of milk and such for now. That all right?"

Arthur nodded excitedly. "Spot on, Fred. Lovely stuff. Thanks."

"All right, I'll take the keys and be back in a bit," he turned and made for the exit.

Arthur stood and made his way to the doorway. He watched Fred shuffle briskly towards the stairwell. The tall man looked as if he was in something of a hurry, and he took several half-glances over his right shoulder *en route* to the stairs. Arthur frowned and stepped out of the doorway and onto the platform as Fred briefly – ever so briefly – halted, took a final glance over his right shoulder, and disappeared into the flickering amber glow of the narrow stairwell.

It didn't take Arthur long to unpack his things. By the time Fred had huffed and puffed past the halfway mark of the stairwell, all his clothes and provisions were in a neat line on his new bed, and he had lit the small brass lamp on the table.

"Lovely jubbly," he whispered to himself, rubbing his hands together as the lamp tossed dull shades of yellow about the dark brick room. He made his way over to the stool beside the bed and scooped up the large stack of dusty hardback books. He flopped onto the bed with a hearty sigh and began to shuffle through them.

Arthur didn't read so well, but he recognised a few of the titles. Having spent his whole life in Portsmouth, the works and wonders of Charles Dickens had been hammered into him from an early age, and although he never went to school, his mum used to read to him most nights until he was ten or so.

Great Expectations, *Bleak House*, *Hard Times* – there were a few classics in here, including his all-time favourite, *Oliver Twist*. There were a few other books he recognised too; *The Picture of Dorian Gray*, *The Jungle Book*, *Treasure Island* and *Alice's Adventures in Wonderland*. That one always gave him the willies. There were also a few books he'd never heard of: *The Fall of the House of Usher*, *Dracula*, and a pretty short-looking one called *The Turn of the Screw* by Henry James. For some reason, this last one interested him, and Arthur began to flick through the flimsy pages with interest. *Maybe I should try and give this one a go one night*, he thought, starting to feel right at home some hundred-and-fifty feet beneath the surface of Whitechapel.

He was just about done skimming through the thin book when he heard a series of short, sharp thuds from somewhere outside the room. He frowned, put down the book, grabbed the hammer, and made for the narrow doorway. Suddenly, something small and white shot past the door towards the platform, and his heart tensed up.

"What the..." Arthur stepped forward and placed both palms either side of the wooden frame. He leant out, looking right then left then right again. The rabbit – *was it a rabbit?* – was gone.

There was nothing; no sound, no echo, no movement of any kind. No nothing. Silence.

Arthur listened.

"Probably just a far-off train or something," he murmured into the suffocating gloom as he slowly walked out of the tiny room, taking a sharp turn onto the platform, "maybe it was a big white rat."

You've no idea what you're talking about, you fool.

Arthur ignored the voice of scepticism in his mind, sweeping his eyes along the length of the poorly-lit stretch of dust, brick and rubble. Scanning it for any sign of life. Finding nothing. He squinted east in the direction of the fresh, three-foot wall some fifty yards ahead.

That's where that weird giggling sound was coming from.

"Shut up," he muttered under his breath.

There was nothing there. Just a bunch of shifting shadows and a paradigm of dancing amber lights, that were being tossed around the tunnel by the flickering wall lanterns. Arthur turned from the short brick wall, heading back to his quarters when, suddenly, a blast of impossibly bright light consumed the entire underground as all the bulbs that lined the ceiling came to life.

Arthur screwed his eyes shut and grimaced.

"Ohh," he grunted, throwing up a hand to his brow, "Jesus Christ." He could see hundreds of bright red blood vessels on the inside of his eyelids, and then they were gone.

Darkness.

Blackness.

Nothing, he thought, *Nothing* –

Giggling again.

What the fuck? Arthur's eyes shot open.

The platform was just as it had been before the burst of electric light, but he was certain he'd heard laughter coming from the east.

"What is this?" he whispered, focussing his eyes on the short wall again. Something moved. Something pale and small, just behind the wall.

The white rabbit?

"What the fuck?"

A dryness in his throat, Arthur spun the hammer around a few times in one hand, reaching for a brass lantern from the pillar just in front of him with the other. He swallowed hard.

Wait, the voice of reason spoke up in his head.

Arthur took a step. There was an echo.

He took another step. Another echo.

Another step. Yet another echo – a mere fraction of a second later – that seemed to reverberate up the length of the empty tunnel.

"There's nothing there," he told himself, "there's *nothing* there."

Arthur Gladstone took a deep breath and approached the wall.

He was maybe twenty paces from where he thought he'd seen a flicker of movement when he heard the sound of laughter again. Clearer this time.

His heart froze.

That sounded like a fucking little girl.

"Hello?" his voice echoed through the tunnel and into the void. "Hello, who's there?"

Nothing.

He edged towards the wall, holding the lantern aloft in his left hand, the hammer cocked and ready in his right.

What you gonna do if it's a little girl, bash her brains in?

"Shut up," he rasped under his shaky breath.

More laughter, and more than one little girl this time. He was sure of it.

It does get a little weird down there sometimes, I'll admit. Rob's distant voice echoed in the dark chambers of his mind. Those words couldn't have been spoken more than an hour ago but, to Arthur, it felt like an eternity.

"Hello?" he called out again, edging closer and closer to a sound that would've seemed normal – pleasant, even – if it wasn't coming from a gaping black hole hundreds of feet beneath the city of London. What Arthur Gladstone heard next would haunt him for the rest of his days.

Singing.

Soft, gentle singing.

Slow, melodious, almost hypnotic.

"Ring… a-ring… a-rosies…"

The sound filled Arthur with creeping fear.

"A-pock…et-full… of-posies…"

His lungs tightened.

"Ring… a-ring… a-rosies…"

This doesn't make any sense. Just turn around and go. To hell with this.

"A-pock…et-full… of-posies…"

He gasped for air. He was paralysed with disbelief and ice-cold terror. The hammer, the lantern, everything was completely frozen in time.

"Ring… a-ring… a-rosies…"

Everything but the singing of the invisible little girls.

"A-pock…et-full… of-posies…"

Movement.

A small, diseased hand slowly folded its black fingers over the top of the brick wall.

"Atishoo."

Arthur's mouth fell open as another hand appeared, gripping the top of the wall.

And then another.

And then another.

There must've been at least four sets of tiny, wraithlike fingers all clutching the top of the three-foot wall. Arthur stood motionless, looking on in horrified incredulity. The yellow lantern in his left hand rattled violently. He was far enough from the waist-high wall that despite looking down from the platform, he couldn't quite see over it. And that was fine by Arthur.

Run!

"Atishoo!"

Run!

"We... *all*... fall... down... *DEAD!*"

The choir of childish singing suddenly turned into a deep, booming roar that detonated in Arthur's core and sent him sprawling backwards.

"FUCKING HELL!" he screamed, breaking into a run, not wanting to know who or what lay beyond the wall.

"Fuck! Fuck! Fuck!" he spat into the cold, rushing air as he bolted down the platform, dodging and leaping over mounds of rubble and brick at a blistering speed. He made it to the corner of his makeshift bedroom and then – inexplicably – turned back to face the sounds behind him.

What the fuck are you doing?

There was nothing there.

The wall was pretty far away now, but there was nothing there. No fingers. No little girls. No singing. No nothing. The only thing he could see was the flickering amber wall and tunnel as it was before. The only thing he could hear was the rattling of the brass lantern over the *thudthud, thudthud, thudthud* of his drumming heart. *Sod the eight pounds and jellied eels. Grab your shit and let's get out of here!* Arthur shuffled along the wall to the small room, but when he motioned to enter the doorway, the door was shut.

We didn't shut the door, did we?

"No," he hissed. The hot air from his thundering lungs came into contact with the now-frigid air and was instantly chilled. His eyes nailed to the door, Arthur slowly knelt down, placing the lantern on the ground.

Don't go in there.

He gradually rose to his feet, reaching for the door handle with his left hand, raising the hammer with his right, ready for what may or may not lie behind the door. He took a deep breath and slowly, tentatively, twisted the handle. The latch clicked and he thrust open the door.

Nothing. The room was exactly as he left it.

Or was it?

The lantern on the table was still lit, his stuff still in a neat line at the foot of the bed, and he could see the creases on the sheet where he'd been sitting just a few minutes earlier. *But what about the books?* The books were in a pile on the floor to the side of the bed. *We definitely didn't do that.*

Arthur felt an ice-cold fingernail graze the back of his neck.

Go! Sod this! Get out of here go!

And then he heard the echoes of childish giggles once again.

He nodded, stepping to the side of the fucked-up book stack and reaching for his things.

He was packing up his duffel bag as quickly as he could when he caught a glimpse of something tall and white out the corner of his left eye.

He stopped.

He slowly twisted his head in the direction of the white. And then back. He did a double take, and his whole body went numb. He gasped.

On the small wooden table was an enormous house of cards.

"Oh… my…" and then a terrible thought slid over his mind like a black and venomous snake. A thought – a question – so grim and unsettling and mad that it made these unexplainable events seem tame.

What if Fred's locked us down here?

"No," he said aloud, frantically shoving his belongings into his bag, unable to tear his eyes from the jagged tower of cards.

What if he's not coming back?

Arthur shook his head.

What if he isn't even real?

"Hello?"

Arthur froze.

"Hello, who's there?" A strange and strangled voice he didn't quite recognise, coming from the platform. He grabbed the hammer and turned.

What the fuck are you doing? Just go!

He slowly made his way through the doorway once

more and onto the dusty platform.

"H-hello?" Arthur's voice this time.

Silence.

He edged along the side of the small building, his back scraping along the course bricks – *sssssccrrrcccckkkk*. The lightbulbs flickered.

"Hello?" the invisible voice seemed to respond. It was distant but clear, and coming from the direction of the hideous wall. Arthur closed his eyes and breathed a long, trembling breath into the cold air. Then he heard the far-off laughs again.

This was a mistake.

He slowly opened his eyes and peered around the corner.

This whole fucking thing was a mistake.

What Arthur saw should have scared him a lot more than it actually did, but his overwhelming emotion was confusion. There was a man. A tall, well-dressed man, standing maybe halfway down the platform. He was holding some sort of briefcase and had his back to him. He was facing the eastern end of the tunnel and the cursed wall that lay just in front of the eternal blackness.

"Who's there?" the man seemed to ask of the wall, "What the bloody hell is this nonsense? Who's there?"

He seemed angry.

Did he hear the little shits too?

"This isn't funny, you know."

That answers that question.

"Why don't you get a bloody life, you little wankers?" the man shouted into the wall.

Under normal circumstances, the posh man's

outburst would have made Arthur laugh – but this whole situation was about as far from normal as you could get.

Arthur inched towards the man.

What are you doing?

He took a few nervous steps.

What are you bloody doing?

The man seemed to hear Arthur coming and he suddenly turned from the wall. Arthur froze; he couldn't quite make out the man's face, but something was wrong. Something was very, very wrong. The laughter, the singing, the fingers, the books and now this man, this face. *It does get a little weird down there sometimes, I'll admit.*

Arthur felt a dark surge of fright inside him and was about to open his mouth to say… something, when a blood-curdling howl tore down the platform, causing him to flinch and snap his head back in the opposite direction.

"What the fuck –"

The guttural howl – or roar or scream – was still reverberating through the tunnel; but there was nothing there. Just the large brick wall that blocked off the west side of the tube some ninety yards or so away. Arthur squinted, but there was nothing.

Absolutely nothing.

He turned back to face the man. He was a little closer now, but the young drifter still couldn't make out the features of his face.

"H-hello? Who's there?" the man asked, he sounded worried.

"What… what are you doing down here?" Arthur yelled down the platform. It wasn't a shout, but there was just enough venom in his voice for the question to sound imposing.

Suddenly there was another howl from the west. Louder this time.

Closer.

Arthur instinctively spun his head back towards the awful sound, then back towards the man. He was stood dead still.

Did he hear that too? Is-is he even here?

Another dreadful howl filled the icy, underground air, and the man suddenly broke into a run towards Arthur. But it wasn't a run at all. He was rushing towards him without even moving his legs.

Fuck! Arthur gripped the hammer tight and was just about to turn and bolt for the stairs when he noticed the man was missing the bottom half of his bloody, gaping face.

RUN!

He wheeled away and sprinted as fast as he could for the stairwell.

"Fuck! Fuck! Fuck!" he spat as he darted past the minefield of tools and metals and piles of rubble. He was closing in on the flickering entrance to the stairs when another demonic roar seemed to shake the entire platform. It was followed by the sound of running footsteps on the stony ground.

"Fucking Jesus!" Arthur cried as he burst into the spiral stairwell, hurdling up and around the crooked steps three or four at a time, still clutching the hammer in his taut right hand. He never knew he could move so fast. But the man with the horrible, smashed-up face and the invisible thing from the west were both gaining on him. He huffed and puffed and powered his legs with everything he had up the never-ending stairs. Another ear-splitting roar from below filled the air and Arthur Gladstone – tears streaming down his red face – dug as deep as he could dig.

"You best behave yourself Arthur or Jack'll bloody get ya!" his late mum's voice ran through his racing mind as he cleared another three steps.

"It does get a little weird down there sometimes, I'll admit." the ominous builder's throwaway comment coming back to haunt him as he cleared three more, surely nearing the gated entrance now.

The gated entrance.

He cleared three more steps.

The gated entrance.

Four more steps.

The locked gated entrance.

"...a man was brutally murdered on that stairway you passed on your way in." Fred's grave words rang in his head.

"No!" Arthur screamed, a terrifying cluster of howls and grunts and scratches and clambering footsteps bearing down on him. He cleared three, six, nine, twelve more steps. He couldn't possibly run any faster but he could now hear a cacophony of dreadful, confusing sounds all around as the world honed in on his short and penniless life.

We're not gonna make it! We're not gonna make it!

Arthur Gladstone was maybe twenty seconds from the top of the stairs when he felt a jolt. A violent, heart-stopping jolt on his right ankle that sent him sprawling face first onto the hard stone steps.

He cried out in terror, dropping the hammer with a *chinkchhinkchnk*. He snapped his head around as he clambered to his feet and he saw the hammer tumble, disappearing down the dark, winding stairs.

He cried out in terror, hearing another guttural howl and a series of awful thuds and screams. Arthur was just about to turn and run when a large hand slammed down on his shoulder and pulled him to his feet.

"Move!" Fred Peters shouted into the insane, growling air as he tugged the petrified drifter up the stone steps. There were maybe twenty seconds of frantic huffing and puffing and stumbling and scrambling when the two finally made it to the top of the stairs. The gate was open, and Fred hurled an exhausted Arthur through the entrance. He turned and swiftly unfolded the collapsible gate, slamming it shut and closing the padlock in one frantic move. The tall man fell against the tiled wall beside the gate and breathed.

"Fuck me!" he panted into the sour air, glancing over at Arthur, who stood leaning forward with his hands on his knees.

Their eyes met.

Fred grinned. "Still want that eight quid?"

Arthur shuffled towards Fred and put a hand on his shoulder.

"Where's my jellied eels?"

They laughed, turning towards the amber glow of the long and winding stairwell.

The terrible sounds had stopped.

There was nothing but the flickering of the lamps and the heavy breathing of the traumatised men. The escapees.

All was silent. All was still.

"Let's get out of here," Fred said, patting Arthur on the shoulder, "you can stay with me and the wife tonight and I'll sort you out some work in the morning, all right?"

Arthur nodded. "Thanks Fred. You won't get in trouble or nothing for this?"

"Nah, the missus ain't that bad mate."

They shared another nervous laugh, and were just about to turn from the gate when a large, wraith-like shadow began to grow and fill the bend of the winding staircase.

"Come on," Fred said, guiding Arthur towards the exit of the Whitechapel Underground, "I've seen this one before."

OLD MAN ABBERLINE

"That's Old Man Abberline's place," said Henry, running, "why the bloody hell are you taking us there for?"

"The Beast!" puffed Tom.

"The Beast?" asked Nick.

"That's right, *The Beast*," said Tom, grinding to a halt just in front of the bushes that lined the old beach house. The three boys crouched into a tight, shivering huddle. "I bumped into Mrs. Abberline the other day, and she must've clocked my big old Sherlock Holmes book because she started talking about how her husband had this story that would put *The Hound of the Baskervilles* to shame."

"I love that one," panted Nick through chattering teeth, "I never knew the old geezer was a writer."

"I heard he was a clockmaker," said Henry, fighting for his breath.

"No, you've got it all wrong," said Tom, "my old man says he was a copper. A proper inspector in London back in the days of Queen Vic' and that."

"No way," Nick and Henry breathed into the chilly December air. The sharp winds had picked up something fierce and the three musketeers were poorly dressed for the occasion.

Henry asked, "So what the bloody hell is *The Beast*, then?"

"No idea," said Tom, shaking his head.

"Eh?"

"All the old dear said was that Mr. Abberline has this brilliant monster story about "The Beast", and it's got The Ripper in it and stuff!"

"Jack the Ripper?"

"How many other Rippers d'you know?"

The boys looked at each other and shrugged.

"Anyway, she said I should come on up to their house one day coz he could use some company so I asked if I could bring you two and her eyes proper lit up."

"So, what? We just knock on the door?" asked Henry.

"No," said Tom, "we break in."

Henry looked dully at him.

"Of course we knock on the door. What's up with you?"

"How old are they?"

"I dunno. *Old*. Come on."

Tom and Nick tiptoed up the front porch steps arm-in-arm. Henry snorted and shook his head, rooted to the side of the rustling hedge.

"Come on, Henry," said Nick, "might be a laugh. What else we gonna do on a horrible day like this?"

"They're old," said Tom, "they'll probably have hot

cross buns and tea," he took Nick's elbow and turned with a grin on his face.

"And biscuits," said Nick as Tom knocked on the big brown door.

Henry joined his friends.

"Oh, hello boys," beamed the old woman, the corners of her narrow mouth turning up into a welcoming smile, "I was wondering when you'd pop round. Come in, come in," she slid to the side, ushering in her red-faced visitors, "'ere, Fred, look who's 'ere."

The three boys all stepped into the warm, peering down a long, dark hall towards a room that seemed to be glowing. The crackling of an open coal fire covered the sound of the howling winds berating the rear of the house.

"What?" A guttural growl came from up ahead. "Who's 'ere?"

"Go on boys," Mrs. Abberline encouraged, flicking her warm eyes to the room at the end of the hall, "his bark's bigger than his bite."

They shuffled forward a few inches before the old woman burst ahead of them. "It's that young lad Tom I was telling you about – and his friends," she said, making her way towards the amber glow.

"'Ere," she turned, "you boys want some tea and biscuits?"

"Oh, yes please Mrs. Abberline." Tom spoke on behalf of his nodding cohort.

"None of that," the old woman said, waving her hand, "call me Emma. Right," she turned back towards the room, "Fred, you want a cuppa and a couple of biscuits?"

"Ohh, *fancy* that," the old man in the rocking chair said with a wry smile on his face, "I was just about to ask whether *you* wanted a cuppa, dear. I best stay sat down now, ain't I?"

"Oh, shut up you," the old woman said, laughing, "Right; you boys sit yourselves down in front of the fire and make sure he behaves himself," she scowled at the wily old man.

Tom, Nick and Henry all inched towards the fire then sat – legs crossed – on the musty Persian rug with their back to the flames. They looked around the cosy room then up at the old man.

His golden face was full, yet tired, lined and cracked like an old oil painting, a scattering of ancient pockmarks and liver spots, black rings under the puffy blue eyes and a two-inch scar on his right cheek.

"Don't listen to her, boys," Abberline said, leaning forward as if he was about to reveal some big secret. "She's had it in for me for years," he winked.

They sniggered.

"How many sugars you boys want in your teas?" Emma bellowed from the kitchen.

"'Ere, listen boys," Abberline rasped over the blazing fire, "she tends to put a little more sugar in than you ask for, so make sure you round up." His dark blue eyes glinted with mischief.

"Uhh, one please, Mrs. Abberline," said Tom.

"One for me as well please," said Henry.

"Three for me, please," Nick snickered.

Tom punched him in the arm. "Nick!" he said,

chuckling.

"That's alright," Abberline whispered, grinning, "Nick's got the right idea," he winked again. "Two for me please, dear," he shouted, sitting back in his rocking chair. "So, Emma tells me you boys like detective stories. Sherlock Holmes and such."

The three boys nodded in unison.

"Oh yeah, Mr. Abberline. We've got this huge book of Sherlock stories we all share between us. It's like," Tom spread his tiny hands out wide, "this big!"

"Is that right?"

The boys all nodded excitedly.

"I remember when the first of those came out. They were all the rage around the station. I could've used a clever dick like Holmes on my unit, I tell you."

The old man's miniature audience chuckled.

"Did you used to be a copper, Mr. Abberline?" Nick asked.

"Nick!" Tom and Henry snapped their heads to the boy in the middle.

"Ha, that's all right, boys. It's no secret," Abberline rocked in his chair, "I joined the Met when I was... bloody hell," he lowered his eyes in thought, "twenty years old. Yeah, twenty. Back in '63 it was."

Three pairs of wide eyes looked up and on in disbelief. The old man *was* old.

"I grew up round here like you boys and worked as a clockmaker for a few years before I decided I wanted something a little more exciting than boring old Bournemouth. Packed up my bags, moved to North London, and enlisted in the police the very next day."

Old Man Abberline continued to rock back and forth

in his squeaky chair.

"Anyway, I worked my way up over the next fifteen years or so before I got my big break and was made an inspector in charge of the Criminal Investigation Department in Whitechapel."

The boys all looked at each other. *Whitechapel*, they all mouthed. So it was true. Nick turned to Old Man Abberline and asked "So... you was like a proper inspector? Like Lestrade?"

Abberline laughed and slapped his knee.

"Yep, sure was," he coughed, "although, like I said, I didn't have no genius detective at my disposal like that lucky so-and-so."

The boys laughed.

"No, it was just little old me and a few good men. A few *bloody* good men."

Mrs. Abberline came rattling around the corner slowly with a tray of teas and biscuits. The three boys stirred, rising to their knees.

"Right," she said, angling the tray towards the old man, "we got two sugars for his Lordship."

"Thank you kindly," Abberline said, sitting forward and plucking his cup from the tray along with two chocolate digestives.

She turned towards the three eager boys. "The two on the right are the one sugars – and who's the cheeky sod who wanted three?" She looked up from the steaming hot teas. Nick's face had turned a bright shade of red.

"Oh, well I think we have our answer, Inspector," she said playfully.

"The boy acted alone, I reckon, Sarge," the old man

said through a mouthful of biscuit.

Nick smiled, nervously reaching for his sweet drink.

"Go on," the old woman said, "help yourself to as many biscuits as you like." The boys, cups in hand, swarmed on the fresh packet of crumbly brown discs.

"Right, I'll leave you boys to it," she said, straightening up, "if there's anything you need you just give us a shout, alright?"

"Thank you, Mrs. Abberline," the boys said as the old woman turned, shuffling out of the warm room with the empty tray.

The teas were a little too hot to drink just yet, so they took to dunking their biscuits into the swirling pools of light brown. At this moment, with a mouthful of sweet, warm chocolate in front of a dancing fire on a miserable winter's afternoon, the waves crashing on the not-so-distant shore, Christmas just around the corner, all three boys figured there was nothing better in the world.

"So," the old man said, swallowing a hunk of biscuit, "what did the missus tell you boys before you came round?"

"Nothing much, Mr. Abberline," Tom said, "just that you had a story about some beast or monster or something."

"Ahh, *The Beast,*" Abberline said. He pursed his lips, lightly blowing into his cup. "Well, that certainly is a story. Not much of a detective story, mind, but it's still a corker." He took a sip of his tea.

Nick and Henry tried to do likewise but theirs were still a little too hot.

"Well, as I was saying, I was made an inspector in Whitechapel around the summer of '78, and I was there for maybe nine or ten years or so before I transferred to the Central Office at Scotland Yard. There, I was soon promoted to Inspector First-Class." He took another sip of his tea. "I could've only been there maybe five or six months before an old friend reached out and pulled me back into the East-End." The old man's cheerful demeanour suddenly darkened. He shifted his gaze towards the coal fire and frowned.

The boys all looked at each other.

"Anyway," the old man said, tearing his eyes from the flames, "around the same time I was being called back to my old stomping ground, a man – a scientist – by the name of Dr. Edward Kessler was on the verge of an incredible discovery. And this tale I'm about to tell you boys is his story, not mine."

"What's it called?" asked Nick.

"What's it called?" The old man seemed confused.

"Yeah," said Henry, "all good stories should have a name."

"Ohhh... I see. Well, It's been a long time since I told this one, and since it's a *true* story... I've never thought about giving it a name, really," Abberline shuffled about in his chair, "but all right, all right, how about we call it... *"The Strange Case of Dr. Kessler and Mr. Merrick."*"

The boys' eyes all lit up instantaneously.

"You mean like *The Strange Case of Dr. Jekyll and Mr. Hyde*?" Tom asked, unable to contain his excitement.

"Not exactly," Abberline said, the wry smile

returning to his face.

The howling winds, laced with rain and ocean spray, continued their assault on the back of the old beach house as the tiny fire raged on. Tom, Nick and Henry all took a sip of their hot drinks and scooted an inch or two closer to the old man.

Frederick Abberline took a deep breath, turned his gaze back towards the fiery coals, preparing to do something he'd seldom allowed himself to do these past forty years. He took a long slurp of his tea, sat back in his chair, and cast his mind back to the summer of 1888.

"They say he was some sort of genius," Abberline said, rocking back and forth in his chair and cradling his warm mug, "a brilliant scientist who was right at the very top of his field. In the summer of '88, he was only in his late twenties, but Dr. Kessler was making all sorts of leaps into the future with his work on genetic engineering and something called *performance-enhancing stimulants.*"

The boys looked stumped.

"Oh, don't worry," said Abberline, acknowledging their puzzlement, "I never understood much of it beyond the fancy name – and I'll admit, I actually found a lot of this out after it happened – through interviews and journal entries, you see. Anyway, Kessler was basically interested in increasing human strength, speed and agility, but also manipulating the body's genetic make-up so's to ward off illness, disease and physical deformities and such." Abberline coughed several times into his fist, nearly spilling his tea. "Ohhh, 'scuse me boys. Anyway, I believe they call it "cellular change". This interest, this *passion* of Kessler's would develop into an obsession, and it was this obsession that would bring about The Beast."

He paused, taking another sip of his tea to soothe his throat.

"Ohh, blimey. Where was I...? Oh, yes. So, Kessler did most of his work out of a basement he leased over on Tooley Street, just off the south bank of the Thames. It was like a mad scientist's laboratory, exactly the kind you'd imagine Dr. Frankenstein had: bottles and beakers of green and yellow potions and serums everywhere, all sorts of weird and wonderful devices and contraptions shooting off tiny forks of electricity here, there and everywhere; there were drawings and equations and diagrams plastered all over the walls, and lots of cages and glass tanks of rats and mice squeaking and scurrying around."

The boys watched on in wonder as the fire warmed their hunched backs. Old Man Abberline was like an old, seasoned fisherman reeling in his catch.

"Yep, he spent a lot of hours in that basement, but he had a small office and quite a few contacts at the Royal London Hospital over in Whitechapel, including his fiancée, Elizabeth, and his good friend Dr. Frederick Treves," Abberline glared into the fire again. "It was Treves who would introduce Kessler to Mr. Merrick towards the back end of that summer, and the two would strike up a friendship that would inspire Kessler to push his work and experiments to the limit."

The old man leant towards his little side table, reaching for his second biscuit. "I'm guessing you boys probably know Mr. Merrick by his stage name?"

Tom, Nick and Henry looked at each other, shaking their heads, perplexed.

"The Elephant Man," Abberline said, snapping his biscuit in half with trembling fingers.

The boys' mouths all fell open.

"Is… is he the…The Beast?" asked Nick.

"God, no!" Abberline bellowed through a mouthful of crumbs, causing all three boys to flinch. "Merrick was one of the nicest people I ever met."

"You… you knew The Elephant Man?" asked Tom, his mind practically blown.

"Well, I wouldn't say I *knew* him – but yes, we shook hands a few times."

Nick dropped his biscuit into his tea. The boys couldn't believe what they were hearing. Up until this moment, they'd always thought The Elephant Man was just a myth like The Loch Ness Monster or Bloody Mary or Father Christmas.

"What… what did he look like?" asked Nick.

"Hard to describe, really," said Abberline, remembering the face of a man he could never forget, "he certainly didn't look like no flaming elephant, though, put it that way. His name was Joseph Merrick, and all that matters is that despite looking different to everyone else, he had a heart of gold."

The old man, sensing the boys' scepticism, saw an opportunity to impart some wisdom.

"Lads, before we get onto The Beast, let me tell you something. I've met a lot of monsters in my life, and take it from me, nine times outta ten, they don't look like monsters at all. It's all up here," he tapped the side of his balding head, "that's where the real monsters are. Never judge a book by its cover, all right boys? It's how people act and what people do what defines them. Not how good they look in a bloody mirror."

They all nodded.

"Anyway, where was I? Ahh, of course, Merrick. He really was a lovely bloke, and based on the way a lot of people treated him, he had every right to act like the beast everyone made him out to be. But he was made of stronger stuff," Abberline smiled, rocking back in his chair, "*better* stuff. Anyway, when Treves introduced Kessler to Merrick, something happened to the scientist. Something strange."

The boys looked at each other again, leaning forward, listening close.

"He cried. He cried, and he cried. And then cried some more."

The boys' collective confusion had returned.

"Treves later told me this sort of reaction to Merrick's appearance was not *that* uncommon, but he said he'd never seen such an outpour like that day."

"Wh-why?" asked Henry.

"Pity, I suppose – perhaps some sense of misplaced guilt – but mostly because Kessler wanted to help him, boys. He believed there was a chance his work on cellular change could reverse the effects of Merrick's severe deformities. Both Treves and Kessler's fiancée Elizabeth later revealed to me that the meeting with Joseph Merrick gave his research new meaning. He felt like what he was doing was now of the utmost importance, and from that day forth, everything else in his life was kicked to the curb. He could help Joseph.

He could cure him. He was sure of it. Treves disagreed, believing that Merrick's condition was simply incurable. Irreversible. And he told me that he instantly regretted letting Kessler meet Merrick, because he had finally settled after years of unimaginable cruelty and neglect. Treves felt like the unstable scientist's presence could cause unrest. But, as the weeks went by and Kessler continued to visit, often smuggled into Merrick's quarters by Elizabeth – she was a nurse, you see – the two became closer, and Kessler became convinced he could cure Merrick. Maybe even improve him."

Abberline shovelled another biscuit into his mouth, chasing it down with another wave of sweet tea.

"You see, Treves was very protective of Merrick, and over time, a great deal of friction developed between the two doctors. Treves felt that Kessler was starting to give Merrick false hope, and while he didn't necessarily disapprove of Kessler's research, he believed he should've refrained from sharing his reports and findings with Merrick."

"But, he was only trying to help him. Wasn't he?" Asked Henry.

"Absolutely. But that doesn't make it right. Kessler was what some people call an "eccentric", boys. He'd often behave quite strangely. Aggressively, even, and I was told he could come across as quite intimidating when he didn't get what he wanted. As summer turned to autumn, he would turn up uninvited to Merrick's quarters at all sorts of hours. One time when Elizbeth wasn't around, Kessler was refused entry and he became enraged and viciously attacked an orderly, fracturing his skull, his eye socket, and breaking his jaw in two places."

Three pairs of captivated eyes all widened with horror. With fear.

"It took four men to finally restrain him. Treves – as you can imagine – was furious. He somehow managed to convince the orderly not to press charges against the hysterical scientist, but he barred Kessler from the hospital grounds, forbidding him to ever see Merrick again. He soon severed all ties with the mad scientist, and even Elizabeth later admitted her feelings towards her fiancée had started to fray in the lead up to the assault."

"Why was Kessler so angry, Mr. Abberline?" Tom this time.

"Well, he'd developed this serum, you see. One that he'd been testing on his lab rats that was shown to not only shrink tumours and other abnormal growths, but significantly enhance the rodents' physical strength and speed."

"How did he manage to find sick rats with tumours and stuff?" Nick asked.

"He didn't," Abberline finished his tea, "according to his journal, he captured as many as he could over a series of a few days – god knows how – and he induced the growths himself through a series of injections and stuff."

"That's pretty cruel," said Henry, shaking his head.

"Yeah, it is. *It was.* I mean, they were only rats, but I agree it's not nice. Anyway, this all happened around late September, and with the exception of what we later gathered from Kessler's journal and a few eyewitness testimonies, what exactly went on in the laboratory between then and the night The Beast came to the East-End is anybody's guess."

A sudden gust of wind growled down the chimney chute, causing all three boys to flinch and turn. The old man smiled, then continued.

"What we know is that the effects of Kessler's serum were short-lived. The rats soon reverted to their original states in a matter of days, the growths and tumours returning, their increased motor abilities vanished. It turns out that Kessler had actually consumed some of the serum himself the night he damn near killed that poor orderly and, judging from his notes, he fell into a deep depression soon after. But he was not discouraged by the failed experiment – he wouldn't give up. He was far too invested in his mission to stop, and so he kept on working. Kept on experimenting – and towards the back end of October, he felt as if he was nearing a solution."

Abberline paused for a moment, turning his head towards the grey window.

"I must've replayed the contents of Kessler's journal in my head a hundred times over the years, and what always struck me was how he began thinking only of others: of Merrick and Treves and Elizabeth; how he could make them proud by bettering the life of one poor man and perhaps even millions. But, as the entries went by, it seemed to become all about him," he turned his gaze back towards the boys. "The surge of power he felt when he ingested that serum must've been incredible, and over the following weeks, he took more and more of it. He became addicted, dependent, and was experimenting with various ways in which the serum could be delivered into the body's nervous system. Based on his notes, it didn't seem to have any positive impact on his intelligence. If anything, you could argue it may have had a negative effect as his spelling and diction were far more basic throughout his final few entries. I actually had it confirmed later that a lot of what Kessler was scrawling into his progress reports towards the end was complete nonsense. The "erroneous ramblings of a madman" was how one professor put it, if I remember. Anyway, throughout the whole of October, Kessler completely shut himself off from the outside world, refusing to see or speak to anybody –"

"Even Elizabeth?" asked Henry.

"*Even* Elizabeth. And as the air turned cooler and the days grew shorter, Dr. Kessler worked away long into the cold and unforgiving nights, unseen, unheard and – I suspect – completely unrecognisable. Then, on 11th November, 1888, The Beast was born." Old Man Abberline paused for dramatic effect as the three young boys watched on, clasping their empty cups tight in their laps.

"Now, we could never be a hundred per cent certain, but we had it on good authority that Kessler had begun to combine a number of elixirs and experimental methods in a bid to perfect the lasting impact of his serum. Electricity and something called trepanning were involved, but based on something mentioned in Kessler's notes, we deduced that he planned to inject a large dose of a new serum he'd been working on into his spinal cord. Apparently, he had tested this on several of the rats and the results were "most intriguing"."

Tom and Nick and Henry all leant forward.

"The last entry in Kessler's journal was made at half past nine on the evening of November 11*, and it was as strange as it was short. It said *"He who makes a beast of himself, gets rid of the pain of being a man."'"*

Abberline looked again to the fireplace, which was now a smouldering pile of red and orange coals resting beneath a charred and peeling grey log.

"He didn't come up with it. It was actually a quote from some old writer called Samuel Johnson, but it stood out – not only because it was the last thing Kessler ever wrote, but because it perhaps showed a glimmer of understanding or recognition or something amidst what had become a sea of mad scrawlings," he paused, scratching his thin grey beard.

"At around ten fifteen, a few neighbours heard a series of howls and screams and bangings and crashings coming from below, and an old man who lived just above the basement went down to check on the mad scientist..."

Abberline's tiny audience could sense the story was about to get really interesting.

"...turns out, this old man had always gotten on pretty well with Kessler up until that autumn, and he actually had a spare key to the basement – presumably in case of any emergencies. He tentatively made his way down the steep stone steps to Kessler's lab, and knocked on the door. There was no answer. He knocked again. Still no answer. The screams and clatterings had all ceased. There was nothing. Silence. He tried again, but there was still no answer. So he pulled out his spare key, and slowly, cautiously, made his way inside..."

Abberline took a deliberately short pause before suddenly rocking forward in his chair with his hands contorted into claws. All three boys screamed and jumped out of their skins. If they hadn't already finished their teas, they would've ended up on the walls.

"Kessler leapt onto the old man in a flash and tore him limb from limb. Ripping and biting and crushing his head and chest with sickening ease, turning bone and cartilage and tissue into thick red jelly. He was Dr. Edward Kessler no more. He was *The Beast*. An enormous, ferocious, impossibly strong beast."

Tom, Nick and Henry were all huddled together, their eyes glued to the old man in the rocking chair.

"The Beast devoured what remained of the old man, scooping up and swallowing chunks of flesh before scrambling out of the basement doorway with a mouthful of hot blood and brains, moving swiftly along the southern bank of The Thames, with only one thing on its mind: *more. More. MORE!*"

The hot coals hissed as tiny spatters of rain made their way down the chimney. It wasn't quite dark outside, but the light from the fire had faded and the room was extremely dim. The boys watched on, and the old man continued.

"The Beast formerly known as Kessler didn't know what it was doing, it didn't know where it was going, but its brain and senses were on fire. It was a bitterly cold night, but The Beast didn't care. It was bearing down on London Bridge when it heard a noise coming from the north – a middle-aged couple on an evening stroll across the old bridge. The Beast howled and hurtled towards them. The couple tried to run but it was no use. They couldn't outrun The Beast – nobody could. It made light work of both the man and the woman, slaughtering them in a matter of seconds to a chorus of howls and cries and guttural screams. It took the man first, beating his head to pulp before it turned on the woman and tore into her throat. Two brave police constables heard the awful screams coming from the bridge and ran towards them. They ran and they ran as fast as they could, not knowing who or what lay waiting for them; but by the time they got to the scene of the crime, it was too late. The couple were dead and The Beast had disappeared into the underground station just at the end of the bridge. They gathered themselves, took a deep breath, and gave chase –"

"More tea boys?" Emma burst into the room.

All three boys and the old storyteller nearly hit the ceiling.

"Good God!" the old man exclaimed, breaking into a chuckle, "You scared us half to death, woman!"

"I hope you're not being too graphic, Mr. Abberline," Emma said, raising her eyebrows and tilting her head down. The old and accused man shook his head vigorously. The three boys came to his rescue.

"No, Mrs. Abberline," Tom said, "we like a bit of blood and guts." Nick and Henry both nodded in agreement, looking up at the dubious old woman.

"Well, all right then. But nothing too violent, okay?"

All four shook their heads.

"All right. Who wants tea?"

The old man held out his cup and smiled but the three boys declined. They were far too invested in the story now and couldn't wait for Abberline to get back to it.

Emma wheeled out of the room and the trio readied themselves for the next instalment. The old man leant out of his chair, gave the fire a few pokes and threw a fresh log onto the smouldering coals. He fell back into his chair with a groan, then returned to 1888.

"The Beast had a taste for the red stuff now, and it moved frantically through the underground tunnel towards Whitechapel."

Tom looked at Nick. Nick looked at Tom. Henry looked on.

"It was only a couple of stops away, and the last train of the day had just pulled away from the Whitechapel platform when The Beast caught a whiff of its next victim: a reporter. An out-of-town reporter had just stepped off the old steam train, and he was making his way towards the long spiral stairwell when he heard the roars of The Beast echo through the underground. He ran. He ran and he ran as fast as his legs would power him up those never-ending steps, but – well, you boys can probably guess what happened."

"The Beast got him?" Henry blurted out.

"Sure did, and made light work of him too. Bashed his chest in something awful, and he died a horrible death."

"What about the constables? The policemen?" asked Tom.

"They weren't too far behind, but they couldn't save the reporter. They heard the howls and thrashings of The Beast and his helpless victim as they ran along the tracks, but by the time they got to the reporter, he was long gone. And so was The Beast."

Emma shuffled in, flipping on the table lamp next to the old man and setting down his fresh cup of tea. She briefly put her hand on his shoulder, smiled warmly, then made her way back out of the room.

"Fortunately, the constables knew where The Beast was headed. Well, no: that's not right. They had a trail to follow, put it that way. A trail of blood. It was thick and hot and there was plenty of it, far too much to be coming just from the victims The Beast had devoured. No, it had to be coming from The Beast itself. Either way, it didn't matter. The constables had a lead, and they followed it."

Abberline leant forward, grabbing a hold of his cup of tea.

"They followed it up and out of the station and into the empty cobbled street. The trail of blood led south on Fulbourne Street, and can anyone guess what was at the end of Fulbourne Street?"

The boys all stared at the old man in silence.

"The Royal London Hospital," Abberline revealed.

"Merrick," said Tom.

"Treves," said Nick.

"Elizabeth," said Henry.

Abberline nodded, taking a sip of his tea.

"Yes, yes and yes. But, whether The Beast formerly known as Kessler was *actually* headed for the hospital shall forever remain a mystery."

The boys all frowned.

"Four young boys – a little older than yourselves – had spotted The Beast coming out of the station and, in their infinite wisdom, decided to follow it."

"What!?" they all cried in unison.

"I know," said Abberline, "I know. But they didn't know what it was or what it had done of course, and they were just thrill seekers. Little scamps were out far too late at night, just looking for a bit of adventure."

Abberline glared into the fire and smiled.

"Although, they did do something pretty special towards the end of the year. Anyway, it was a peculiar time, boys. A mad time. A lot of folks were acting weird, and take it from someone who was there and thought he had seen it all: it was a very dark time. The district was gripped by a kind of fear, a mass hysteria I'd never seen before. I'm not sure too many places have. The Beast wasn't the only strange and vile fiend to pass through Whitechapel that autumn." Half a dozen images that clung to the back of Abberline's mind like blood-soaked leaves came clearly into view for the first time in years. He winced. "Anyway, lads, The Beast was fading –"

"F-fading?" Henry rasped.

"Wilting, weakening, shrinking. The extreme effects of Kessler's serum were wearing off. Whether he knew this would happen, whether he knew *any* of this would happen, we'll never know."

He paused.

"As The Beast scrambled down the dark and gloomy street – blood pouring from its eyes, ears, nose and mouth – four stupidly curious boys were hot on its heels. It must've become aware of their presence somehow, because it suddenly turned and clambered down a narrow alleyway. It was a dead end, and the boys approached the entrance to the alley with caution.

One of them later told me he thought it might've been The Elephant Man himself. Whatever it was, they had to have a look. They had to see. They had to know,"

Abberline took another long sip of his hot tea.

"To this day I don't know whether they were brave or just plain stupid – I don't think the two are mutually exclusive, in all honesty. Anyway, the boys slowly made their way down the alley, inching closer and closer to the cornered beast."

Neither Tom, Nick or Henry had ever been so encapsulated. So hooked. The old man had them now.

"What was waiting for them at the end of the dark alley was neither beast nor man. It was something in between. It was a writhing, hissing, slimy mess of bone and muscle and hair. It was an abomination. It was death, and upon seeing the approaching shadows, it threw back its head and cried out into the night, thrusting its giant arms to the side and scurrying right for the four boys, who soon realised they'd made a huge mistake. They turned and ran. They ran, and ran, and ran as fast as I imagine any boys have ever ran. They spilled out onto the street one after the other. The first boy, the second boy, the third and finally the fourth…"

The old man stopped.

The trio of kneeling boys looked on through wide and transfixed eyes.

"…The Beast got him. It hurled itself onto the fourth boy's back and they both fell to the ground in a bloody heap. The boy cried out, squirming and struggling with everything he had to get away, but The Beast was still too strong. There was no escape. The Beast raised its pulsing arms high above its horrible head and was just about to smash them down into the boy's tiny skull when a barrage of gunshots filled the air – and The Beast went down."

Tom, Nick and Henry all cheered and whooped and in the room next door, the old woman smiled. Abberline maintained his composure, his game-face, and the boys soon fell silent again.

"The Beast went down, and the two constables approached, their rifles still smoking. The terrified boy scrambled from beneath the beast, and his friends scrambled to his aid. They all gathered around the fallen beast, looking down and on in absolute terror as it crackled and shrivelled and pulsed before their very eyes, gradually dissolving from an enormous monster into a once-brilliant scientist. Dr. Edward Kessler opened his mouth, looked up into the starless sky and uttered his final word...."*Elizabeth.*""

"Oh my God," said Tom.

"He *was* going to see Elizabeth," said Nick.

"Or was he just, like, calling out for her or something?" asked Henry, peering up at the old man.

"We'll never know, boys. We'll never know. To this day, I still don't believe he was aware of just how badly the experiment would go. Treves believed that although Kessler may not have been of sane mind, he was not a bad man – and that there's every chance he had no control over what happened that fateful November night. We can never be sure, but from what I found out over the following days and weeks, I came to the conclusion that Kessler tapped into something he didn't truly understand and something else took over. The Beast took over, and five people lost their lives that night."

"What happened to Elizabeth?" asked Henry.

"She wasn't at the hospital that night. Again, we'll never know if Kessler knew this. Probably not. But she was devastated, of course. She couldn't believe *her* Edward could do such terrible things, regardless of how distant or indifferent he had become in recent months."

"What about Merrick?" Nick asked.

"He was distraught. We never disclosed the full details of what happened to Kessler and his victims that night, but the loss of a friend, the loss of a man whom Merrick believed was genuinely trying to help him, was upsetting enough," Abberline rolled his glassy eyes to the ceiling, "Merrick had a lot of trouble speaking and he'd actually taught himself to read and write over the years. When Treves and I broke the news to him, he was very upset and scrambled for a piece of paper – on which he wrote the words *"Was it because of me?"*"

Abberline felt his throat clench.

"Boys, I've no shame in admitting to you I damn near cried my eyes out when I read that," the old man took a long pause and steadied himself. "Eighteen months later, Merrick unfortunately passed away in his sleep having shouldered more harm, more scorn and ill-feeling than a million far worse people could have endured in an entire lifetime. He was twenty-seven years old. Treves went on to have a long and successful career. He died only five years ago, and I hope he will forever be remembered not only as one of the country's greatest ever surgeons, but as a man who showed compassion and heart in a time and place where there was a lot of darkness."

Abberline finished his second cup of tea, looking down and smiling at the mesmerised boys.

"Listen to me," he said, "I've turned into a right sappy old geezer, haven't I?" he smiled.

"M-Mr. Abberline," Nick said nervously, "w-what about... Jack the Ripper?"

Abberline's smile disappeared.

The room fell silent.

"What about him?" The flickering light of the gentle fire danced across the right side of his face; the other side was shrouded in shadow.

"Mrs. Abberline said your story had The Ripper in it," said Tom.

"I see," said Abberline, rocking back in his chair, peering into the depths of the fiery coals once more. "You remember me saying earlier that I was called back to the East-End by an old friend?"

The boys nodded.

"Well, everything I've just told you boys actually happened around the same time as a series of brutal murders in Whitechapel. The last of which, in my opinion, occurred a couple of nights before The Beast's rampage."

Another growl of wind could be heard creeping down the chimney and through the cavity walls of the old brick building. The old man continued down a road he rarely cared to visit.

"In the days following Kessler's demise, the dogs in the local press tried to connect him to the other killings – and I'm sure there are still all sorts of nuts out there who believe they were related in some way. It's a load of old nonsense, of course, but like I said before, there was enough fear and paranoia going around to fill a hundred cities. No, this wasn't the same as the murders of those poor women. What that monster did was far worse."

"W-worse?" Nick couldn't possibly see how it could be worse.

"Yes," croaked Abberline, "much worse. To this day, I don't believe Kessler knew what he was doing, boys. I don't believe he ever meant to hurt anybody, let alone kill them. What happened was awful, but – in the end – it was a failed experiment. He had no real control. But The Ripper," Abberline paused again, "boys, let me tell you something… I always thought I knew what evil was. I figured I'd maybe brushed shoulders with it once or twice in my career up until that dreadful autumn. Twenty-five years on the force is a long time, and I'd seen a lot of terrible things. Things that clung to the wall of my memory like shreds of an old circus poster. Things nobody should have to see. Things I wished to God almighty nearly every night I could unsee. I'd seen a lot of terrible things," he leant forward, lowering his voice, "but I'd never seen anything like this. This was a new kind of evil – a new breed. And most of what I saw, I've never even shared with Emma. Which means it ain't for your ears, boys. Not yet." Abberline leant back in his chair.

By refusing to reveal the finer details of the evil that terrorised Whitechapel that dreadful autumn, the old man had inadvertently caused the hairs on each of the boys' necks to stand on end. Their imaginations did the work for him, and that was far more terrifying than anything he could've told them in that moment.

"All I will say is this – then we best call it a night, boys," Old Man Abberline leant forward in his chair. He didn't know it then, but this would be the last time he would ever speak of the famous case that would forever haunt the annals of British criminal history. The case that would forever have his name woven into its hideous fabric.

"Every bad thing I'd ever dealt with, every violent and vicious attack – The Beast's included – all paled in comparison to the demonic violence I saw that autumn. I didn't understand it then, and I still don't understand it now. For years after, I struggled to sleep. Something I'd never truly experienced in my life… but I'd often lay awake long into the cold and endless nights, staring up into the eternal black and wondering whether God even existed. If he did, well, I'd come to the conclusion that he abandoned Whitechapel in 1888. It didn't take no inspector to work that one out – and yet, that didn't stop me from knocking on the big man's door every single night asking why things went the way they did for so many. There were other things going on too. People went missing. Other vicious crimes, poisonings and such. Whitechapel was no Garden of Eden, boys, but for a three-month period, a giant snake slithered unseen through the streets at night and inspired some unspeakable acts."

All three boys had gone completely numb. And then Tom asked, "Did-did you ever catch him, Mr. Abberline?"

"No. Maybe. It…" Abberline frowned, "…it was never proven. We had theories. We had suspects. Lots of theories and suspects; we were lost in them really and, looking back, it's possible it may've been the work of more than one man. But...there was this one man in particular. A Polish immigrant – born Seweryn Klosowski, but he went by the name of *George Chapman*. We never had enough to charge him with but, without going into it too much, I liked him for the murders. There was just something about him," Abberline paused, "Anyway, back in '03 he was hanged for poisoning three women. Could he have been The Ripper? It's possible, but it was so long ago now, unless something miraculous were to happen, I don't think we'll ever truly know *who* he was. But there can be little doubt as to *what* The Ripper truly was, boys..."

Abberline paused.

The boys leant forward.

"...evil."

The boys turned to look at each other. Listening to the old inspector talk these past few hours had been like stepping into a time machine. A warm yet eerie time machine that could take you way back to a time where the world was on the brink of exciting yet terrifying possibilities. To a time where electricity was in its infancy and the gaslit streets of London were haunted by a faceless fiend and a horde of savage beasts.

Tom, Nick and Henry all rose to their feet, thanking old man Abberline for his time and Emma for the tea and biscuits. The old man willed himself out of his comfy chair and joined his wife in seeing the three boys to the door. He had enjoyed their company.

"Thank you, thank you, thank you," all three boys

said, nodding and smiling as they stepped out onto the front porch and into the chill of the dark and blustery night. It had finally stopped raining.

"Thank you, boys," Frederick Abberline said, "it was nice to meet you all."

"You boys be careful getting home, all right," Emma Abberline said cautiously.

"Be safe boys," the old man added, "be safe."

"We will," said Tom as the boys made their way down the steps and headed for the rustling bushes that lined the old beach house. When they stepped out onto the street, they turned and waved to the old married couple who still filled the open doorway. They waved back, bellowing their goodbyes.

Tom, Nick and Henry made their way along the pavement, not talking, still reeling from the old man's incredible story. Was it true? Was it all true? They didn't know. They didn't care. It was an excellent story and a hell of a way to spend an otherwise miserable winter's day.

In the weeks, months and years that followed, they would often come back to Abberline's story and reminisce about that cold December afternoon in front of the fire.

They stepped out into the road, crossing the street towards the small stone path that would lead them inland, and home. The distant barks of a large and angry dog could be heard howling on the biting wind.

They slowed. They stopped. They all looked at each

other.

They ran home, laughing.

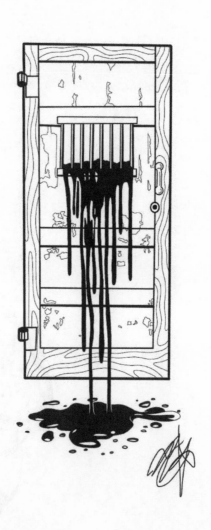

RIPPER COUNTRY

"Tell us a story, Grandad."

"Yeah, tell us a story, Grandad!"

"*A story?*" feigned the playful old man to the two small children, the yellow light from the old lamp dancing in their bright and eager eyes.

"What kind of story?"

"A scary story," said Rebecca and Paul together.

"A *scaaarryyy* story," said Grandad in his best Count Dracula voice. The twins giggled and clutched their mother excitedly. The old man's impression was actually pretty good.

"Well," the old man whispered, leaning forward into the light, "it is rather spooky down here, so I suppose a scary story would be just the ticket, wouldn't it?"

The twins nodded.

The old man lifted his gaze to their mother – his daughter – who rolled her eyes and smiled, nodding her approval. She'd heard them all before and knew the old magician would soon be mixing all manner of lies and truths to suit his rip-roaring narrative, but she couldn't deny that the kids could use a distraction. She tilted her head and raised an eyebrow at her own mother, who was already shaking her grey head, grinning. She'd heard them all before as well – even starred in a few. It was just a question of *which* tale her husband was going to conjure. *Double, double, toil and trouble*, she thought.

It was a cold and stormy night in the East-End of London. Another Christmas had just sauntered by, and the small family unit – minus Father – were all huddled around the old paraffin lamp in the damp, dark space. Their bedding and blankets were all bundled together and formed a small ocean of thick, wavy cotton. It was quite nice, all things considered. Comfortable. Cosy.

It had been an unusual Christmas. A dark Christmas, in a way, for there had been a lot of storms lately. Mostly during the day, but this particularly heavy downpour had reared its ugly head at night and the crashing and drumming of thunder could be heard all around. The children stirred, angling their eyes to the wailing heavens. The shrill, nerve-shredding cries of the howling winds rose and fell, rose and fell, rose and fell. Grandad, sensing their alarm, grabbed the handle of the brass lantern. He took a deep breath. He cracked his neck, and held the lantern gingerly beneath his chin. This was what he lived for.

"Right," he started, demanding Rebecca and Paul's full attention, "once upon a time, the beast moved swiftly along the riverbank with hot blood pouring –"

A chorus of groans filled the musty air.

"Nooo, not that one again!" cried little Paul, giggling.

"Why not?" asked Grandad, puzzled, "It's a classic. Just the thing for a *spoooooky* night like this, surely?"

"Noo," cried the little girl this time, "you've told that one before, Grandad."

"Yeah, Grandad," said Grandma. *I bloody hate that one*, she thought.

"All right, all right," he conceded, putting the lantern back in the centre of the blankets. He sat brooding for a moment. Gazing deep into the flickering yellow, mesmerised by its colour, pondering his next move.

Maybe it's time to bring out the holiday special, he thought. *It's hardly* A Christmas Carol *but it'll certainly do for a cold December night like this.* He smirked, peeling his eyes from the dim light, spreading his arms out wide.

"'Twas the night before Christmas," he said leaning forward again, "and everyone in Whitechapel thought that Jack was gone –"

"Bill," the old man's wife interrupted, "I'm not sure that's such a good idea."

"No, it's all right, Mum," her daughter said, leaping to the old man's defence. She actually liked this one. "Just keep it clean though – all right, Dickens?"

"Of course, of course," the old man smiled, "I know my audience dear, don't you worry."

Rebbeca and Paul shared a look of excitement then turned, grinning, to Grandad. If his story came with a warning, it *had* to be good.

They leant forward.

"'Twas the night before Christmas, and everyone in Whitechapel thought that Jack was gone. Everyone except for one little boy, and his three best friends. There had been…"

283

*

There had been a change in the air. Maybe it was Christmas. Maybe it was the weather. Maybe it was the promise of a new and better year; a fresh start. Or maybe, just maybe, it was finally over.

It had been a little under seven weeks now. The dust hadn't quite settled, but it was trying. There had been a change in the air, but it was still early days. Forty-five, to be precise. Forty-five days of peace. Forty-five days of quiet. Forty-five days of sanity – whatever *that* was nowadays. There had been no more letters, no more poems; no more kidneys in the evening post. No more women taken in the middle of the night and ripped to pieces by the faceless fiend. The fiend with a dozen different names; the fiend with no name. There had been no more poisonings. No more stabbings. No more *beasts*. A handful of locals were still missing, but nothing new had been reported for a while now. For forty-five days.

Yes, the autumn of terror had finally passed, but it had given way to a winter of misgiving. Of that, there could be no doubt. The entire district had been living under a shadow of mass neurosis since the night of the big storm back in late August. Now, it was cautiously beginning to wriggle free from clutches of fear and out into the cold, but it was still mourning, still despairing, still reeling from three mind-bending months of unspeakable cruelty the likes of which Whitechapel had never seen.

Children had lost mothers.

Mothers had lost daughters.

Countless people had lost their friends and faith; their faces, hearts and minds. It was the season of darkness. It was the winter of despair. These were dark times – hard times. But hard times make hard people, and the people of Whitechapel were harder than most. They would go on. Time, after all, heals all – but, for now, the wounds and memories were as fresh as the cold, crisp air this Christmas Eve night.

There had been a change in the air. It had been forty-five days, and maybe – just maybe – Jack The Ripper was gone.

Young Bill Talbot didn't buy it. Things had gone quiet, sure, but nobody had been caught. Nobody had been hanged. The fiend was still out there somewhere.

Watching.

Waiting.

Bill Talbot knew it. He just *knew* it. And as he sat beneath the flickering yellow glow of a wrought iron streetlight, his eyes fixed on the black front door across the grimy cobbled street, listening but not listening to his friends chew the fat about this, that and the other, his mind wandered off into the dark maze of speculation once more.

Bill supposed it was possible that the Ripper might've left town. Even the worst, most violent storms eventually move on. He supposed it was feasible that the lunatic could've been thrown into an asylum or maybe even killed. That was what his friend Joe thought, and he had to admit those theories did make sense. But in his heart, Bill Talbot truly believed that in some way, shape or form, Jack was still here. Even if he had moved on, his malevolence – his poison – still coursed through the veins of Whitechapel. The man and his knife had changed things forever, and there was no going back. Not now, not ever. This was his district now; his Borough, his dismal slice of London. This was Ripper Country, and there was something in the air. Something terrible. Bill's heart was filled to the brim with the ice-cold conviction that it wasn't over yet… and my oh my oh my, didn't it feel terrible?

Bill had always had trouble sleeping – one of the many drawbacks of an overactive mind – but these past few nights had been ridiculous. He had a bunch of hunches; a flurry of ideas and theories and suspects, an arsenal of what-ifs that he'd act out in his mind time and time again. He'd grown accustomed to lying awake long into the early hours of the morning, his fully-charged mind lost in the labyrinth of dark and terrifying possibilities; *What if he's still out there? What if he's just biding his time? What if he's not done? What if he's just down the street? What if he's protected by a higher power? What if he's more than one? What if…*

After hours of deliberating and exhausting all kinds of imaginary scenarios, Bill would eventually fall asleep only to wake up a few hours later crying and screaming. Just like he knew he would.

Bill and his three best friends had all seen a lot of strange and inexplicable things these past few months. Things they couldn't understand. And yet, Joe, Gordie and Fred had actually started to mellow towards the madness. But Bill's imagination wouldn't let go. A barrage of questions raced through his mind night after night as he tossed and turned in his uncomfortable bed, his mind teetering on the edge and inevitably falling down the rabbit hole: *Has everyone just forgotten? Does nobody care? Is it really over? What about the poisonings? What about all the missing people? What about that kidney in the post? What about all those messed up letters? What about the door? What about The Beast? What if they're all linked somehow? What if I could stop him? What if...*

"I still think it might've been that beast thing all along, you know," said Gordie, leaning back against the damp brick wall, blowing long strands of cloudy white vapour into the chilly air. The *Fab Four* had been hanging around on Lamb Street for the past hour, messing around and killing time before the Christmas Eve fête over on Brick Lane got into full swing.

"Are you bloody mad?" said Joe, "The *Daily Star* said all those poor birds – includin' Mary Jane – were sliced up with a knife."

"Ohh if it's in the *Star* it *must* be true!" said Fred.

Gordie and Joe chuckled. But not Bill.

"No, seriously," said Joe, "the beast couldn't have done any of that. You saw it. We all saw it."

Fred grimaced, remembering the thing's writhing face and red-veined eyes for the thousandth time.

"Joe's right," said Bill, chopping the palm of his left hand with his right, "just look at the facts: each and every one of those women had their throats cut and was carved open by someone who *knew* what they were doing. I'm bloody telling you."

"I thought Martha just got stabbed a bunch of times. She didn't have her throat cut, did she?" said Gordie.

"Read that in the papers as well, did you?" said Fred, rising to his feet. "Look, can we talk about somethin' else for once? We always end up on this shit."

"Yeah," agreed Joe, "I think I'd rather see Bill act out *A Christmas Carol* for us again like last year than sit around talking about all this nasty crap."

"Gawd bless us, everyone," said Fred in a high-pitched voice. Joe and Gordie both laughed, but Bill was not amused.

"Whatever," he said, getting to his feet, stretching his back.

"Alright," said Fred, mimicking his agitated friend, "what's your bloody point, Sherlock?"

"My bloody point is that the beast was just a freak event. A one-off. A coincidence. I think the Ripper is still out there and he *has* to be a butcher or something."

"I thought you reckoned he was a doctor?" said Gordie. "A surgeon?"

"What about the actor?" said Joe with a wry smile on his face.

Gordie put his hands to his face and pulled down on his cheeks.

"Nah, that was last week," said Fred, grabbing a hold of Bill, "a new week, a new suspect. Looks like Holmes is about to blow the lid right off this one, chaps. Gather round."

Bill didn't care for Fred's tone.

Joe chimed in "So, what? You reckon it might've been old *Leather Apron* after all then?"

"Exactly!" said Bill, "And do you know who my

money's on?"

Joe, Gordie and Fred all rolled their eyes and groaned. *Here it comes.*

"That creepy fucking cat's meat man!"

A series of boos and scoffs filled the frosty air. The jury were not impressed.

"Well it's a good job you don't have a pot to piss in, Billy boy," said Fred over Joe and Gordie's jeers, "because if that's the new horse you're backing then you're shit outta luck, mate."

Bill's wild accusations never went down particularly well, but this was one of the worst reactions yet. Worse than when he accused scary Mary Pearcy on the grounds that she "gave him the creeps".

"She gives *everyone* the creeps," Gordie had said, "how the bloody hell would she be able to overpower all those women?"

Worse than when he suggested it might've been old man Tandey, the barber, because he'd been acting strange lately: "Everyone's been acting strange lately. Geezer lost his wife and daughter, for God's sake," Joe had cried.

Even worse than when he'd outrageously pointed the finger at the stage actor Richard Mansfield who happened to be in London performing in a production of *The Strange Case of Dr Jekyll and Mr Hyde*. When Bill unleashed that corker last week, Gordie had laughed so hard he'd nearly wet himself.

Fred grabbed Bill in a headlock, laughing. "What did the poor old cat's meat man ever do to you Billy boy, aye?"

"Get off me," panted Bill, trying not to laugh. Fred

always knew how to cheer him up.

"Does he give you the creeps as well, does he? Been skimping on your old dear's cat meat, has he?"

"Get off!"

"Grab his legs boys," Fred said to the rest of the jurors, "time to cart this one off to Broadmoor. He's finally cracked."

Joe and Gordie swarmed on the flailing boy, hoisting his little legs up in the air and spinning him around, laughing.

In a way, this little moment of theirs was the most fun they'd had since before they crossed paths with the beast that fateful November night. They were still scared, but they were dealing with it in their own way – and when they came together things always seemed to get that little bit brighter. Even if for just a few hours. This was their little support group, their boys' club. They were the *Fab Four of the East-End*. It wasn't much, but for Bill, Joe, Gordie and Fred, it was enough.

"Put me down, you wankers," cried Bill, kicking and squirming.

"No can do, Inspector Talbot," said Fred in his finest regional accent, "you've simply gone *too* far this time."

"Ve vill haz to give you zie leeches, Mister Talbot!" said Gordie in a terrible German accent. The sound of raucous laughter filled the street.

"Listen-listen to the Russian professor," said Joe, still laughing, "ve must save you from yourself, Mister Bill!"

They spun the helpless inspector around a few more times before finally releasing him. Bill, Joe and Gordie all stumbled back into the nearby wall. Fred clutched the cool black lamppost, chasing his breath.

"The bloody cat's meat man," Fred rasped, shaking his head, "Jesus, Bill. Who's next? The Queen? Prince Albert?"

Joe and Gordie cackled.

"Seriously," said Fred, "have you seen the state of the bloke? Geezer must weigh less than you, Gordie."

Gordie held out his arms and flexed his non-existent muscles.

"There's something about him," Bill insisted, the grave look on his red face returning, "he's a dodgy bastard, I'm telling you. Don't act like you ain't noticed."

"I'm not even sure I know who the bloody hell we're talking about," said Joe.

"Yeah you do," said Gordie, "skinny, pale geezer with the fucked-up teeth. Horrible looking bastard, to be fair. Seen him down the lane a few times. He's always covered in blood and guts and wheels around a shitty looking handcart."

"He's a fuckin' butcher! A cat's meat man! Of course he's covered in blood," Fred cried.

"Yeah, well, I've been watching him," said Bill, "followed him home the other night from the slaughterhouse over on Buck's Row." He paused. "Ring any bells?"

Joe, Gordie and Fred all looked at each other blankly, shaking their heads.

"You're joking?" Bill couldn't believe it.

"Just spit it out, Holmes," said Gordie.

"That's where they found Polly Nichols," Bill declared, his arms spread wide in disbelief.

Joe, Gordie and Fred all groaned.

"Oh come off it, Bill," said Joe, "that sorta thinking narrows it down to like… five hundred people. What's so special about this geezer?"

"There's some–"

"–*thing about him*," they all joined in, finishing Bill's sentence.

"Whatever. I'm not wrong about this bloke. I'm telling you, something's going on in there," Bill raised his eyebrows, nodding his head to the house with the black door across the gloomy street.

Fred spun his head around.

"Oh, bloody hell," he spat, turning back to face the others, "is that why we've been hanging around here for the last hour?"

"He had a roll bag on him the other night," said Bill, gravely, "one of those knife bags –"

"He's a fuckin' butcher!"

"Why would he be taking it home with him, then?"

"I don't bloody know. It's Christmas. Maybe he's got a big old turkey in there –"

"Or a body!" spat Bill.

A chorus of groans filled the air.

"You're mad," said Joe.

"Maybe. But I ain't wrong," he pushed himself off the wall, gesticulating at the house opposite, "I've been sat out here the past few nights and the only light I've seen coming from that house is from that tiny basement window," Bill pointed to the dull glow just above the pavement –

Suddenly the light went out.

Bill froze.

"That doesn't mean a bloody thing, Bill," said Joe, stepping towards the frozen boy, "what, you think he's got a load of those missing people down there or something? Carving them up and feeding them to the cats? This ain't one of your Penny Dreadfuls."

"I know. I mean, maybe. I don't... I don't –"

Bill's eyes were glued to the black door.

"So what's your plan then? Knock on matey's door and ask if he's the Ripper?" Gordie scoffed.

"I don't... I don't..."

The door opened.

A short, hunched figure shuffled out of the black, pulling the door shut with one hand, locking it with the other. Bill suddenly spun to his dubious friends.

"Don't look at him," he hissed, "don't look!"

"Oh come on," said Fred, still leaning against the lamppost, "let's go ask him. Oi, *Jack!*"

Bill grabbed hold of Fred. "What the fuck are you doin'!?" he hissed.

The twisted shadow didn't seem to notice the tall boy's heckle. It pocketed the keys, turned, and shuffled off down the pavement into the cold night.

"You're such a dickhead, Freddy," chuckled Gordie.

"Oh shut up, he didn't hear nothing."

"You don't know that," spat Bill, "this ain't one of your bloody games, Fred."

"Look," Fred pushed off the lamppost with a serious look on his face, "do I think the Ripper's gone...? No. Well, maybe. I don't know. But you need to ease up accusing every Tom, Dick and Harry, alright? Especially little weasels like that loser. It's getting old now, mate."

Bill looked down at his feet.

"Yeah," said Joe, "I know me and dickhead here don't agree on much" – Fred put a hand to his chest, feigning a broken heart – "but there's a lot of shady bastards around here, Bill. You know that. And even if the Ripper's still alive, it ain't our job to find him. We tried it one night, and look how that bloody turned out."

Silence.

"Look," said Fred, stepping towards the three boys, placing a hand on Bill's shoulder, "a lot of fucked up things have happened these past few months. You know it. I know it. And I know I joke around and that, but that… thing… that *beast* thing, the Ripper, the bodies, Mary Kelly, they all keep me up at night, all right. There, I bloody said it."

Bill looked up. He'd never heard Fred Peters sound so sincere. None of them had.

"Me too," said Gordie, stepping towards Bill, "I… I can't seem to shake what happened to Mary Kelly. Can't seem to get her face out of my head, you know."

"Me neither, mate," sighed Joe, patting Gordie lightly on the back, "me neither."

"I keep on having this dream," said Bill, struggling to hold back the tears, "I ain't been sleeping much lately but when I do, it's always the same… bloody… dream."

He paused.

"Go on, mate," said Fred, "we're listening."

Bill took a deep, cold breath.

"It's the summer. Back before all *this* started. I'm sitting on some bench in Mitre Square. Just sat there. Looking out at all the people rushing around, minding their own business. Some of them I recognise. Most of them I don't. But I nearly always see Mary Kelly and Cathy."

"Eddowes?" asked Gordie.

Bill nodded. "They always smile and wave and I wave right back. Some old man is sat next to me but for some reason, I can't face him. No matter how hard I try. It's like I'm paralysed or something, but I know he's there and I know he's old. He's talking about a load of stuff I never seem to remember. I got a feeling it's about a boat or something. I don't know."

Bill looked up at Fred, then back down at his shuffling feet. He grimaced.

"After a while, I look down at my feet and they're covered in blood. I look up and it's everywhere. The whole square, it's all flooded in blood. It's, like… ankle deep, but nobody seems to notice. Nobody seems to care. Everyone just goes about their business, trudging through the red stuff like it was nothing."

Bill sniffed and shook his head. He was half expecting the boys to have burst out laughing by now, but they were listening. They were *actually* listening.

"The sky clouds over, it turns all black and stuff, and I always hear a big clock off somewhere followed by a loud crack of thunder. All of a sudden, there's a big black door in the middle of the square. All the people have disappeared. There's nothing but this door and the sloshing blood. *So* much blood. The old man then puts an icy hand on my shoulder. I turn to face him, but he has no face. It's kinda like, blurred or smudged or something. It's weird. It's fuckin' horrible. And then he opens his mouth, and his voice is so deep and loud it seems to fill the entire square…"

"What does he say, mate?" Fred was trying his best not to shake.

"...*We're all mad here,*" Bill croaked, a single tear trickling down his cheek. "Just like the fucking creepy cat in *Alice in Wonderland,*" he shook his head, expelling a sharp blast of air from his nostrils.

"Then... then the man points towards the door. I follow his long finger, and the door has changed. It's all rusty and beaten and it's got, like, a small window in it with a load of bars running down it... it's red, now. It's a big red door. All the people are back – except they're not people anymore, they're skeletons. The blood is gone. Then the door starts to throb and thump, and then they all start screaming. They scream and they howl and they scream. There's so many of them and it's so loud. Like a hundred fingernails on an old chalkboard, and they won't stop screaming. I try to put my hands to my ears but I can't move and the red door bangs and shakes and then blood starts to pour through the bars and the man with no face just laughs. And that's when I wake up. Screaming."

Silence.

There was a moment of eerie, deafening silence.

"What do you think it all means?" asked Joe.

Bill shook his head, "I don't know."

"D'ya think, if they caught him – if... *we*... caught him – the dreams would stop?" asked Gordie.

"I don't know," Bill wiped away a single, lonely tear, "I just want them to stop screaming."

"Me too, Bill," said Joe, gripping his friend's shoulder.

"Yeah, me too," said Fred.

They all put a hand on little Bill Talbot, squeezing him tight and ushering him away from the light of the tall gas lamp. He twisted his head, glaring back at the bleak house. At the black door.

"Come on," said Fred, ruffling Bill's shaggy brown hair, turning his head back and away from the row of houses, "let's have a night off from Ripper hunting with Inspector Clueless here for once, aye? It's bloody Christmas, after all."

They smiled.

Gordie put his arm around Bill, leading him out into the grimy cobbled road, "Yeah come on. Let's get down the Christmas market. Was a good laugh last year."

"Sure was," said Fred, "maybe even swing by the old underground after, yeah?"

"Nooooo!" they all cried, laughing.

Bill managed the glimmer of a smile. Fred always knew how to cheer him up.

The four boys arrived on Brick Lane just ahead of the snow. It was an unpleasantly cold yet calm evening. It was just before seven. The full moon, clear-edged and vanilla, hung just above the tip of St. Paul's Cathedral. The crisp, cold smell of approaching snow, combined with the warming scent of roasting chestnuts and mulled wine, was almost enough to drive the ghosts of Whitechapel out of their damaged minds. Almost. As they headed north along the wide and muddy road, edging deeper and deeper into the warmth and safety of the night's festivities, the sound of carol-singing over the crackling of a dozen open fires consumed the bittersweet air. Yes, it was Christmas all right. A black Christmas. Blacker than any in living memory, but still Christmas.

"Beats sitting around on Lamb Street outside a creepy old butcher's house, don't it lads?" said Fred, ruffling Bill's hair again and pushing him playfully to the side, forcing another smile.

"It will as soon as I get me some bloody chestnuts," said Gordie, scanning the nearby stalls.

"Yeah," said Joe, joining the frail boy in his search, "where the bloody hell are they? I'm starvin'."

"I can smell 'em but I can't see 'em anywhere."

"Yeah me too, where the fuck are they?"

"I'll check this side, you boys go have a look over that –"

"Bloody hell, will you two shut up?" Fred chuckled, "we've only just got here, calm yourselves down –"

Fred suddenly slowed. Frowned.

"'Ere, what's… what's going on over there?" He motioned to the side of one of the stalls off to the right. A large group of maybe twenty or so boys and girls were all huddled around something, jeering and shouting and rocking back and forth. A small gap opened up in the melee of dark cotton, revealing Ben Draper – the local bully – holding a much smaller boy up by the lapels of his coat.

"Fight!" Gordie shouted, breaking into a run, his craving for roasted chestnuts gone. The rest of the *Fab Four* followed suit and they were on the crowd in a flash, clattering into and instantly becoming one with the pulsing cluster just as the timeless chants of "Fight! Fight! Fight!" consumed the frosty air. They all but drowned out the nearby choir.

Nobody liked Ben Draper. Nobody outside the little pack of rabid wolves he hung around with, that is. And they were all here tonight, probably making up at least a quarter of the crowd.

Like all bullies, Draper was known for having a mean streak and a short fuse. Nobody messed with him. He messed with you. And like all bullies, he was big, he was strong, and he was – in the words of Fred Peters – "a complete and utter knobhead". He was more of a man than a boy, really, and the *Fab Four* had always done their best to steer clear of the brute and his gang. Even if they all shared the opinion that, if it ever came down to it, Fred could probably take him.

It soon became clear that what they were watching wasn't a fair fight. It wasn't even a fight. The small boy's nose was bloodied; his pink cheeks streamed with tears and snot; his coat was torn. He was utterly defenceless. He could've been no more than eight years old, which would put him around four or five years younger than Draper.

Bill, Joe and Gordie all looked at Fred. The last thing he wanted was to lock horns with Ben Draper. Especially after the way he'd been feeling since his encounter with the beast. Especially tonight – of all nights – but this was low, even for Draper.

He rolled his eyes with a look of damned acceptance. *Ah, bollocks*, he thought. He knew what had to be done. Fred was a lot of things, but a coward wasn't one of them. He put his hand on one of the brown coats just in front of him, pulled him to the side, and began to make his way through the crowd.

Gordie grabbed both Joe and Bill and said, "It's happening!" over the rising chants, "It's fuckin' happening!"

"No," said Bill, "no, we have to stop him, Gord."

"What?"

"Bill's right," said Joe, "we go together. Maybe we can calm it all down."

"Oh for fuck's sake," sighed Gordie, "Freddy can take him!"

"Yeah," agreed Bill, "maybe, but we gotta have his back, mate. Come on."

Bill and Joe grabbed a limp Gordie, and wriggled through the sea of brown coats towards their tall, brave friend.

"What you crying for, you little prick? Had enough have ya?" Draper snarled into the little boy's wet face.

"I'm... s-s-s-sorry," he snivelled.

"Yeah, you already s-s-s-said that, you little –"

"Put him down, Ben," roared Fred, emerging from the crowd, placing a firm hand on the shivering boy's shoulder.

"Oh piss off Peters, this aint got nuffin t' do with you!"

"Look at the fuckin' size of him," Fred growled, attempting to pry the boy from the bully's grasp, "put him down, mate, for *fuck's* sake!"

"Or what?" spat Draper, yanking the boy away, tossing him to the ground like a child's plaything. Fred clenched his fists and took a purposeful step forward. *Fuck it,* he thought.

Draper craned his head and spat a white glob of phlegm into the little boy's face.

"Little maggot ran right into me and made me spill my bag of nuts everywhere. Didn't you, maggot!?"

The little boy sobbed.

"Someone needs to teach you a fuckin' lesson, don't they –"

Out of nowhere, Bill shot out from behind Fred and shoved Draper in the chest. It didn't do much, but it was enough to send the giant back a couple of steps. The mob broke into a chorus of sardonic *ooooooooooohhhhhhhhh*s.

Draper looked down at the point of impact, confused.

Aw, shit, Bill thought.

Joe and Gordie grimaced.

Fred, smirking, put a hand on Bill's shoulder and pulled him back behind him. He'd never known the little guy had it in him. *Bill* had never known he had it in him.

"Talbot," Draper snarled, tearing his eyes from his chest, his face had turned an alarming shade of red, "come to save your lanky boyfriend, have ya?"

Suddenly, a dark-haired girl burst from the crowd just behind the boiling giant. She wheeled around to face him, put her hands on his shoulders then thrust her knee into his groin with sickening accuracy. Draper let out a high-pitched yelp and went down like a tonne of bricks. Everyone gasped and for the briefest of moments, everything seemed to stop, suspended in time and motion. Even the carol singers seemed to halt. The first flakes of snow floated on the inky black sky and Ben Draper squirmed and clutched his crushed bag of nuts, whimpering. It was then that Gordie Cooper burst out laughing, sending three quarters of the crowd into a frenzy.

"Come on, Jake!" the girl bellowed over the insane cackling, hoisting the crying boy from the muddy ground and running off through the rabble.

"I… I… think I'm in love," said Fred, turning to his friends, dumbstruck.

"Come on!" cried Bill, grabbing the bemused boy, "Let's go!"

The *Fab Four* bolted through the crowd after the giant slayer and the tiny boy, away from the fallen bully and the gathering wolves.

Lucie Wright was furious. Riled, scared and furious, and she ran like the wind. Ducking and diving through the throng of rushing bodies, dragging her little brother Jake by the hand. His tiny feet slapped against the muddy stones as he fought back yet another river of hot tears, trying his best to keep up with his big, brave sister.

"I can't leave you alone for five bloody minutes, can I!?" she screamed.

"I'm sorry Lucie," cried Jake.

"Not a word of this to Mum," she snarled, rounding the corner onto Hanbury Street, heading west and away from the Christmas fête, "not a bloody word, you hear?"

"Yes –"

"'Ere wait up!" cried Bill.

Jake, still running, twisted his head to the distant call.

"Slow down!" Fred shouted.

Jake began to slow, but Lucie refused, tugging at her

little brother's arm, forcing him back up to her speed.

"What about my chestnuts?" cried Gordie.

"Sod your bloody chestnuts," panted Fred.

"How's she running so fast in that dress?" said Joe.

"Slow down!" Gordie this time.

"Come on," said Fred to his relay team, "dig in, chaps!"

The *Fab Four* picked up the pace and closed the gap.

Lucie, hearing the fast-approaching footsteps, slowed, stopped, and turned to face the boys, shielding her brother.

"What d'you bloody want?" she spat.

"Woah, woah, woah," said Fred, grounding to a halt, sticking out his arms in a gesture of peace, "we ain't…we ain't with that lot, we swear."

The other three boys nodded, hands on their knees, furiously panting.

"Yeah," Lucie said, chasing her breath, "I know you aint. But what… what do you want?"

"You all right, mate?" Bill said to Jake, leaning to the side.

Jake poked his head out from just behind Lucie's shoulder and nodded.

"What happened?" said Lucie, hurling the little boy around from behind her, wiping his bloody nose with the sleeve of her petticoat.

"That fuckin' lump Ben Draper was pickin' on him," said Fred.

Lucie looked up at Fred, and then at Jake. "Yeah, I figured that out. What'd you bloody do this time, aye?"

"N-n-nothing," the little boy stammered into Lucie's sleeve as she continued to dab at his scarlett nose, "I was just w-walking and that big boy b-bumped into me then he p-pushed me and p-p-punched me."

"He's such a knob," snarled Gordie.

"Then what happened?" asked Lucie, turning to the boys, "you boys step in, did ya?"

"Well," said Fred, stepping forward, beaming with pride, "I mean, we can't have bullies like Big Ben picking –"

"Actually it was Bill who told Draper to do one," said Joe. The look of betrayal on Fred's face was priceless.

"Woah, hang on a minute –"

"Yeah," said Gordie, seizing the opportunity to get one over on Fred, "Bill swooped in and gave the big wanker a proper good push."

"Yeah, I saw that," said Lucie, meeting Bill's eyes and smiling at him warmly, an act which turned his face the same colour as Jake's nose. "Thanks," she said, "a lot of wronguns round here, but I appreciate you lookin' out for this little pain in the arse."

"Oh, uh, that's all right," Bill scratched the nape of his neck, returning an awkward smile, "as long as you're both okay."

Jake nodded again. He was all right. Fred Peters wasn't, but he instantly recognised that just one look from the feisty girl had brightened Bill's dark mood, and that pleased him.

"Yeah, we'll survive," she sighed, "anyway, I'm Lucie," she said, curtseying sarcastically, "This little troublemaker 'ere is my little brother Jake."

"All right, Jake," they all said.

Jake smiled, "All right."

"Gets yourself into all sorts of bloody mischief, don't ya?" Lucie said, shaking her head. Some of her hair had come loose from her dark blue hair tie.

The boy looked down at the grazed, dirty pavement.

"Honest to God, I can't leave him alone for five minutes on that bloody lane," she wiped his dirty face.

Jake, embarrassed in front of the older boys, tried to bat his sister's hand away, but Lucie persisted.

"Well, I guess that's our Christmas fête over for another year, ain't it?" she cursed, "Can't exactly go back there now, can we?"

Jake shook his head. He didn't want to go back to Brick Lane ever again.

"To be fair, I don't think anyone's gonna mess with him again after seeing what you can do to the old crown jewels," said Fred.

A flurry of nervous laughter rang out through the snowy street.

"Yeah, I suppose you're right," she said, ruffling Jake's greasy hair.

"Yeah, and you got us to look out for you now anyway," said Bill, smiling.

"Yeah," Joe, Gordie and Fred agreed, nodding. Gordie flexed his show-stopping muscles again. Jake laughed.

"Nah, seriously, I appreciate it," Lucie smiled again, "Right, well I guess we best be off home then. You... uhh... you boys fancy walkin' us back?"

They all nodded; they definitely did.

*

Lucie released Jake and swiftly crossed the road, heading west down the damp pavement and into the swirling sheet of sleet and snow. The boys trailed, absorbing Jake into their little gang.

"'Ere, Jake," Gordie whispered out the corner of his mouth, "don't suppose you managed to swipe any of Draper's chestnuts did ya?"

Joe and Fred groaned. Jake, bewildered, shook his head and laughed at the skinny boy with the funny face.

Bill quickened his pace and caught up to Lucie.

"So, where do you live?" he asked.

"Dorset Street," she muttered, fixing her hair.

"Oh," Bill slowed ever so slightly.

"Mmmh," she sighed, "there are nicer places. And before you ask, the answer is yes: I knew her."

"Yeah?"

"Yeah. Well, me mum did. Always seemed like a nice lady," she paused, "very pretty."

"Yeah, I know."

"You know?" Lucie asked, twisting to face Bill, confused, "How the bloody hell did you know Mary Kelly?"

"Well," Bill's face had turned red again; he was surprised the flakes of snow didn't turn to steam as they touched down on his roasting cheeks. "Well, we didn't *know* her, but we always said 'ello and stuff when we saw her and that."

Lucie raised her eyebrows, "Oh right," she said with an air of suspicion, "you boys fancy her, did you?"

"Well… well… no… I…"

Lucie grinned, flicking a playful jab to Bill's shoulder, "I'm only teasing, Bill."

"Oh," he chuckled, stepping off the curb, pretending the stiff jab didn't hurt.

"Yeah, she lived opposite us. Jake swears blind he saw her that night, but he sees a lot of things."

Bill turned to Jake but he was too far back to hear their conversation.

"Me mum was friends with Polly Nichols and all." Lucie looked to the sky, squinting into the snow, "She cried her eyes out when she found out about her. I did, too, if I'm being honest. Me and Jake always liked her."

Bill didn't know what to say.

"That's really shit."

Smooth, he thought, *real smooth*.

"Yeah. I'd love to get my hands on the evil fuckin' bastard," she seethed, "Not that I'd be able to do much, but I'd have a bloody good go."

After seeing her in action less than ten minutes ago, Bill had no doubt. He smiled awkwardly, looking down at his shuffling feet on the snowy pavement. He'd never really spoken to a girl for this long before and his stomach felt all strange and fizzy.

"So you're those boys what had that run in with that scientist bloke, right?"

Bill looked up.

"You... you know about that?"

"Everyone knows about that –"

"Everyone knows about what?" asked Fred, appearing from nowhere.

"The beast," said Bill, motioning to the tall boy who'd positioned himself on the other side of Lucie.

"The beast?" frowned Lucie.

"Yeah," said Bill, "it's a long story, but put it this way: it was more of a beast than a man when we crossed paths with… it."

"Oooooooh, how mysterious," she turned to Fred, "he always like this with the words and stories?"

"You've no idea," Fred grinned.

"Well, you'll have to tell me all about it one day, won't you!" she said. It was a proposal that hatched a dozen large butterflies in each of the boys' empty stomachs. They walked on through the falling snow.

"'Ere, that's where Annie Chapman was killed weren't it?" Lucie asked, pointing across the cobbles to 29 Hanbury Street.

"Yeah," said Bill, "well, yes and no."

Lucie frowned. "Yes and no?"

"Oh no, here we go," Fred groaned. The other boys had caught up just in time for Bill's inquest.

"Apparently she was actually found round the back of the building in the backyard up against a fence. Just in front of the steps to the rear entrance."

"Is that so?" Lucie said; the tone of her voice suggested mild interest. "What else do you know?"

The chorus of groans echoed down the street. Jake and Lucie smirked.

"Well," said Bill, "two penny farthings were found next to her body. Her throat had been cut and she'd been disembowelled with a large chunk of flesh from her stomach placed above her left shoulder and bits of her small intestine above her right."

Jake screwed up his face.

"Jesus," muttered Lucie, turning to Bill, "how the bloody hell do you know all this?"

"He reads too much," snapped Fred.

"Waaaay too much," said Joe and Gordie in unison.

"That's not all," said Bill. He was on a roll now and his friends knew it. They all moaned again, dragging their feet and flapping their arms in dismay. Bill ignored their protests. Lucie smirked again. "A leather apron was found just a few yards from Annie's body. Apparently, it belonged to a bloke named Richardson – but the nature of the crime, along with how the other women were killed, suggest that maybe the killer has some sort of knowledge of anatomy. Perhaps a butcher or –"

Gordie interrupted, "What Inspector Clueless is trying to say is that he thinks it was the bloody cat's meat man."

Fred and Joe laughed and meowed, messing up Bill's hair for the umpteenth time this evening, giving him an innocent, playful shove.

Jake's heart froze.

The others carried on for maybe eight or nine paces before they realised they were a man down. Joe glanced to his side and did a double take.

"'Ere," he said, turning to face the frozen boy, "you all right, mate?"

They all stopped.

"Come on Jake," Lucie yelled, "what're you doin'? It's bloody freezin'."

The boy stood dead still. His once-pink face had turned as white as the snowy rooftops.

"The-the-the ca-ca-cat's me-meat man," he

stammered into the cold, crisp air.

"Yeah," said Fred, "you know who we're on about?"

Jake nodded vigorously.

"Oh, for God's sake," groaned Lucie, rolling her eyes, "not this again."

"What happened?" asked Bill, turning to Jake, then Lucie.

She sighed, "He got lost one day out in the lanes and reckons this mad, ugly cat's meat man threatened him with a knife."

"A b-big knife," Jake added, "c-c-covered in b-b-blood –"

"Was he *really* skinny?" asked Bill, oddly excited. "Did he have an evil white face?"

"And fucked up teeth?" Gordie jumped in.

"Y-yeah."

A horse and cart suddenly rattled past the gang along the slushy cobbles, defrosting the young boy who scampered towards the others.

"What'd he say to you?" asked Joe.

Jake's eyes darted back and forth between the cart and Joe.

"Huh?"

"What did the cat's meat man say?"

"He s-said if he ever s-saw me again he'd cut my n-n-nose off and feed it to the f-f-f–"

"Fuckin' dogs," Lucie finished, "he said he'd feed it to the fuckin' dogs."

"Blimey," said Gordie, "you must've pissed him off pretty bad."

Jake shrugged nervously.

"I told you there was something about him!" said

Bill, "Didn't I bloody tell you!"

Joe, Fred and Gordie all waved away Bill's latest claims, but with far less vigour than before. Joe still couldn't place the cat's meat man and Fred had only seen him once or twice, but Gordie... Gordie had to admit the bloke did look pretty shady. But a murderer? The Ripper? No – that was ridiculous. Wasn't it? *Wasn't it*?

"Oh don't take no notice of him," Lucie said, leading the boys away from the site of the third Ripper murder and towards the busy Commerical Street junction.

"Was he wearing a leather apron, Jake?" asked Bill, walking between the two siblings, gazing down at the shuffling boy.

"Yeah I th-think so," he said, "I can only r-remember the kn-kn-knife and his f-face, his t-t-teeth."

Lucie rolled her eyes again. She had heard *that* much about Jake's boogeyman the past few months, she felt as if she *knew* him. But after hearing and – more importantly – seeing Bill's reaction to her brother's tall tale, she felt intrigued. Guilty, and intrigued. Maybe Jake *was* telling the truth after all. And Bill seemed like a bright lad. She'd only known him all of twenty minutes, but there was... something about him. He seemed smart and sweet and brave and caring and boys like that – people like that – didn't exactly grow on trees around here. He spoke differently to the others, and he had kind eyes. Nice eyes.

Chuckling, Lucie leant across Bill to Jake and asked: "What is it you say, Jake? Reckon the horrible bugger has a smile like the chester cat from Alice in Wonderland?"

"Cheshire Cat," said Bill and Jake together. They looked at each other with wide and excited eyes.

"Would you look at that," said Fred, placing a pink hand on Bill's shoulder, "looks like Holmes finally has his Watson, chaps. Maybe we should take a detour via Lamb Street and let the dynamic duo loose."

Tweedle Joe and Tweedle Gordie baa'd like a couple of sheep. Fred, towering above the rest of the gang, lightly squeezed a bemused Jake on the shoulder and said: "Oh, you're gonna fit right in mate. Inspector Bill reads a lot of weird and wacky books when he's not helping out Scotland Yard."

They all laughed. Jake didn't get it, but he laughed anyway. Even Bill chuckled at that one and yet, there was a strange amount of truth in the tall boy's joke. Bill shook his head and feigned a sarcastic smile. He had no comeback. No witty retort. Nothing but a stupid grin and a face red with embarrassment. And then something totally unexpected happened: Lucie grabbed his hand and began to swing it back and forth.

"Don't listen to them, Bill," she said, their arms cutting through the falling snow like a pendulum, "they're just jealous of you and your big old brain."

Fred, Joe and Gordie's mouths nearly hit the frosty pavement. Bill Talbot figured this was the happiest he'd ever been in his whole life. He'd forgotten all about the snap and bite of the inclement weather, the morbid monkey he'd been carrying around on his back for weeks on end. He felt so warm and excited and good that he briefly forgot where he was. He smiled. *It's all downhill from here,* he thought.

He wasn't far wrong.

As Lucie continued to skip and swing their arms in a smooth yet frantic motion, three jealous pre-teen boys and one shuffling eight-year-old looked on as the pair pranced towards the edge of the busy crossroads; towards a chain of events that would follow them all to their graves.

"So come on," Lucie said, preparing to cross the slushy road, "what's on Lamb Street then?"

"Oh that's where he lives," said Bill, stepping out into the road.

"Where who lives?"

"*The cat's meat man*," said Fred, sending a cold prickle of terror down Jake's spine.

Lucie turned to Fred and then back to Bill and smirked, squeezing his hand tight, then letting go. Their fingers brushed ever so slightly as they parted. Bill felt dizzy.

Lucie raised her voice to the rest of the gang behind, craning her head slightly to face them but keeping her eyes fixed on Bill's: "We gonna swing by there then or what?"

Silence.

"No-no Lucie," said Jake from behind the three taller boys, "no, no, he's m-mad."

"Oh don't be silly Jake. It's only a couple roads down from home."

Fred, stepping out into the road, turned to Jake and said: "There's nothing to be scared of mate. Well, not unless you're a cow or a horse or whatever the hell it is they cart around in those wooden box things."

"Are you serious?" a dubious Bill said to Lucie, frowning as they negotiated the slippery stones.

"Yeah, why not?" she said, the harsh yet brilliant light from one of the district's only arc lamps sparkled in her green eyes, "We ain't expected home for a while yet and I'd like to have a butcher's at the so-called Ripper's house."

Everyone except Jake giggled. They stepped up onto the pavement.

"Unless, of course, you boys are a little... oh, what's the word I'm lookin' for?"

They all frowned.

"...Chicken!" She grinned, slowly raising her wrists to her armpits.

Fred, Joe and Gordie all sneered, clutching each other in pretend shock and outrage.

"Woah, woah, woah," cried Fred over his friends' jeers, "I ain't no chicken, luv."

"Oh I dunno, Fred," said Joe curiously, "you seemed perfectly happy to let Bill do your dirty work earlier."

Fred screwed up his face and gave Joe the finger.

"Come on then, chickens, show us where Jacky Boy's been hiding all these months."

"Fine," said Fred, riled, "lead the way, Inspector."

Bill, puzzled by the sudden turn of events, shrugged and headed north along Commercial Street. Maybe he was going to get a closer look at the cat's meat man after all. The gang followed and Lucie smiled, her reluctant, cautious little brother trailing just behind.

*

314

The tumbling snow had turned to sleet and was falling a little harder now. The frigid night's sky was a splattered canvas of whites and greys on black, no colour. The icy rain had combined with the ash in the air to form something resembling a hazy, phosphorus waterfall. Silver on black, black on silver. There was no wind.

The large moon was still visible but covered in waves of dark and broken clouds. A black forest of brick chimneys spewed long and winding tendrils of dirty, thick smoke into the night. The smell of coal and burnt wood charred the air. It was oddly pleasant and, in many ways, an idyllic winter scene. Vivid. Picturesque. The kind of bleak yet undeniably beautiful image that would feature on Christmas cards for a millennium.

It was only a ten-minute walk – give or take – to the cat's meat man's house. Commercial Street was far quieter than usual this evening, and Bill Talbot led the gang along the treacherous pavement, paying the cold flakes of sleet no mind. He was on a mission; a mission to find out what was lurking behind that black door once and for all. A mission to prove his best friends wrong. A mission to impress a pretty, dark-haired girl called Lucie Wright. He marched on through the falling ice, an eager, twelve-year-old girl at his shoulder and a pack of straggling boys at his back.

Little did they know they were now minutes from a series of dire decisions that would make them all the stuff of local legend.

*

As the gang turned onto Lamb Street, the great clock struck eight and Bill began to count. Fred, still reeling from Lucie's taunt, turned to Jake and asked: "Your sister, she always this mean?"

Jake nodded, but he didn't hear the question. Not really. He was only half listening. If the boys were right and this was where the cat's meat man lived – the *actual* cat's meat man; the one who had shoved a red knife in his face a hundred times over, the one who haunted his dreams and clung to his memory like a blood-thirsty leech – well, then they didn't know what they were letting themselves in for. He was bad news. He was dangerous. He was mad. *"We're all mad here,"* the fabled words of the Cheshire Cat slid across his mind like an icy river. He wouldn't go near that house. Not for all the cake and chocolate and Grimm books in the world. *What are they gonna do?* He thought to himself as he shuffled behind the pack. *Knock on the door? Break in? That would be mad!*

"We're all mad here..."

"...ten... eleven... twelve... thirteen..." Bill was counting.

Everyone frowned at the boy in deep concentration.

"...sixteen... seventeen... eighteen... nineteen... twent–"

"Bill, what the fuck are you doing, mate?" asked Gordie.

Bill suddenly stopped, causing a miniature pile-up. Childish laughter briefly filled the otherwise empty street.

"Twenty," he whispered, turning to the others, "twenty houses in."

"Right," said Fred, bemused, "what's the significance of that?"

Bill pointed to the cat's meat man's house opposite.

"Well, first of all: the light from the basement window is still out, and the rest of the windows are dark. So it's safe to say nobody's home."

"I don't like where this is going," Joe muttered nervously.

Jake grimaced.

Lucie's eyes lit up.

Bill continued. "Round the back of these houses is a narrow alleyway. Every house on Lamb Street has a small garden, but they don't join onto the gardens from the houses over on the next road or anything…"

"*Right*… so what you sayin'?"

"Most people don't have locks on their front doors. Agreed?"

Everyone but Jake nodded.

"Well, we know the cat's meat man does. Which is dodgy. Real dodgy. What's in there? What's he hiding?"

They all looked at each other, shrugging and shaking their heads, and then Fred said "It's his bloody house, Bill. I ain't sure I see the connection between some poor bastard locking his front door and his being Jack The Ripper."

Sniggers.

Fred rolled his eyes. "Go on then, Sherlock. We're listening…" The tall boy actually wanted to see where Inspector Clueless was going with this.

"A lock on the front door round here is rare," Bill said, "really rare. But a lock on the back door? No.

Never. Nobody does that."

There was an awkward silence.

"Are you bloody joking?" Joe seethed.

"Well, you're just full of surprises, aint ya?" said Lucie, giving Bill a playful elbow to the ribs and causing him to flinch and Fred to frown with yet more jealousy.

"You... you can't be bloody serious?" Joe again, his eyes wide and darting all over the place. "Fred, Gordie, have-have a word with him for fuck's sake!"

Joe wheeled away, pressing his hands up against the nearby wall.

"So why were you counting the houses then?" Fred asked, echoing Lucie and Gordie's confusion.

"It's the only way we can be sure we get the right house if we go round the back."

"So you wanna break in?" Fred chuckled.

"It's not breaking in if we just go in through an unlocked door," Bill reasoned.

"Oh leave it out, Bill," Joe was losing his mind, "it's against the bloody law and you know it."

"'Ere," Lucie turned to Gordie, "you're awfully quiet, Chuckles, what's the matter? Cat's meat man got your tongue?"

Everyone but Jake and Joe laughed, but Joe did raise a half-hearted smile into the cold bricks. Gordie went a little red but soon fired back: "I'm just waiting to hear the full version of the masterplan before I make a decision, thank you very much." He stuck out his tongue.

Lucie scowled at him. *Smart arse*, she thought.

"All right," Bill conceded, "I know it's wrong, but

nobody's home – and what if I'm right? What if we find something in there? What about those people that are still missing? What if he's been, like, kidnapping them and stuff? What if he's actually the Ripper!?"

A mixture of fear and excitement rattled up and down Fred's spine. Lucie's too. Gordie wasn't sure what he felt. Joe was.

"This is bloody mad," he seethed, completely and utterly beside himself, his hands still pressed against the damp wall the four boys had all leant against no more than an hour ago.

"*We're all mad here...*" the words of the sinister, talking cat slid through Jake's mind again.

Fred chuckled, "I bloody told you boys earlier, we shoulda carted him off to Broadmoor."

"Look," said Bill, "I've got it all planned out, I swear. Just hear me out, all right?"

Fred, Gordie and Lucie all leant forward. Jake was shuffling his feet next to Joe over by the wall, looking nervously between both ends of the empty street.

"Right," Bill started, "so one or two of us can stay out here and keep watch. We need someone who knows what the cat's meat man looks like, so it'll have to be Jake or Gordie or maybe both." He paused. "When the rest of us are inside, one of us goes and stands by the front room window while the others have a look about. If those out here see the cat's meat man coming, then they signal, and we scram. Simple. He'll never know."

"This is assuming the bloody back door's even open," said Fred

"Yeah, course."

"And what if it ain't?"

"There might be a window or something, but we'd probably have to just knock it on the head and leave it."

"And you promise you'll stop with all this cat's meat man shit?"

Bill sighed. "Yes, yes, I swear."

"Swear down?"

"Yes. Swear down."

"So what's your plan if we get in, then?" asked Gordie. "Swipe his bloody turkey?"

Nobody laughed.

"Don't be a fool," Bill rolled his eyes, "we'll just have a snoop around. See what's down in that basement –"

"Even if by some fat chance he is the Ripper," Joe spat into the wall, "I'm not sure what you're bloody expecting to find in there?"

"Well," Fred started, ignoring Joe, "you are right about one thing, Billy boy, it does make sense for Jake or Gordie to stay out here –"

"Woah, Fred," Joe spun from the wall, "you… you ain't seriously considering this, are you?"

"The inspector's plan is pretty mad, but I gotta admit he's covered all bases," he said, turning to Wild Bill Talbot, "How long you been putting this together?"

"Few days," he shrugged.

"Well," said Fred, glancing at Joe, "Joseph clearly ain't got the minerals for it and Jake reckons he knows the butcher by sight, so they can stay out here with the princess and keep watch, which leaves me, you and Gordie to go in-"

"Woah, woah, woah," said Gordie and Lucie together,

"Don't give me none of that Princess shit," Lucie sneered, "I'm in!"

"I... I never said I was in," said Gordie. Bill and Fred both looked at him knowingly and raised their eyebrows. "You're in," they said.

Gordie, grinning, rolled his eyes. They were right. There was no way he was going to pass this little adventure up.

"All right, then," Fred nodded, "so us three will go in, and you three will –"

Suddenly, Lucie turned on her heels and ran across the cobbles. She was heading straight for the cat's meat man's front door.

"What's she bloody doing?!" Joe hissed, "What the bloody hell is she doing-"

Lucie stopped at the door and stared.

She slowly turned to face five sets of disbelieving eyes. A waggish grin on her milky face sent the butterflies in Bill and Fred's stomachs into raptures. She slowly turned back to face the door, hesitating for the briefest of moments, before delivering three sharp blows to it. As she delivered the final knock she bolted from the house and back to the squirming bundle of boys. Both Joe and Jake were ready to turn tail and run but it all happened so fast they didn't have time to react. Lucie spun behind Bill, wrapping her arms around his collarbone, giggling nervously into his ear. The thrilled and besotted boy glued both his hands to Lucie's forearms. He'd never been so excited in his life.

They watched.

They waited.

They watched and waited for the door to fly open.

They watched and waited for Jack The Ripper to burst from the shadows of the black house, screaming and wielding a crimson knife.

They watched for some sign of life or movement or something, anything. But nothing happened.

Nobody was home.

Bill slowly panned from left to right, checking both ends of the street. Lucie, her cheek still pressed against the side of Bill's head, moved with him. The coast was clear. They all breathed a unified sigh of relief into the crisp air.

"You're bloody mad," Joe scoffed under his breath, returning to the wall.

Jake shuddered.

Fred, Gordie and Bill all exerted a rabble of throaty chuckles. The girl had guts. Real guts. Real, *actual* guts. And as she slowly released the reeling boy from her grasp, spinning back around to face the group, Bill Talbot fell in love for the first and last time.

"Well, now we know for sure, don't we boys?"

They all looked at her in shock and awe. She stuck out a bent arm in Bill's direction, "Shall we, Inspector?"

Bill smiled and took a step forward.

"What about the houses on either side?" Gordie said, looking up at the dark row of bricks and windows.

"What about them?" said Lucie.

"What if someone hears or sees us?"

"I'm pretty sure they're empty," Bill said over his shoulder, his eyes fixed on Lucie's, "I took a look the other day and there's no curtains or furniture as far as I can see."

"I… I can't believe this," Joe cried, "are you nutters actually going to do this?"

"Lu-Lu-Lucie, p-please do-don't-"

"Oh don't be silly, Jake, we won't be long. You stay out here and protect Mother Hen."

Fred and Gordie laughed aloud.

Joe was not amused.

Bill took another step towards Lucie, gingerly hanging his left arm out in the air before the girl grabbed it excitedly and the two made off down the street.

Fred, practically boiling with jealousy, turned to Joe.

"We won't be long, all right. Bill needs this. I don't know why, but he does."

"Yeah," said Gordie, "yeah, you saw him earlier. Plus, you know, it'll be a laugh."

Joe shook his head.

"Just keep an eye out, all right?" Fred shifted his gaze back and forth between the two night watchmen, "All right?"

Jake nodded.

"If you see him coming, just give whoever's in that window the thumbs down, all right?"

They both nodded reluctantly.

"All right," Fred muttered, "we won't be long."

They nodded again, both leaning back against the black brick wall.

Fred and Gordie stepped off the curb and away from the two dejected boys.

"There is just one thing though, Fred," Gordie said to the tall boy, a look of grave concern on his face as they walked along the slippery street.

Fred frowned, lowering his head. "What is it, mate?"

They both stopped.

Gordie suddenly fired a sharp right cross into Fred's shoulder and sprinted after Bill and Lucie, laughing.

Fred screwed up his face and gave chase.

Joe and Jake both looked on as the boys vanished into the now dwindling wall of sleet. "They're mad," Joe muttered again, turning back to face the row of bleak houses, "they're actually bloody mad."

Jake slowly tore his eyes from the end of the empty street.

"We're all mad here," he said.

The Cat's Meat Man crossed the road onto Hanbury Street just as four twelve-year-old scamps were scaling the wall of his back garden. The Cat's Meat Man was annoyed. The Cat's Meat Man was angry. The Cat's Meat Man was furious with himself for forgetting his bag of blades. How could he be so foolish? They would be needed tonight. He *knew* they would be needed tonight – and yet, he hadn't realised that he'd left them back at the slaughterhouse until he was bearing down on the pathetic whore.

The Cat's Meat Man had been thinking (*fantasising*) about how he was going to do it all day. The stinkin' bitch was of no use to him now. She had grown weak and despondent and – above all – annoying. She was nothing but a dirty, ungrateful cunt anyway. Her time had come and, for the Cat's Meat Man, Christmas had come but a few hours early.

Such was his excitement, his eagerness and frantic trail of disturbed thought, that the Cat's Meat Man had bolted for the door of the slaughterhouse as soon as he'd finished his rounds, his precious roll of knives still nestled in the drawer of his trusty handcart. The Cat's Meat Man had been terribly forgetful lately. It had been a busy few months, and his head had been a mess of sticky, brown cobwebs; a clutter of sick and twisted notions – diabolical evocations. His mask of sanity – if there ever was such a thing – had all but slid from the bones of his gaunt face. It had been a busy few months, and the Cat's Meat Man had grown careless. Complacent. Foolish.

This wasn't the first time this sort of thing had happened. Just a few days ago, he'd gone hunting for some fresh meat and accidentally left the basement door unlocked. Something – to his knowledge – he had never done before. *Maybe I'm gettin' old*, he thought, as he marched on through the never-ending wall of tumbling ice, his sharp tools wedged beneath his left armpit. *Maybe... maybe I left the basement unlocked again?* His pulse quickened; his thoughts raced, feet slowed. *I definitely locked the whore's door and the front door, I think, but the basement... the basement?*

"Fuck!" he spat into the freezing air, "Fuck! Fuck! Fuck!"

He picked up the pace.

What the hell is wrong with you, boy?! His father's booming voice echoed through the chambers of his mangled mind. *You stupid cunt! You stupid fuckin' cunt! What have I told you about that fuckin' door!?*

"I'm s-s-s-sorry Sir," the Cat's Meat Man stuttered into the sleet, "I'm s-s-s–"

The Cat's Meat Man sniffed and bowed his head

slightly, watching his legs power his body along the dirty pavement. *Stupid*! he cursed himself. *Stupid! Stupid! Stupid!*

It'll be all right, a second voice – a child's voice – suddenly spoke up in his head, *father hasn't been downstairs in –*

Suddenly, the Cat's Meat Man clattered into something big and hard and lost his balance. He stumbled to the side of the pavement and into the row of houses, his bag of blades falling to the ground.

"Fuckin' mind where you're goin' mate," a stocky man growled, never breaking his stride.

The Cat's Meat Man bent to retrieve his roll bag, looking back and up at the back of the man's thick, wet skull with utter contempt.

"Fuck off, you fat bastard!" he rasped, rising to his feet.

The man stopped.

He jerked his thick neck back to face the Cat's Meat Man. "What d'you fuckin say?"

"You heard!" the Cat's Meat Man rasped, removing a large butcher's knife from his bag. The stocky man clenched and unclenched his white-knuckled fists and took a purposeful step towards the seething figure, and then he saw the knife. He froze.

"Woah," he stuck out his hands, "wh-what?"

"What's the matter?" the Cat's Meat Man seethed. "Cat got your fuckin' tongue, has it?"

"M-m-mate," the stocky man stuttered, reduced to the size of a cowering boy in an instant, "just calm… just calm down, yeah? I didn't mean nothin' by it."

"Didn't mean nothin' by it?" the Cat's Meat Man

grinned, tilting his head to the side as he took a slow step towards the wary man.

Gut him!

The Cat's Meat Man took another step forward.

"Look, look, just forget it, yeah?" the man reasoned, "It… it was an accident. Just put… put the bloody knife down –"

"Don't tell me what to fuckin' do!" the Cat's Meat Man roared, spit flying from his cracked lips, steam oozing from his mouth and head as if he were boiling right there and then in the ice cold street. His yellow, bloodshot eyes glinted with spite like a pair of piss-yellow pearls.

The petrified man took a cautious step back. And then another. His face was as grey as the sleet on the grimy cobbles.

"Mate… mate…"

The Cat's Meat Man suddenly raised the knife and scurried towards the man causing him to turn and break into a sprint.

The Cat's Meat Man stopped. Laughed. Lowered his gaze down to the glistening blade. It was flecked with tiny flakes of snow and sleet. He brought the knife slowly up to his mouth and voraciously licked the ice-cold droplets from the sharp object. And my, oh my, didn't they taste sweet?

As the Cat's Meat Man put the large knife back into his bag of blades, something caught his eye. Something to the right. He slowly twisted his head to the side and smiled his hideous smile.

"What a coincidence that would've been," he chuckled, staring at the number on the large black door.

Never mind that! The basement door! Hurry! Move!
The Cat's Meat Man ripped his cold gaze from the door of number 29 Hanbury Street and headed home.

Bill Talbot stepped towards the weathered back door and took a long, deep breath. This was it: the moment of truth. He wrapped his hand around the cold, wet handle and gripped it tight. There was a sharp gasp from behind him as Lucie, Fred and Gordie all drew mouthfuls of frigid air from the frigid night. A blanket of asphyxiating stillness fell over them, and then Bill turned the handle.

The door opened, and four thundering hearts skipped a beat, their eyes wide with fear and excitement. Bill, his hand still clutching the iron handle, turned to his partners in crime and exhaled.

"Here we go, ladies," he said, pulling the door open. Out of the dark and into the darkness.

"So what now?" said Gordie, his eyes darting about the dank, black space.

They stood with their backs to the door, scanning the gloomy kitchen.

"Let's start with the basement," Bill whispered , "then we'll work our way up."

They all nodded, their eyes slowly adjusting to the dark gloom of the house.

"But first, don't forget we need someone at the front room window to keep an eye out," Bill turned to Lucie and smiled, "you up for it, Wright?"

"Sod that," she said excitedly, "I wanna have a look around."

"I'll do it," said Fred, "but as soon as Joe or Jake give the signal, we get the fuck out of 'ere, all right? No messin'."

"No messin'," they all said, slowly following Bill across the creaky floorboards, their eyes searching the shadows as they neared the hallway.

Bill spotted the door to the basement. It was just to the left, directly under the stairs – maybe ten paces ahead. He stuck out his arms and brought the pack to a halt.

"There it is," he said, craning his head back to the others, "the basement."

He paused.

"Right; Fred, you get in that front room, at the end of the hallway. Gordie, you have a look around in 'ere – see if you can find some candles and matches or somethin' – and Lucie, you up for checkin' that back room?" He flicked his head in its direction. "First room on the right?"

She nodded.

"All right," he smiled nervously, "I'm gonna see if the basement's open. Be as quiet as you can and keep your eyes open, okay?"

They nodded.

Fred made his way past Bill and groped his way down the narrow hallway towards the front room door. Gordie turned and began to search the kitchen. Lucie lightly brushed past Bill and gave him a playful jab in the ribs with her forefinger. The boy flinched and returned the gesture. She giggled. She briefly looked back over her shoulder at him before disappearing into the open doorway of the back room. Bill stood for a moment staring into space. *What's going on?* he asked himself, smiling stupidly into the musty, dark air. He'd suddenly forgotten where he was – w*ho* he was. He'd forgotten all about the basement and the Cat's Meat Man and the Ripper and everything that had happened these past few months. All he could think about at this moment was Lucie. Beautiful and amazing Lucie –

"Got some, Bill," Gordie hissed from behind, shaking the besotted boy from his ill-timed daze.

"Huh?" said Bill, turning.

"Found some candles and a box of matches in one of the drawers," Gordied said, "want me to fire 'em up?"

"Yeah," said Bill, his focus returning, "yeah, light one and we'll head downstairs."

"It open, then?" Gordie asked.

"Oh," said Bill, "oh, shit. Let me check." He swivelled on his heels and made for the basement door.

Bill reached for the doorknob, sucking another deep breath from the musty air. He held it tight in his lungs for a second or two before cautiously twisting the cool piece of metal.

He grimaced.

It opened. The door opened. He couldn't believe it. He'd almost been certain it would be locked and they'd have to hunt for a spare key. *Maybe*, he thought, *maybe there's nothing down there – in here – maybe this is a mistake, maybe the cat's meat man has nothing to hide after all.*

"It's open," he muttered over his shoulder to Gordie, his eyes fixed on the black crack between the door and the doorway, "get us a candle sorted."

Bill took yet another purposeful breath and gradually pulled the door open with a loud *rrrreeeeeeaaaaaaaaahhhhhh*. He let go of the doorknob and peered down, down, down into the abyss. Gordie was suddenly at Bill's shoulder.

"Jesus fuck!" Bill jumped. "Don't do that!"

"Do what?" said Gordie, knowing exactly what he'd done as he handed his startled friend a lit candle, a grin stretched across his mouth. The two boys stood side by side, a thin, white candle between them, their eyes fixed on the dark world below.

"You ready?" Bill whispered out the corner of his mouth, his eyes still glued to the black.

"Yeah," gulped Gordie, "yeah, let's go."

They began their descent.

Lucie searched the back room as instructed, but there wasn't much to search. Just a few pieces of janky old furniture, and a stack of old newspapers and books. There was nothing. Nothing but dust and wood. She left the room, shut the door, and made her way along the hallway to the front room. There wasn't much to see in there either; just an old dining table in the centre of the room, a few chairs, an empty fireplace, a display cabinet full of China plates, and a tall boy stood with his back to her. He was holding a net curtain to the side, staring out of the mucky window. Fred hadn't heard Lucie come in, and she smirked and seized the opportunity. She tiptoed towards the oblivious boy – one, two, three, four light and tiny steps – before leaping to his side and digging her nails into his ribs playfully.

"What you doin' mate?!" she barked in a deep, gruff voice.

"Jesus!" Fred hissed, his heart practically in his hands. He snapped his head from the outside world, "You... you scared the shit outta me!"

"That was the idea, silly," Lucie chuckled, peering beyond Fred and out of the window to check on her brother. He was okay.

"Jesus," Fred's heart was still hammering in his hands, "you... you wanna make yourself useful and stay by this bloody window while I go have a butcher's upstairs?"

"No, no, I'll go look," Lucie said, reversing towards the doorway, "you stay by the window and keep watch. Like Joe said, you like other people to do your dirty work for you." She winked.

Fred's jaw nearly hit the ground.

He'd never met a girl so sharp, so mean, so... brilliant.

Silly boy, she thought, shaking her head as she put a hand on the wooden rail and slowly made her way up the noisy stairs. Each and every step seemed to creak a little louder than the last.

Fred watched Lucie disappear up and out of view from the front room doorway, slowly shifting his gaze from the empty stairs to the grimy window, out into the snowy street at little Jake and Joe.

Joe...

"Joe," Fred croaked under his breath, "I'm gonna bloody get you for this. You just see if I don't."

Joe must've seen Fred in the window because he

suddenly waved.

Fred half-smiled and gave him the finger.

At the same time that Lucie was approaching the top of the stairs, Bill and Gordie were nearing the foot of the basement. Down, down, down they went into the black and when they reached the bottom, what they saw – what they smelt – filled them with a mixture of dread and disgust. It wasn't a basement. It was a cesspit. It was a hole, a grimy, filthy hole that was beyond anything any sane mind could conjure. The awful, fetid stench of piss, shit and God knows what else crowded their nostrils. It took everything Bill had to not to turn and run. It took everything Gordie had to not to throw up.

"Jesus," he coughed into the foul-smelling air, scanning the shadows, "what the hell is this place? Smells worse than the fuckin' Thames."

Bill had no answer. No words. He looked about the grime and the gloom, his heart ringing in his ears. He began to survey the dungeon from left to right. The combination of the pale moonlight creeping in through the small, high window with the unsteady candle did just enough to light the lair.

He panned. He scanned. He saw a dust-caked window guarded by a dozen dead spiders. Beneath it lay two metal buckets placed against a stained brick wall. He saw a filthy floor. He saw a dirty mattress covered in a pale green sheet with a few scraps of paper nailed to the wall just above it. He saw an old wooden table with a lantern and some crayons on top, and he saw a chair. And then Bill Talbot felt the cold, firm hand of Gordie Cooper on his shoulder, and his heart stopped.

It was the door.

It was the red door.

"B-B-Bill," Gordie stuttered, "is that... is that..."

"Yes," said Bill, trembling. The unsteady flame from the candle flickered madly beneath their white faces.

The door was identical to the one Bill had seen in his nightmares time and time again. From the deep shade of red and the peeled and rusty texture of the grazed steel, right down to the twelve-inch-square window maybe a quarter of the way down the door itself. The only obvious difference was that the monolith was in the centre of a brick wall and wasn't suspended in the middle of Mitre Square. They stared through the bars in the small, black square.

Go back, the voices of reason and logic spoke up in Bill's head, *leave this place*. Bill ignored them, slowly rounding the last of the stony steps, being extra careful to not knock over the buckets of piss and shit and God knew what else.

Go back. It's not worth it. Joe's voice this time.

Bill took a big, brave step towards the red door. And then he took another. Gordie shuffled in behind him. Their eyes fixed, unblinking, on the space between the bars of the towering red thing no more than ten paces ahead.

They approached with caution. They approached with fear. The world – the underworld – fell completely silent, and everything seemed to slow as they inched towards the rusty red door.

Eight paces.

Seven paces.

Six.

Five –

A sound. A sound from beyond the door.

They froze.

The dim candlelight seemed to stutter with every short, sharp movement of Bill's quivering hand.

"What was that?" Gordie whispered, clutching Bill's left arm. They were in touching distance of the rusted steel now but couldn't see what lay beyond the bars.

They stopped and rose – slowly – to the tips of their toes.

And then they heard the crying.

They shuffled back.

A woman's cry. Or a child's? They couldn't be sure. It was soft and snuffly. A gentle yet haunting concerto of moans and groans that sent chills down the spines of both boys.

Bill and Gordie looked at each other.

The crying continued.

Go back.

The crying intensified.

Leave.

They returned their eyes to the sobbing door.

Bill took a step forward.

Gordie tried to pull him back, but Bill resisted. He shook off the boy's terrified grasp, and took another cautious step towards the sound. He had to see; he had to know.

Abandon all hope, ye who enter –

All of a sudden, there were no more steps left to take. Bill had finally made it to the door. He took another deep breath of the sickly, fetid air - held it tight - and gingerly raised his face to the window. He peered through the bars of the red door. What he saw in there made his skin crawl. What he saw in there would never leave him.

There was a woman.

A ghoulish, highly emaciated woman.

She was chained to a wooden chair in the centre of the dark and gore-splattered room; she was naked and limp, her head was bowed and her long, tangled hair hung down and over her face. She was weeping. Her pale body glowed from the gloom of the cell and was scarred, scratched and stained with dried blood and excrement. The chair looked as if it had been fixed to the floor somehow, and there was a small bucket just beneath it. Her fingernails scraped and scratched against the arms of the chair. Bill Talbot was stunned. Horrified. Little did he know that the unthinkable nightmare had only just begun.

Gordie had summoned enough courage to join Bill at the black window, and he gasped when he saw what lay on the other side.

The woman ceased her cries abruptly and jerked her head up to face the bars. She let out a confused cry and flung her hair back over her shoulders. She was gagged, but her desperate, hollow face – her eyes – spoke a thousand words.

And then they heard the screams from above.

Lucie made it to the top of the stairs and looked about the landing. Again, there wasn't much to see, and even if there was, it would be difficult in this poor light. It wasn't quite pitch black, but it was close. There were no windows, no lamps. Just doors – three doors. They were closed, but the pale white glow from the full moon creeping under each of them offered something in the way of light, although it wasn't much.

Lucie took a step forward, and slowly opened door number one – *reeeeaaaaaaahhhhhhh.*

It was empty. Nothing but four bare walls and a dusty window that overlooked the small backyard.

Nothing.

She frowned, softly closing the door, making for the next one just to her left.

She took a long, deep breath, and twisted the handle.

At first, what she saw gave her a fright, but her shock soon turned to relief, and then to laughter. "Bloody hell," she rasped into the room, releasing the handle and putting her hand to her chest. She leaned against the narrow doorway, chuckling. This was the last thing she'd expected to see. Well, maybe not the last thing, but it was certainly up there.

The small room was full of animals; dozens and dozens of stuffed and mounted animals. Mostly cats and dogs, but there were a couple of foxes and badgers and a few birds. It was like a taxidermy showroom. A pet cemetery. A morbid, moonlit tomb of fur and feathers and claws and small, glassy eyes. It was bizarre. She took a step inside and frowned.

What the hell is this? she thought, looking about the sea of dead animals as she made her way across the floorboards. Each and every one of them seemed to watch her as she slowly moved about the dark menagerie. She reached the centre and turned, taking stock of all the weird and – in a way – wonderful creatures. *Wait 'till the boys see this*, she thought, *Jake would've bloody loved this*.

Lucie carefully crept back the way she came and made for the third and final door. She slowly felt her way along the gloomy landing, inching closer and closer towards the room that overlooked the street.

Towards the room not even the Cat's Meat Man dared to enter.

Lucie grasped the doorknob and suddenly became aware of the eerie silence in the house. She hesitated. Took a deep and deliberate breath of the silent, musty air and opened the door.

The pungent stench of sickly, rotten cheese hit her in the face like a fork of lightning. She threw a hand up to her face and screamed.

She screamed when she saw the old man propped up on the bed, the wasted, decomposing body of an old man whose sunken, leathery face seemed to be screaming right back at her.

"Oh my god!" she howled. Her bulging eyes locked on the cracked holes where the dead man's eyes used to be. They looked wet and almost seemed to shimmer in the moonlight. Like sunken black discs. Numb, she shifted her gaze from the dark circles to the bright, jagged teeth. They were even worse than the eyeholes and stood in stark contrast to the rest of the corpse's ghastly face. It was as if the hairy, brown thing was melted into the stained pillow. It was wearing a light blue pyjama shirt, and the rest of the skeleton – thankfully – lay beneath the discoloured bed sheet.

Lucie flung a hand to the doorway and shrank back in incredulous horror, wanting to look away but unable to. She retched and coughed then vomited onto the floorboards. Her knees buckled. It all happened so fast.

Fred suddenly burst into the room.

"What the fuck –"

And then he saw it.

"Jesus Christ!" he screamed, coughing and reaching for the traumatised girl. Lucie grabbed Fred and buried her wet face into his chest. He put his arms around her and they stumbled back through the open door. "What-what –"

Fred was lost for words. The cold. The stench. The corpse. He didn't know what to say, he didn't know what to do. He wrenched his gaze from the hellish thing on the bed and looked down at the top of Lucie's head.

"It's… it's all right," he said, "it's… it's dead."

"I know it's fuckin' dead," Lucie sneered into his damp jacket, "it's bloody horrible."

"I know…" he said, "I… I know… come on, let's get the boys and get the fuck out of here."

Lucie, nodding, peeled her face from Fred's trembling body. She looked up at the tall boy through a river of tears, and then they heard a muffled, blood-curdling howl deep from below.

They froze.

"What," she said "what the fuck was that –"

"The window!" they both cried, scrambling across the room to the bedroom window.

*

They were gone.

Jake and Joe were gone.

And then they heard the front door open.

The sound of Lucie's screams was perhaps the only thing that could've distracted Bill from the grotesque, weeping woman in the chair. He jerked his face up to the low ceiling and shuffled, tentatively, towards the stairs.

Gordie heard the screams too but was unable to tear his eyes from the red and white thing in the chair. He couldn't move. He couldn't look away no matter how hard he tried. No matter how much he wanted to. The woman croaked again through her terrible sobs. She was clearly trying to say something but Gordie couldn't make it out. He didn't know what to do, but he had to get out of here. He couldn't look any longer. He couldn't stay here. *This is so fucked!* he thought as he finally turned and stumbled from the door towards Bill.

Suddenly, a guttural, bone-chilling cry filled the air and prickled the hair on the back of both boys' necks. It was the most awful sound either of them had ever heard, but it was a cry for help. And they knew it. Bill stopped and turned back to face the red door.

"B-Bill…" Gordie stuttered, tears in his eyes, "Bill, come on, let's get the others and go get the police."

The woman's desperate cries drowned out Gordie's pleas. The chains that held her down rattled and scraped and clattered against the chair and ground as she moaned and wailed through the piece of bloodied cloth. Bill scrambled back to the red door and tugged the handle. Hard. Harder. But it was no use.

"Fuck!" he seethed.

"Bill, come on –"

"Gordie, help me look for a fuckin' key –"

And then they heard the front door slam.

At first, they thought it was thunder; then came the creaking of the floorboards above, and they both knew: Jack The Ripper was home. Jack The Ripper was moving along the hallway. Jack The Ripper was heading for the basement.

There was nowhere to run.

"Did you shut the door?" Bill hissed, turning to Gordie.

Gordie shook his head.

There was nowhere to hide.

A mess of terrible thoughts collided in Bill's mind as he looked about the dungeon in something far beyond panic.

Did he hear the woman scream? Did he hear Lucie scream? Did he see the light from the candle? What's up there? Where's Fred? What the fuck is going on?! What the fuck are we gonna do?!

"What the fuck are we gonna do?" Gordie whispered, crying, "What the fuck are we gonna do –"

"There," Bill whispered, pointing beneath the stairs at a large bundle of sheets and dirty rags, "we can hide under them."

It was a terrible idea, but there was no alternative. Bill blew out the candle and they scrambled for the dirty mound, grabbing and pulling frantically at the large pieces of stained cotton. A rat screeched and scurried from beneath the pile, disappearing through a small hole in the wall to their left.

"Quickly," Bill rasped, cramming his body tightly

into the wedge between the wall and the stairs, pulling Gordie close, "as soon as he goes through the red door we'll make a run for it, all right? Quickly!"

They were frantically burying their small bodies under the pile of sheets when the situation took another terrifying turn.

"IT'S ONLY ME, SIR!" A deep, crisp voice from above. An amplified roar that echoed down the stairs and into the souls of two petrified twelve-year-olds. Bill and Gordie froze beneath the mound of foul-smelling rags, their arms and necks breaking out in gooseflesh.

"NO! NO SIR! I'M S-S-SORRY!"

"Who's… who's he talking to?" Gordie breathed.

"There… there must be someone upstairs…"

Fred and Lucie stood perfectly still with their backs to the dead man's window, their dilated pupils nailed to the gloomy landing just beyond the open door.

"I KNOW SIR! I-I KNOW. I'M S-S-SORRY!"

Lucie slowly turned to Fred and put a quivering hand on his shoulder.

They locked eyes.

"Who's he talkin' to?" she mouthed, petrified.

Fred shook his head, but he had an idea. He was as puzzled as Lucie, but he'd heard enough horror stories from his good old pal Bill Talbot over the years to have an idea who the Cat's Meat Man might be shouting at. He slowly returned his gaze to the wasted, bed-ridden corpse to Lucie's left. He nodded. Lucie frowned, her wide eyes bouncing all over the room until the moment of grim realisation. She craned her head to face the putrid, leathery thing once more.

Jake was right, she thought. *Jake was right this whole time, and I didn't listen. This man is real! And he's mad! He's out of his fuckin' mind! And I didn't listen!*

A large black spider suddenly crawled from one of the skeleton's gaping nostrils. Lucie gasped and threw a hand up to her face, falling back and bumping into the window ledge.

"Don't... move," Fred murmured, grabbing hold of Lucie.

For a breathless moment, they stood perfectly still. And then:

"NO!" a nerve-shredding voice howled from below, echoing up the stairs and into the souls of two petrified twelve-year-olds.

"NO PLEASE DON'T! PLEASE! I'M SORRY!" The voice moved beneath the floorboards. They heard terrible, clattering footsteps down the hallway. Moving fast. And then a loud *BANG* as the Cat's Meat Man slammed the basement door.

They both breathed an unsteady sigh of relief.

"Come on," Fred whispered, "I think it's time to go, don't you?"

Silence.

Stillness.

Nothing.

The Cat's Meat Man stood at the top of the basement stairs for a moment, peering down, down, down into the black. *You're safe*, he reassured himself, *you're safe*.

And he was, because Father could never – would never – touch him down here. But, as The Cat's Meat Man had feared, he had, indeed, left the basement door unlocked again. Although, he couldn't remember leaving it wide open. *Stupid*, he thought, as he threw across the top and bottom deadbolts. *Stupid! Stupid! Stupid!* He headed down the stairs; and as he made his way down, down, down into his dungeon, The Cat's Meat Man cursed himself aloud for being so forgetful. He was angry. Furious. On the verge of tears.

"Stupid fuckin' bastard!" he spat into the dark, despair coursing through his veins. "Cunt," he spat as he shuffled across his chambers towards the table. "Useless fuckin' maggot!" He threw his bag of knives down on the table, unfastening the straps and scrambling, frantically, for his skillet knife.

He sighed, put the knife to one side, and hastily removed his soaking jacket and damp grey shirt.

Good for nothing maggot, his father's voice echoed through his head. The Cat's Meat Man hurled his clothes to the side, grabbed the knife, and began to cut and hack at his left forearm.

"Stupid, stupid, stupid," he sneered into the dark, every word punctuated by a sharp slash of the blade.

Through the tears and holes in the mound of crumbled sheets, Bill and Gordie watched on in horror as the scarred thing ripped into his own flesh.

"Stupid fuckin' boy –"

He stopped.

They held their breath.

The Cat's Meat Man or Jack The Ripper or maybe even The Devil himself slowly twisted his skeletal frame towards the red door, and began to laugh.

He spun back, threw the knife onto the table and removed a match from his pocket. He leant across the table and struck it several times against the wall. One, two, three attempts and then the Cat's Meat Man put the tiny flicker of light to the wick of the paraffin lamp, and a tall orange flame lit the basement in a kaleidoscope of ugly shadows.

"Right," he grinned, rubbing and smearing the blood from his forearm all over his face and chest, coughing and kicking off his shoes as he continued to laugh his diabolical laugh, "no rest for the wicked. Best get to it."

The Cat's Meat Man removed a set of keys from his trouser pocket, grabbed a large knife from his tool bag, and dragged his bare feet across the ground towards the red door. He jabbed at the lock with the large iron key. The woman's desperate sobs started up again, and the Cat's Meat Man mocked her terrible cries through the bars in the doors as he slowly turned the key. Bill and Gordie opened their eyes and carefully released their breaths into the acrid sheets.

Bill gripped Gordie's arm in a gesture that said "this is it" and Gordie squeezed his friend right back. He understood.

"Evening Miss," the Cat's Meat Man slurred as he yanked the large, heavy door open. It scraped and almost seemed to scream across the ground, causing both boys to wince in pain. In terror.

"All ready for Christmas are ya? Ha!"

The woman's muffled cries were music to the Cat's Meat Man's ears, and my, oh my, didn't they sound beautiful? This was the most he'd heard out of her in weeks. He cackled maniacally and sauntered into the room with a smile on his face and a spring in his step. Yes, Christmas had come early indeed. He pocketed his keys and slammed the red door shut.

"Not yet," Bill breathed. There was no way his voice could be heard over the horrendous sounds coming from their right, but he kept his voice as low as he could anyway, "not... yet."

Time had never moved so slow.

Life had never felt so hopeless.

Gordie stirred.

"Okay," Bill whispered, gripping Gordie one last time, "okay, slowly, okay, *slowly...*"

The boys gradually emerged from the rancid pile of off-white sheets. First Bill. Then Gordie. They slowly crawled on their hands and knees towards the foot of stairs. It was a short distance – real short – but it seemed to take forever. The hair-raising sounds, the laughter and the sobbing from beyond the red door filled the entire world. It made them want to run as fast as they could – but they knew they couldn't. Not yet.

Bill reached up and grasped one of the stone steps, slowly pulling himself to his feet as he rounded the foot of the stairs in one smooth motion.

He climbed.

Gordie wasn't far behind but as he turned onto the stairs his trailing foot clattered into one of the metal buckets, knocking it to the ground with a heart stopping *clkcklkckck!*

Gordie froze.

Bill froze.

The laughter from hell froze over.

Silence.

Stillness.

Nothing.

The boys slowly raised their fearful eyes to the red door.

A white-faced demon with blood dripping from its brow was glaring right back at them. The hate. The fury in those terrible, red-veined eyes was beyond anything. Terrifying. Maddening. The Cat's Meat Man suddenly shrieked and hurled himself into the bars with hideous speed and screamed: "You fuckin' bastards!"

They ran.

They ran as fast as they could up the basement stairs and they were at the door in an instant. But it wouldn't open. Bill grabbed the doorknob and pushed but it wouldn't open. It *wouldn't* open.

"Bill!" Gordie cried.

Bill pushed and pulled and thumped and tugged but the door wouldn't budge. Then a terrible thought detonated in Bill's brain like a nail bomb: *he's locked it from the inside!*

"He's coming!" Gordie looked back and down in time to see The Cat's Meat Man scuffling around the bottom of the stairs like an enormous white beetle waving a large red knife.

"Bill!"

"Deadbolt!" a muffled voice cried from the other side of the door. Fred?

"Deadbolts!" Lucie?

Bill suddenly looked down at his feet and saw the deadbolt. He kicked it free, and tried the door again.

Nothing happened.

The Cat's Meat Man screamed.

Gordie screamed.

Bill screamed.

The whole world screamed.

Then Bill saw the other deadbolt just above his head.

Deadbolts!

He leapt up, swatted it across, and the door flew open. Bill fell into Lucie's arms and forced her back into the hallway as the hell-bent Cat's Meat Man slashed into Gordie's ankle. Gordie howled as he fell into the hallway in a heap and went into instant shock. Bill and Lucie leapt forward in a flash and grabbed him by the shoulders, pulling the rest of his body clear from the doorway as the knife wielding fiend scrambled up the rest of the steps. Fred slammed the door hard, trapping the Cat's Meat Man's arm just as he was clambering through the doorway. The feral limb slashed and thrashed about in a mad blur, like some kind of rabid animal caught in a trap; flapping and growling, pounding and roaring at the hollow wood as Fred tried to hold him back. But it was no use: the Cat's Meat Man was slithering through. Bill threw himself against the door, grabbing the grotesque arm.

"Cunts!" the Cat's Meat Man hissed in an unearthly voice, "Fuckin' cunts!"

"Lucie!" Bill cried, "Lucie, run!"

Lucie ignored Bill's pleas and hurled herself into the pulsing, splintering door. Trying to help the boy pry the flailing knife from the wild right hand.

"Run!" Bill screamed in desperate voice again as the bloody hand slipped through Lucie's grasp. The blade caught her on the back of her hand, opening a clean, two-inch gash just below the knuckles. Lucie cried out. There was no blood, but there was pain. Sharp, searing pain. Blinding pain. But the girl kept her eyes open and wouldn't give up. She seized the crazed limb tight just below the wrist with both hands and tried to wrestle it under control.

"Fuckin' little pigs!" the monster snarled with blood-curdling spite through the gap in the door, "I'll kill you all. I'll fuckin' kill you all! Little cunts!"

Suddenly Joe burst from the kitchen and leapt to Lucie's aid. They fought and struggled and finally ripped the rusty blade from the bloody hand.

The Cat's Meat Man roared and spat into Joe's terrified face. "Stinkin' maggot! Fuckin' pig. I see you!" His entire right arm and leg were now through the door and his gaunt, wet face seemed to be oozing through the ever-widening gap.

Joe stumbled back, clutching the knife with one trembling hand, wiping the stringy, foul-smelling spit from his face with the other.

"I don't know how much longer we can hold him off!" Fred cried.

"Run!" Bill shouted over the demented sounds. "This is my fault, just grab Gordie and run!"

"Oh, fuck off Bill," Fred sneered.

The door thundered at their backs and felt as though it could give at any second.

"Joe!" Bill cried, "Joe, you've got to stop him! Stab him Joe! Joe!"

Joe, shaking, looked down at the large knife in his hand.

"Joe! Hurry!"

Suddenly, the Cat's Meat Man contorted his arm and grabbed a handful of Lucie's hair. She screamed.

Bill sprung from the door and the Cat's Meat Man forced himself an inch or two further through the gap and into the hall. Bill grabbed the knife from Joe's trembling hand and drove it deep into the madman's thigh. He cried out in a guttural blend of pain and anger, releasing Lucie and reaching for the knife. Lucie fell forward and the door finally gave way. Bill charged at the Cat's Meat Man and pushed with everything he had. The Cat's Meat Man fell back and down the hard stone steps, tumbling down, down, down into hell.

Fred slammed the door and everything stopped.

A smothering stillness fell over the hallway as five shell-shocked children stared at the closed door and listened close.

There was silence.

There was nothing. Nothing but a cluster of terrified twelve-year-olds, all panting and rasping. Gasping for air. Gordie clutched his bloody mess of an ankle and moaned. Joe went to him. Bill, Fred and Lucie stood gripping one another tight in front of the basement door, looking at each other in horrified disbelief.

Bill suddenly reached for the doorknob. He had to see. He had to know. Lucie put a hand on his shoulder but it was too late. Bill was already pulling the door open, and he peered down into the abyss. Fred and Lucie reluctantly joined him, and what they saw would haunt them for the rest of their days.

In the feeble amber light, the Cat's Meat Man lay crumpled in a growing pool of scarlet. A steaming, broken heap of bone and flesh and hair and blood.

Deformed.

Defeated.

Dead –

A hideous, dislocated arm rose from the bloody pile and slammed itself down on the stoney steps with a sickening, almost defiant slap.

"No," Bill, Fred and Lucie all caught their breath in horrified unison as the Cat's Meat Man began to writhe and crack and crunch and moan. He slowly looked up with a face that was a reddish snarl, a sticky mask of venomous fury and undying hate. He was frothing at the mouth, bursting at the seams and two bulging, yellow eyes seemed to throb and twitch out of the redness as they stared up and into the souls of the three paralysed children. They were snake eyes from a terrible, reptilian nightmare. Indescribable. And then the Cat's Meat Man unleashed a gurgled hiss that seared the cold and rotten air like molten lava as he uncoiled his twisted mess of a body like a demented serpent.

Revived.

Renewed.

Reborn.

And then the Cat's Meat Man began to claw and slither and drag his mangled frame up the stairs.

"Kill... you... alllll –"

Bill slammed the door.

Suddenly, a deafening barrage of thumps and bangs echoed down the hallway before the front door exploded from its hinges. A handful of policemen came stomping into hell house, a little boy called Jake trailing close behind.

It was over.

It was finally over.

There had been...

"There had been a change in the air. It wasn't Christmas. It wasn't the weather. Nor was it the promise of a new and better year – a fresh start. No, it was The Ripper. His reign of terror was finally at an end. And so it went, that on the night before Christmas in the year of our Lord 1888, six brave children came together to stop one big bad monster..."

The twins' eyes were glued to the old man as he brought the scariest, most incredible story they'd ever heard to a close.

"...The *Fab Four* had become the *Super Six*, and every Christmas Eve thereafter, they would come together and remember the night they brought light in a time of darkness. They would remember the night they saved Whitechapel. They would remember the night they stopped and caught... Jack The Ripper. The End."

A tiny chorus of cheers and claps filled the air, and the old storyteller stuck out his arms and bowed. He had done it again.

"Shhh," their mother said, chuckling, "sshh, keep it down my lovelies, keep it down."

"That was the best story ever Grandad," Rebecca gleamed.

"Best story ever," Paul echoed.

"What happened to Bill and Lucie, Grandad?" the little girl asked.

The old man smirked. "Ohh, well they lived happily

ever after of course."

The twins giggled.

Paul turned to his mother and asked, "Can we go and tell George and Rachel, Mum? Can we please?"

"Yeah, can we, Mum?" Rebecca jumped in.

"Oh… go on then," she said, "but don't be long and try not to mention the parts about Jack The *Bloomin'* Ripper, alright?"

"Yes, Mum," they both started to their feet.

The old man swept his eyes along the platform as they turned and ran and dove into their friends' blankets up ahead. He was sure their retelling of the old tale would be every bit as good as his. He smiled.

"Gets better every time you tell it, dear," the old woman grinned, poking him ever so gently in his ribs.

"Oh thanks very much," he said, turning to the old tease.

"Nice of you to add that little part with The Ripper at the end for them as well," his daughter smiled.

"Well, it was only a minor alteration," the old man held up his thumb and forefinger a few centimetres apart, "after all, the moral of the story – if there ever was such a thing – was never about the kids thinking they'd actually caught The Ripper. The point is that they stuck together. Six brave souls stood strong and tall to overcome something evil. It might not have been *the* big, bad wolf everyone was scared of, but it was still a wolf."

He shifted his gaze back towards his grandchildren and sighed.

"These are dark times, girls, and those kids have got some long nights ahead of them. We all have. I guess I just wanted to give them... something. A little bit of hope. A little bit of light, you know? A happy ending."

The two women smiled ruefully.

"We need to stay strong," he said, "we need to stick together."

"But..." the young woman hesitated, "but what if he doesn't come back, Dad? What if he bloody dies out there like Uncle J–"

"You can't think like that Polly," the old woman broke in, leaning forward, gripping her daughter's knee.

"Positive trumps negative every time, love," the old man added, "we know it's hard, but there's no use thinking like that, okay? Just try and stay positive. Stay strong. You listen to your old mum and dad."

Polly sniffed, wiped away a tear and turned to her mother. "So, was that really how you two met?"

Lucie Talbot smiled at her partner of fifty-two years, "Yeah, as a matter of fact, it was. Although I can't remember being so flirtatious."

Bill grinned. "Your memory's not what it was dear. You just leave it to the professional storyteller, alright?"

Lucie stuck out a hand and gave the cheeky old man a light tap on the cheek.

"Most of that story is actually true, love," Bill smiled at his daughter, "well, except for the part about us actually thinking we caught The Ripper, of course. Inspector Abberline was quick to rule that out."

"So... so who was the cat's meat man then? You never really told me."

Bill sighed. "Just some lunatic, Poll. His old dad made him what he was, no doubt. Not like that's any excuse, but evil breeds evil. I truly believe that." He paused. "You know, they reckon he'd been dead up in that room for a little over a year –"

"Wait… that… that actually happened?"

Bill and Lucie nodded.

"Afraid so," he rubbed his brow, "that old man must've been one hell of a bastard for him to think he was still alive up there. For him to do the terrible things he did. He'd had that poor woman down in that horrible basement for nearly two months. She wasn't the first, and I'm sure she wouldn't have been the last," he took a long pause.

"Her name was Rose Clarke and she was a barmaid in the White Hart pub. We never knew her but she was a lovely girl by all accounts. She took her own life a few months after we found her that night. Turns out the sick bastard cut out her tongue and force-fed it to her. Kept her alive by feeding her bits of other people he'd butchered down there and stuff. I honestly can't remember seeing anything else beyond the bars of that red door that night. Or maybe I just don't want to."

Polly's eyes widened.

"Yeah," Bill said, nodding, "I left that part out when you were a little girl too. Like I said earlier, I know my audience, love."

Bill stared into the light of the small lamp.

"They found the remains of three people down there. Two vagrants and a man named Johnny who lived over on Thrawl Street. They hanged the Cat's Meat Man the following month. You know…I can't even remember his name."

The three all stared into the light for a moment. Then Polly asked: "What…what do you think really happened to him, Dad?"

"Who?"

"You know who," she rolled her eyes.

"Jack?"

She nodded.

"He never left."

She frowned.

Bill took a deep breath.

"There're Rippers all over London, Poll. All over the world. Always have been, always will be. He was nothing new. Nothing special. Murdering bastards like him never are. They get far too much attention and they never really go away. It's just a question of when and where they're going to strike and what their bloody name will be. Only difference is, we never found out who our Ripper really was…"

There was a loud rumble above. A few gasps.

"…and I suspect we never will."

"Are you still not curious though? About who he really was and stuff?"

"Oh, I thought about it for years," he glanced at Lucie, "we all did. But, in time… I don't know, you just grow to see things differently."

Polly frowned.

"Put it this way: maybe a man's name doesn't matter all that much. Especially his kind: cruel, narcissistic monsters who think they know best. Think they ought to mould and twist the world in their bloody hubris simply because they can. He was a murderer, Polly, nothing more."

Bill slowly swept his gaze back to the trembling world above.

"Take this Hitler fella, for instance," he raised a stern finger to the cracked ceiling, "is he really all that different to what we had back then? Oh, he's much worse, of course but, in a way, if you think about it, they're much the same: both madmen, both self-entitled murderers. Bastards. Only difference is this one has a name and a face and an evil army to do his evil work. Obviously that makes him infinitely more dangerous. But I think our Ripper, in a way, had an army too and no doubt inspired some of the other madness we saw back then. Evil breeds evil. Maybe your mum and I were in on it somehow: the madness. Maybe we all were. I don't know. But the fact remains: men like him reckon they're above everyone. Reckon they have a right to control and kill people who are just trying to get by. Brainwashed a load of others with a bunch of nonsense so they can do his bidding. What gives him the right to pass judgement, aye?"

Lucie put a hand on the old man's shoulder. He was rambling again.

Bill sighed. "But…then again, he's nothing special. There'll be more like him, I'm sure. What worries me is how people will probably look back on all this in years to come. Once all the dust has settled on the countless bodies that'll no doubt pile up, you think the world will remember them? Or will they only remember the man with the knife?"

He bowed his head.

"You've become awfully morbid in your old age dear," Lucie said, putting a gentle hand on the old man's knee.

Bill stared into the flickering yellow of the old

paraffin lamp, transfixed by its soft, buttermilk glow. He forced a smile. He put an arm around his wife. He pulled her close. He slowly plucked her cool, wrinkled hand from his knee and lightly kissed the old pink scar just beneath her knuckles. She smiled. She squeezed the old man's hand tight and nestled her cheek on his thick, warm shoulder. Bill tilted his head, resting it against his darling Lucie's. There was a sadness in his eyes but he winked at his daughter who returned the gesture. She started to her feet, making her way down the platform to check on her two children, leaving the old Victorian couple in peace.

Bill slowly raised his eyes to the grey, cracked ceiling of the underground tunnel. The nightmare of that dreadful autumn combined with the grave concern he now felt for his family settled on the old man's mood like a dark, melancholy haze.

He thought of Lucie. He thought of Polly. He thought of his two beautiful grandchildren, and their brave, brave father. He prayed for his safe return, and then he thought of Fred. He thought of Gordie. He thought of Joe and the little boy called Jake who would grow up to fight and die for his country in the Great War. Bill Talbot never saw what was so *great* about it. He closed his eyes and listened to the wailing storm, searching for a word that would best encapsulate it all; the murders, the monsters, the victims, the phantoms, the ghosts, the ghouls, the love, the loss, the fear, the facts, the fiction and, now, the terrible, terrible war…

"Madness," he whispered, "madness."

*

From above, a dozen air-raid sirens cried out into the cold and unforgiving night. Their terrible screams lifted high above the black smoke on the river, echoing out and across the torn and empty streets of Whitechapel as the bombs rained down on the city of London.

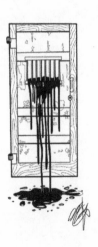

THIS HAUNTED LAND

The following poem was received by the Central News Agency at their premises in the city of London on the 15. February 1891. Two days prior, 32-year-old Frances Coles had been found with her throat cut beneath a railway arch near Swallow Gardens. She died on the way to the hospital.

Experts believe the poem to be a parody of the prefatory verse to Lewis Carroll's *Alice's Adventures in Wonderland.*

The true origin and authenticity of the poem are debated to this day.

This Haunted Land

And in the silver winter's night
Half hearted he returns;
Look upon his work with open eyes,

JACK HARDING

Look close and you shall learn,
Their filthy hands make poor pretence
Those dirty whores still burn.

Oh, dear five, have I lost count?
An apron made of leather?
They begged for mercy, but he said "No!"
Beneath that dreadful weather,
Rejoice at what one man can do
Against ten tongues together.

But then, a sudden silence came,
No reason, rhyme or clue
Delusions passed across the land
Of suspects old and new,
In friendly chat with man and beast,
And half believed it true.

Alas it went, his fine work drained
The river had run dry,
And faintly strove that vengeful one
His work will never die,
"To be –" "No! Not to be!"
Their stupid voices cry.

Thus grew the tale of Ripper Country:
Died swiftly, one by one,
Its mad events were chiselled out
And now the tale is done,
And go I ride – that stone white horse,
Beneath the blood red sun.

RIPPER COUNTRY

Jack! A timeless story given,
And with a vengeful hand,
Forget me not, there will be more
Their work will be most grand,
I am eternal, I shall live on
To haunt this haunted land.

THE NEMESIS OF NEGLECT.

" THERE FLOATS A PHANTOM ON THE SLUM'S FOUL AIR,
SHAPING, TO EYES WHICH HAVE THE GIFT OF SEEING,
INTO THE SPECTRE OF THAT LOATHLY LAIR.
FACE IT—FOR VAIN IS FLEEING!
RED-HANDED, RUTHLESS, FURTIVE, UNERECT,
'TIS MURDEROUS CRIME—THE NEMESIS OF NEGLECT!"

ACKNOWLEDGEMENTS

This book would not exist without the help and guidance of several people.

Firstly, I'd like to thank my partner, Rachel Wassell. Without her, I would not have made it past the first paragraph let alone the first page. Rach, thank you for not calling the men in white coats when I first told you about my crazy idea and thank you, also, for putting up with all the madness. You encouraged me to do something I never thought I would find the courage to do.

Secondly, I would like to thank my publisher and editor, Jay Alexander. When I originally pitched my vision for *Ripper Country* to Jay, I was nervous as hell but his response to and ultimate passion for the project gave me the energy and desire required to bring this book to life. Without him, this book may still exist but it would be considerably lacking in about twenty layers of polish and sheen; it would be nowhere near as good nor would it look so damn easy on the eye. Jay, thank you for taking a chance on me, I am eternally grateful for the opportunity.

It would also feel wrong if I failed to acknowledge the legendary author whose timeless tales inspired me to pick up my laptop in the first place. In the lockdown summer of 2020, I fell in love with the short stories of Ray Bradbury, and without his words, I'm not sure I would have found the inspiration to attempt a single sentence. Thank you, Ray.

And how can I forget my small team of proofreaders? Many of which have become dear friends over the course of this strange and not-so-beautiful journey. Matthew Siegal, Callan Brunsdon, Christopher Badcock, Benjamin Pritchard, Lauren Bruce, Sara Hay and Samuel Hallam, you've all been immense and your feedback has been invaluable. Thank you for giving me and these stories a shot, and thank you for your honest and constructive words.

I would also like to thank the three incredibly talented artists who quite literally helped bring my vision to life. From Joe 'Khanage' Worrall's showstopping cover art to Nicola Spencer's stunningly grotesque back cover and, of course, Portsmouth's very own Tim Childs for thirteen sharply etched beauties which all help give the tales in this book that little bit extra…something…I was looking for. It's been a pleasure working with you all.

Lastly, I would like to thank my parents for their undying support and belief that, one day, this little pipe dream of mine could come true – I could actually have my very own book published.

And now I do.

Thank you.

Jack Harding
December, 2021

CONTENT WARNINGS

Here you will find a comprehensive list of situations or themes within this book that may be triggering. If you have found anything that you think deserves warning, please contact me at bloodritespublishing@gmail.com.

Beware of spoilers.

In all/most stories:
Gore, violence, language, harm and threat of harm. Prostitution and discrimination against prostitutes (by antagonists).

In *Funny Little Games*:
Harm to an animal.

In *The Barber*:
Antisemitic language (used by antagonist).

In *Night Terror*, *Beast of the Thames* and *Ripper Country*:
Harm or threat of harm to children (also implied in moderation in other stories).

CPSIA information can be obtained
at www.ICGtesting.com
Printed in the USA
BVHW040554070223
658034BV00023B/235